King James' Aversion

Betty Younis

For RDL

with all my love and gratitude

Betty Younis

Chapter One

Robert Devereux, Earl of Essex and Elizabeth's favorite, has risen against his sovereign and is marching upon London in an attempt to overthrow the aging queen by main force and surprise.

Informed of the plot, and in a desperate bid to warn the queen, Coudenoure sends its only heirs – Anne and Henrietta – on a wild midnight ride to reach Elizabeth before Devereux is able to declare himself king of all England.

But Anne's journey is cut short. She now lies on the far side of the meadow abutting Greenwich Wood. Her mount, Galahad, stands beside her, keeping guard over her unconscious figure.

All hopes now ride on with Henrietta alone, but as she gallops through the streets of London, she is caught up in the fighting between Elizabeth's loyalists and Essex' traitors and wrongly arrested. Taken to the Tower of London and facing immediate execution with no chance to clear her name, Henrietta boldly attempts a desperate escape, but as this final gambit fails, she is forced back down into the dungeon.

February 1601:

The Tower of London

A guard with a torch came running, and as he held it up to identify the prisoner who was brazen enough to try and escape, he also lit up the face of the man who had caught her. It was the guard from the morning, and again, as Henrietta looked into his intelligent eyes, she thought she saw a slight flicker – was it pity?   On impulse, she reached beneath her dress and in a single hard jerk broke the chain with the ruby cross which hung there. Before anyone could touch her, she seized his hand and placed the cross and chain securely in his grasp.

They began pulling her away.

"Give it to the queen, I beg you! She will recognize it I promise! Sir – I beg you!"

Chapter Two

February 1601:

Whitehall Palace

She lay as they had placed her the previous evening. Her hands – white and waxy with cold – were folded across her midriff, adorned only by her most treasured possession: a small locket ring which she never removed. She rubbed a finger across it now, feeling its bejeweled surface, and closed her eyes as her hand sought its familiar clasp. It no longer sprang open as in her youth, but gently parted, inviting its owner into a world long since faded. She held her hand close to her face so that she might view the two miniature portraits revealed within the secret confines of the piece. One, of herself as a young woman, made her smile. Yes, she had been quite handsome in her youth. There she was, in profile, bedecked in all the glory of England and her kingdom. Funny, time had not dimmed the feel of the high, ruff collar Holbein had insisted she wear for the sitting. Composed of multiple layers of tightly rolled and starched lace, it had proven difficult for her ladies to secure – the buttons were too small and the lace too stiff. Once in place, however, it had continued to irritate her – she had immediately begun to itch beneath its gossamer folds. Holbein had ignored her whining and she had been forced to allow him to do so. Artists were a strange breed, a tribe apart, and she had been warned that if she did not cooperate to his satisfaction, well . . . several patrons, having rebuked the great painter, had noticed that he ultimately failed to capture their beauty, focusing instead on such trivial faults as a prominent mole or multiple chins, or even an unfairly renowned nose.

So she had remained quiet, there before him, with her wig of tightly coiled curls, her high proud forehead, her dignified aquiline nose. She studied the painting for several more minutes before turning her gaze to its opposite, a miniature of her mother, Anne Boleyn.

They were right, she had not been classically beautiful. Her complexion was too dark for that, her eyes too hard. But even in the tiny portrait, across time and circumstance, she had the ability to captivate, to mesmerize all who looked upon her. Her deep brown hair was drawn back in a caul, held in place by a French hood, the headdress she herself had made fashionable. Placed far back upon her head, its ends framed her face as they curled gently forward. Holbein had perfectly captured her intelligence and bravery, and in moments of extreme pain, or when fear perhaps overtook her or depression ate at the very fabric of her soul, Elizabeth always sought and found comfort in the calm visage of the one who had loved her first and most.

A knock on the door of her chambers interrupted her reverie. She closed the ring and kissed it, knowing she would need all the strength it might offer over the coming days.

"Majesty, did you not sleep last night?" It was Robert Cecil, son of her beloved William Cecil. Like his father before him, he kept her kingdom in order, her world orbiting smoothly around its contentious base of jealous courtiers, hungry nobles, aspiring ladies, gossipy servants, able and not-so-able administrators, nosy clerics, scheming bishops, and a host of others who inhabited her court, following her from palace to palace, always watching, waiting, wanting. And Robert Cecil, like his father before him, believed he should have constant access to her, whether she was dressed and ready for the day or not.

He barged into her bedchamber now and she amused herself with the thought that the fashionable at court need never worry about their place being usurped by her chief minister of state. Long, black woolen robes and tunics, stuffy ruffs and little, round black caps perched eternally upon both of their balding heads appeared as throwbacks, haunts from another era. She was not even certain that Robert did not wear the robes and cloaks left behind by William upon his death. It was not that the pair of them – father and son – had ever been averse to riches or sumptuous and elegant living. It was more a matter of not drawing attention to the wealth one was busily accruing by wearing it on one's back. Better to spend one's fortune on priceless books and antiquities, things enjoyed in the privacy of home with friends and family. Of all Elizabeth's ministers and courtiers, she knew for a fact that only the Burghley's managed to avoid debt, even so far as paying in full for the delightful manner house the elder had built upon being made a baron, a rare honor seldom bestowed by Elizabeth. Her kingdom was in good hands, and she occasionally thought upon how fortunate she had been throughout her reign in having such capable ministers. She sighed as her ladies began rustling in behind Robert, gently pushing him aside as they raised her from her bed. He ignored their ministrations towards her and rattled on about the day's agenda.

"'Tis important today of all days, Majesty, that you show yourself to your people."

Marian, her senior lady, looked at him and twirled her finger in the air. He nodded and turned so as to avoid seeing Elizabeth in too great a state of undress, but never slowed his speech.

"Majesty, did you hear me? We must make certain today that the populace know that the knave Essex did not succeed."

"Yes, Lord Robert, I heard you and I understand your point. To belabor it is tiresome."

"Yes, Majesty, but 'tis important . . ."

'*Robert*! Fie!! Leave me in peace! My ladies shall dress me appropriately and in my own good time I shall call for you to discuss the day's schedule."

Jane, a junior maid, took his elbow and began guiding him towards the door.

"And Majesty, as soon as we have determined how best to deal with the traitor . . ."

The guard closed the door behind the loquacious minister, leaving Elizabeth and her maids in blissful silence. She moved closer to the great fire which now burned brightly in the hearth and raised her arms to a ninety degree angle from her body. Her ladies, able to sense her mood from years of routine and protocol, proceeded quietly in their familiar morning ritual, leaving the queen to her own thoughts. She closed her eyes, feeling their gentle, caring hands upon her body. Catherine, yet another junior lady, entered the bedchamber from the wardrobe room. In her hands she held two gowns, one of lustrous pale blue satin with pearl beading running in parallel lines to its tightly cinched waist, the other a warm amber velvet with a wide necklace of topaz and garnet cabochon stones sewn directly on to its front. Elizabeth glanced at them before turning away.

"The amber, for the blue is too light for such a somber occasion. You! Careful with the chemise!"

The dress was finally settled upon her thin frame, and Catherine brought forward the puffy sleeves which accompanied it and began buttoning them to her gown. Each sleeve bore an inset of heavily embroidered cloth of colors similar to that of the gown. As each maid completed her task, she stepped back, allowing the queen to inspect the results in the gilded looking glass which sat nearby. The effect of the tiny waist, accompanied by the billowing sleeves, accentuated her feminine form, and she nodded with satisfaction. She indicated she was ready to be made up.

Since her bout with smallpox just after her coronation, Elizabeth had worn wigs and makeup. For all noble women, an alabaster complexion was de rigueur as a symbol of class and taste, and Elizabeth achieved hers using ceruse. She found that the white lead provided the pale, almost ghostly hue of white which she preferred, while the emollients mixed with it, such as vinegar, ensured a smooth application. Finally, a wig of auburn red curls was put in place. She brushed away the woman with the final piece, the ruff, which would offset her gown and set her face afloat on a sea of expensive lace.

"I shall eat my breakfast first, and alone. When I am done, I shall call for you."

Each of them bowed in turn, backing towards the door as they did so. As they left, Elizabeth sat at the small table near the diamond-paned window. A meal of fruit and bread was brought in, accompanied by a jar of honey, slices of ham, a small cup and a ceramic jug of tea. She waited patiently until once again she was alone. Her thoughts returned to the melancholy theme which had kept her awake most of the night, and she realized that perhaps she should not have been made up quite so soon. She fought back the tears, closed her eyes, and thought of young Devereux. What a fool he was. And what a fool she had been to trust him.

Trust him? She laughed aloud and sipped her tea. No, she had not trusted him for many a year. But she had loved him all his life. That was at the heart of her sadness. He had come to her court as a mere youth, and his charm and good looks, his quick wit and exaggerated romantic overtures towards her had given her warmth, had made her feel alive. Thirty odd years separated them, and yet he treated her as a woman of his own age. He courted her as only a young man could – with poetry, with song, with declarations of love as big and eternal as all of heaven. It may have been ridiculous, it may have made her court twitter, but she cared not. He courted her.

His manly attentions towards her had allowed her to pretend, not just to her court but also to herself, that some semblance of youth still clung to her old bones. She had found reason in his amorous poetry to rise in the mornings and pay attention to her dress. In his song she had heard youth, eternal youth, and believed that she could possess it even now. For years, only he had stood between her and her own mortality. With care and deceit, she had positioned herself always so that his bright presence stood between her and the grave, lest she be forced to see it, acknowledge it, peer into it.

But that was gone now, for hubris had claimed him for its own. We all spin our own narrative, she thought dolefully, carefully crafting our thoughts to present ourselves *to* ourselves in the best possible light, but only a fool never saw beyond that thin veil of illusion. Oh Robert, what have you done? You have forced me to act on your treason, to rid the earth of your footsteps, to cast your soul into darkness, to deny you life.

She was not hungry and started to stand.

"No, no," she muttered to herself, ". . . that will not do. You cannot parade through London without sustenance. You might faint, and that would only fuel panic amongst your people."

She reached down and plucked a dried fig from the shallow plate on the table. Her gesture was met by an odd metallic clinking sound in the bottom of the dish. Cocking her head, she moved the remaining fruit aside to see what on earth might be rattling round in her breakfast bowl. After a moment, a shrieking scream escaped her lips. Again and again she cried out, until her bedchamber was filled with guards, ladies and courtiers. Robert Cecil fought his way through the crowd.

"Majesty! Majesty! What is it? What has disturbed you thus?"

Queen Elizabeth pointed to the table in front of her.

"Bring me the person who put *that* before me!" she screamed in a blind panic, unable to hide her fear. "Bring them to me *now*!"

Chapter Three

Matthew Collins knew wool. He had risen to middle class status primarily for two reasons: he seldom thought of anything but his trade, and he worked harder than any other ten men put together.

He knew that a hot summer followed by a warm winter would result in coarse wool, while cooler climes would ensure a finer, warmer fleece. He knew also, however, that pasturage was more important than climate and that ewes and rams grazed upon poor land would produce short staples but that a luxuriant, full pasturage would yield staples with more bulk and length. All who traded England's most important commodity knew those basic facts, however. That knowledge alone did not mark Matthew Collins out as a man of distinction within his world.

What made Matthew Collins an expert was his deep, almost reverential knowledge of and respect for the varying grades of wool produced by specific regions and his ability to acquire them. If someone wanted the finest wool available, Lemster Ore, produced only by the Ryeland sheep of the west country, he could oblige. If, however, Lemster Ore was out of reach financially, he might direct a buyer to the March wool of Shropshire. Or perhaps he had learned that Hertfordshire had had an exceptional year for fine, short fleece. If so, he would not fail to secure such as might be needed from that locality. And aside from any financial considerations, he would firmly and religiously dissuade all and sundry from wool produced in Lincolnshire, for the salt marshes of that region meant that sheep grazed there produced vastly inferior staples of the coarsest wool known. A network of agents, of small tenancies and large estates, were at his beck and call, for if Matthew Collins was interested in your wool, you were assured of a fair price and an honest appraisal.

He could not remember a time when his life had not revolved around the yearly cycle of shearing, washing, carding, and spindling. Matthew Collins had begun as a simple wool merchant, selling the raw product to those who would refine it into cloth. Eventually, however, the market began to turn, for superior wool from Spain was allowed to compete with the English product. Realizing he must change with the times, he had taken up the secondary processing of wool himself and finally, just recently, had started to make a small business of producing woolen broadcloth for export. Earlier in his career, he had looked only to the commodity itself for a living, but now he began to delve into the bifurcated world of finished woolen products – the clothing branch and the worsted branch. Within each of these were a myriad of materials graded according to fineness and weight: bayes, sayes, penistones, kersies, bombasines, shalloons – the list was almost endless. If wool had made him blissful, woolen products now made him delirious and complete.

Matthew Collins was self-made and well established, and his family lived a comfortable middle class life in the heart of London's wool district. During the most recent economic downturn, he had purchased a fine house from a brogger – a wool retailer who dealt in small lots on the fringes of the main trade. The house, built in the time of Henry VIII, still retained the 'H' layout popular during Henry's reign, with a set of courtyards front and back. Each evening, upon his return from his small shop near the fleecing yards, he paused before entering his home, partly to admire it but mostly to give thanks for all he had received, for despite what some might think, his rise had been difficult and he could not forget his beginnings.

Born the oldest son in a long succession of tenant farmers on the Althorp estate of the Spencer family, he had started life in his father's footsteps as generations before him had done. Indeed, as he liked to point out to his sons, their line could be traced back deep into the Middle Ages when serfdom was the law of the land.

From the start, the elder Collins had loved the wool industry in all of its facets. He lived for market days in the spring, when he and the other tenants would drive their sheep into town for shearing. The wool was bundled and sold to a middleman, usually a brugger, who would clean it, take a profit, and pass it along. Down the chain of vendors each bundle would go, until finally, having been carded, spun, and dyed, it was sold for cloth. The industry was at the heart of England's economy, and Collins lived and breathed with its every pulse. And he was bright, bright enough to understand that wool was not just the secret to bread on his table, but also his means to a better life. He dreamed of becoming a merchant, of buying and selling the commodity of which he knew so much.

Gradually, the grand earl of Althorp had given him an increasing measure of responsibility. A kind man, and an astute one, he had recognized early on the young boy's talent for mathematics and business along with his exceptional drive, and had seen to having him schooled along with his own children.

Collins' chance to break out of his tenancy had come with the birth of his first child, a daughter. By fourteen, the girl was widely known to be one of the most comely in the county. Having observed the ways of the wealthy for years as he dealt with them in various markets, he ensured that the girl could read, sew, manage a household and was sufficiently charming in her conversation. These efforts paid a handsome dividend when the earl's son fell in love with her. But the lack of a proper heritage proved an enormous obstacle – to marry beneath one's class was one thing; to marry the daughter of a tenant upon one's own land quite another. And it was at this juncture that Matthew Collins' true genius had shown through.

Over the years, and with soul-searing economies, Collins had managed to put aside a small amount of coin. If the earl would loan him what he might lack, to be paid back of course with a handsome interest, then a fig leaf could be placed across the nuptials. The earl, sensing the business acumen of Collins and being pushed by his heir, finally agreed. A great deal of pride was bound up in the agreement for Matthew, but more was to come, for his daughter initially refused the great man's son, saying that unless her family were set up in London, far from the tenancy upon which she had been raised, she could not logically nor reasonably be expected to assume her duties with them still in their tenancy. In the end, the old earl gave in, secretly happy that if his son had chosen to marry a woman of no social standing, at least he had chosen a woman of substance. The situation, while not perfect, was manageable, and she was right – without her family on the grounds reminding all those round about of her origins, the story, while it might not die, would at least become a muted strain within the chorus of life on the ancient estate.

The elder Collins was overjoyed. A suitable house, small but limestone built, was chosen in the inner city, not far from The Wool Exchange. It was here that he would conduct his business. Each morning, he joined other staplers at the exchange. Prices were set, negotiated, changed and renegotiated on a constant basis throughout the day. He had finally arrived.

*****

Roman Collins opened the door to his family's home. There was a furtiveness about his movements as he pulled the door behind him, making certain not to release the handle until the latch had slid over the doorplate. Turning with the stealth of a practiced burglar, he began zigzagging across the wide-planked floor, first dancing to the left, then leaping to the right, and finally, stepping gingerly on the floorboard nearest the stairs. He winced as it let out a tired, loud squeak. His one mistake.

"Roman?" a woman's voice called from the parlor just off the hallway. "Roman, son? Is that you?"

Roman sighed, let out his own tired noise, and abandoned his quest for a silent trip to his bedchamber.

"Mother, yes, 'tis me." He strode into the room from whence the call had come.

It was rather grand for Roman's taste, reflecting too much his father's determined climb into the middle class. He loved his parents deeply, and knew the struggle they had endured to give him a better life. He found his own attitude towards material wealth, therefore, strangely out of step with the very things they had sought so desperately to provide for him, the very things which he found lovely, interesting, and mostly unnecessary. Roman loved simplicity, and contrary to what his father wished, he loved the wool trade. But that was gone for him, gone because his parents wished a better life for him; one not tied to such middle class pursuits. Despite these differences, however, they loved him and he loved them unconditionally.

The sitting room was rigidly square and laid out with fine, proper furnishings. His mother, dressed in a soft, silken gown of brown and blue, rose from the straight-backed chair in which she sat. He strode to her and after bowing, kissed her on the cheek. She was older, with the face of a woman who knew struggle. It was a kind countenance, though, with soft brown eyes and a small upturned nose. The pride she felt towards her son was almost palpable. He turned to the overweight gentleman bundled into silken hose, tight pants and a doublet which had the look of a small dam attempting to hold back the sea – its buttons had a Herculean task set for them. With the aid of a cane, Matthew rose to greet his son. He, too, felt nothing but pride and as always, made a ceremonial inspection of Roman in his fine Tudor uniform.

"My son! Mother, look – our boy as a queen's guard. What do you think?"

His mother clasped her hands together in joy before reaching out to touch her son's black curls. Roman had to smile despite his weariness with the daily ritual. He glanced about and his mother, sensing his every need, called sharply for tea and dinner. It appeared almost instantly, for while Roman's stealth was nearly great enough to get him past his parents' failing hearing, it was insufficient to allow him to go unnoticed by the servants. Besides, he arrived home at the same time each evening and cook always had a servant child watch for him so that dinner might be ready when called for.

The talk amongst the three of them turned to their daily lives, and Roman listened intently to his father's description of the trading events at the Exchange.

"And do you think the price of Shropshire will hold? For if Althorp does not produce enough . . ."

Matthew Collins caught the tone of fascinated interest in his son's voice and as always, changed the subject, much to the ire of Roman.

"Father, why must you do that? I am born of a woolsman, and I see nothing wrong with following in his footsteps!"

Matthew shook his head violently and waved his cane with feigned menace.

"No, no, boy, 'tis not for you. Did you get an education only to sell wool? Did I not pay handsomely for your small commission with the queen's guard? Eh? We shall work that circumstance, and in good time, God willing, you may marry a woman of noble birth. Your sister, after all . . ."

"Yes, yes." Now it was Roman's turn to change the subject.

"Did you hear of the uprising? 'Twas over before it began."

"Yes, we heard as did all of London. Those men risked all, and they shall pay the ultimate price," his father declared while his mother tsk-tsked.

"Oh, not just men," Roman said as he slathered butter on his bread and reached for another thick slice of ham. "There was a girl as well."

"A *girl!*" exclaimed his mother, her face mirroring her disapproval and surprise. "What on earth?"

Roman nodded.

"Indeed. She even tried to escape. In fact . . ."

He had almost forgotten the necklace Henrietta had so frantically given to him as she was dragged back down to her cell. He stuffed a bite in his mouth, stood, and began frisking himself. Finally, he pulled forth the necklace which had been surreptitiously entrusted to him by that remarkable girl.

"Roman, what is *this*?" His mother reached out tentatively, gently taking it from him. She turned it over and over in her hand, feeling its weight and rubbing her fingers against the large, inset rubies of the cross. "'Tis a most expensive piece of jewelry, son – and you say the prisoner gave it to you? The rebel girl?"

Roman gave a confirming nod, and as his mother passed the piece to Matthew, he told his tale.

"She claimed to know the queen, or at least, that the queen would recognize the necklace should I show it to her. She begged me to do so." He paused, thinking. "She seemed to think that the queen would intervene, I believe, and perhaps save her, should she be made aware of the necklace. 'Twas strange."

His father looked at him.

"What did you say to her?"

"I did not have any opportunity to answer, as she was taken away most abruptly."

The old couple exchanged a wary look. They were proud of Roman. Like his father, he was making the most of the few opportunities and resources available to him. With the education they had provided and the commission, he had found a place for himself in the queen's own guard, and, like all men who wore her livery, he had begun his career at the Tower, learning carefully the lessons taught by those who outranked him. Despite his relative newness to the corps of guards there, Roman had already moved several ranks above those who labored in the dungeon. He was not of the noble class, and could therefore never serve at court, but given his background and his heritage, the role of serving the queen in any capacity was a mark of ambition and ability. Yes, they were proud of him, and confident about his future.

But the tale he had just spun for them had ominous undertones. Who was this girl? Where did she get such a necklace? Was she simply attempting to buy time or favor by entrusting it to Roman with such a desperate plea? His father spoke first, and slowly.

"Roman, this has a bad feel to me. What do you make of it?" He passed the necklace back to his son.

"I do not know, father. I do not know."

His mother interrupted.

"Tell us what manner of girl this rebel is – how she looks, how she spoke and dressed."

It was Roman's turn to finger the ruby cross now. He studied it closely for the first time, and realized that his mother was correct – it was indeed a very expensive piece. As he examined it, he recalled Henrietta's face and demeanor.

"Roman?" his mother prompted him.

"She was bold, as a noblewoman might be," he began thoughtfully. "She had a manner which brooked no nonsense. She was . . . imperious. It was clear she was frightened, but equally clear that she was brave. And intelligent. I saw in her eyes that she was gentle, but through her actions that she was also courageous. I have worked at the Tower only a short time, but I have seen many men, both brave and cowardly, pass beneath its portals. Yet I have never seen one – not one! – attempt to escape. Yes, she is brave indeed."

His voice took on a slightly dreamy tone, and the look of alarm on his father's face was matched in full by the concern written across his mother's countenance. It was clear that Roman had some nascent feelings for this girl. A traitor! Their son – their beloved son whom they had raised so well was in dander of falling under the spell of a witch who would see the queen, nay, the entire kingdom,

overthrown! God in heaven! His mother wanted
desperately to cross herself and ward off whatever
evil might be spreading itself over their family like a
veil of foul and boggish air, but she was afraid
Roman might take notice and grow silent. So she
remained still so that he would continue on – better
to know one's enemies, she thought as her heart
beat faster.

"She was quite beautiful. No, no, I must change
that – I must say in truth, she was the *most* beautiful
woman I have ever seen. Her hair was long and
flaming red, like streaks of dawn on a sailor's
stormy horizon. Her eyes, father, they were not
blue, but yet not gray. They were the color of a
deep and cloudy ocean, one that could only be
penetrated . . ."

"Roman, are you describing a prisoner
condemned for treason or are you the woman you
would marry?" Matthew Collins stood and laughed
uncertainly. His mother wanted to kick him for
putting such a notion in their son's mind. Roman
laughed, but his mother noticed he did not answer
the question.

"'Tis the necklace we must worry about," he said
finally. "What should I do?"

His mother shuddered even as she spoke.

"You must do as the rebel girl asked, my son,
though I think no good will come of it. If you do

not, and she speaks the truth and does indeed know the queen, then much more harm might befall us all if it comes to light that you had ignored her plea. No, you must do as she has asked." She hesitated before standing. "But Roman, know this – no noble maid of good intent would ever have been arrested by the queen's men in the midst of a rebellion. I am not certain who this young woman is, but I have little doubt that she is not as she appears. Tread carefully, my son, for our fates may well depend upon it."

They bade him good evening and disappeared up the darkened stairs. For some long time Roman sat by the fire, fingering the necklace and remembering Henrietta even as he pondered his mother's warning. Yes, there was something strange here, and he must be extraordinarily careful. He knew full well that there was no safe harbor for him or for his parents – should the queen take displeasure with any one of their small family, all would suffer, and none would have recourse. And should a single wrong move be made, they would be lucky if they came out of such a situation with any future at all. Care must be his watchword, but also speed, for the rebel girl would surely be executed on the morrow with no fanfare and no one to hear her pleadings. He began pacing as he formulated a plan. An hour later, he put the fireguard in place and followed his parents up the stairs. The morning was not far off, and there was much to be done.

Chapter Four

The privy kitchen complex of Whitehall Palace was a world unto itself. The days of constant progresses on the part of the monarchy were almost gone, a faded remembrance of times past. Early in her reign, Elizabeth had followed the routine laid down by those who ruled before her, travelling from palace to palace on a constant spray of arcs which straddled the country north to south, east to west. The long rides through the countryside, boring at first, had become times when she could marshal her thoughts and develop her plans strategically. As they passed through hamlets and villages, the progress allowed her to be seen and just as importantly, to be gracious. England had great wealth and a growing merchant class, but such riches as might accrue to those in that situation had not filtered down to those who lived beyond the pale as tenants and independent farmers far removed from the cities where money and wealth were commonplace. These long treks became embedded in her way of life and thinking. And her court had appreciated the novelty that such travels bring as well. That she received adulation and acknowledgement from her subjects as she went forth, well, these had always been welcome. Some said such signs of loyalty inevitably renewed her spirit. And her vanity.

Gradually, however, over the course of her long reign, these progresses had become fewer. Her government had become larger, more cumbersome. No longer was it feasible for the monarch to move from palace to palace with courtiers and administrators in tow, even if such changes greatly benefited sanitary conditions and the problems of supply. Gradually, all branches of her government had become centralized and settled in London. Most were housed in or near Whitehall, while Parliament and its members met in Westminster. Along with the issues associated with her encroaching age, the progress had become an archaic way of life. Her subjects still flocked to see her, but such opportunities were more limited than in the past. Whitehall became her primary abode.

Long before dawn, the privy kitchen of that great wooden palace was abuzz with activity. Unlike the larger, main kitchen which served the court generally, Elizabeth's meals, and those of her close associates, were prepared in a smaller, separate facility. Put in place by Thomas Wolsey when Whitehall was still York Place, both the privy kitchen and quarters for its staff were built over the Thames to aid sanitation – its drains emptied directly into the river below. A gabled window looked out over the river and brought in light, while great hearths lined each wall. Like others in the queen's employ, the privy kitchen staff had begun their royal careers in the main kitchen, and only with years of training and considerable luck were they even considered for the queen's personal retinue.

Roman knew the main kitchen well, for as a Tower guard he routinely took his mid-day dinner there. Over time, he had noticed that on certain days, when a certain cook's maid served, his food portions were of a higher quality and more plentiful than those of his colleagues. His comrades had noticed as well, but their teasing meant nothing to him. The maid, on the other hand, did. Small in stature and quick-witted, her name was Alice. Again, as time progressed, their relationship had blossomed into a friendship, but never anything more for the simple reason that Alice was married. Recently, when her mentor had moved on and up to the privy kitchen, she had taken Alice along with her.

In the early morning fog, on the day following his discussion of the necklace with his parents, Roman presented himself at Holbein Gate and was waved through into the main courtyard of Whitehall Palace. As he strode with suppressed deliberation towards the entrance toward the privy kitchen, intent on seeing Alice, he was relieved to hear her call out to him from a nearby bench. Roman stopped short and gave her a kind smile.

"Ah, so the queen pays her cooks to sit idle under her fruit trees, does she? 'Tis quite the job you have there."

Alice grinned.

"What brings you this way, Sir Roman? That young maid you were eyeing two days ago? Hmm? She asked about you as well."

Roman shook his black curls and sat down beside her.

"No, something more serious, my friend."

Alice was fair, with blonde hair and barely visible brows. They became more evident as she narrowed her eyes and stared at him, waiting.

"I wish to add something to the queen's breakfast tray."

Alice jumped up.

"Do not say such scandalous, treasonous things young friend. Men have been hung for less! And with traitors still roaming about . . ."

"No, no. Sit down and I will tell you a strange story, Alice."

She listened intently as Roman once again told the tale of the ruby cross. At the key point in the narrative, he produced the necklace from his coat pocket. Checking to make certain they were not being observed, he passed it to her for examination and continued in a low voice.

"Alice, I believe this girl is telling the truth. I must, for there is no other reason or explanation for her tale."

Alice said nothing and stared at the cross.

"Alice, do you hear me woman? I must put this cross before the queen. If it be not hers, I am not certain what will happen to me, but you will not be blamed. I will claim that I slipped it onto the tray myself when you were not looking."

She looked at him with concerned blue eyes.

"Why not just give it to a guard to place before her? Or better, pass it to Cecil, her favorite toady – he will surely give it to her."

Roman shook his head vigorously.

"No, I cannot be certain. Look at the piece, Alice. It has great value. Anyone I might give it to would be sorely tempted simply to pocket it and deny its existence. And if they should do that, they will be condemning to death someone who I am almost certain has been mistakenly taken to the Tower."

"Mistakenly?" Alice gave a knowing chuckle. "No decent maid would have been swept up in the net thrown over such rabble as would do the queen harm, Roman. She would not have been there at all had she not had some purpose, some scheme, in which she was engaged."

Roman sighed.

"Will you help me, Alice? Please? 'Tis no harm to anyone. Just slip it onto her plate, perhaps beneath her fruit – does her Majesty eat fruit and bread for breakfast?"

"Why no, Roman, she eats cheese from the moon and nectar from Olympus."

He smiled weakly.

"What do you think the poor woman eats? Of course she has breakfast much as we all do."

She stood and dropped the necklace into the deep pocket of her apron.

"I shall do this for you, Roman, and if it ends well, you will remember my husband and me. If it ends badly, then I will pray for your soul. Now wait here, upon this bench."

She turned and walked towards the privy kitchen, uncertain purpose evident in her gait.

Despite the tension he felt in every fiber, Roman was tired – he had stayed awake late plotting his actions, and had only slept fitfully afterwards. His eyes grew heavy as the sun rose and warmed the bench, heavier yet when a ray of warmth fell directly upon him. He would close his eyes for a moment, but only a moment. Such respite would restore his energy for the coming day he was certain.

*****

The hands were rough upon him, the voices loud.

"This one? Is this the nit?"

"Yes, that is the one."

Was that Alice's voice? He was fully awake now, and tried in vain to brush the guards' hands from him. It was no use, and his feet barely touched the ground as they hauled him unceremoniously across the courtyard through a small, inner door. With two of the burly men in front of him and two in back, they shoved and pushed him up a narrow, spiral staircase. The irony of being handled in the same way as the rebel girl had been earlier, of being drug up a staircase similar to the one she had been forced to tread, was not wasted on him.

By the time they reached the summit of the stairs, Roman had given up all attempts to talk to the unresponsive men and now waited for fate to unfold his circumstance. Would he be deemed a traitor? Or perhaps a hero? A door opened and he was shoved through, only to be met by yet more guards. They closed crisply round him, forcing him to walk lockstep with them down a long, narrow gallery. On one side of the great hallway were floor length windows, looking out over a garden. On the other, great squares of wood paneling supported portraits of long deceased royalty. The guards stopped suddenly, and the two immediately in front of him stepped aside. All bowed, and Roman found himself staring at her Majesty, Queen Elizabeth. He found himself dropping to his knees under pressure from the guards' strong hands.

The queen said nothing. She had used the intervening time between her discovery and the present moment to complete her dress. The end result, as she well knew, was one of regal splendor and isolation. Great strands of pearls hung about her neck and reached to her waist. Stones set in gilded glory adorned her fingers. Atop her curled wig she wore a small yet elegant tiara, placed there for added emphasis of her royalty.

A menacing quiet settled over the scene. From the corner of his eye, Roman now realized that there were others in the room. They stood near her yet apart and neither moved nor spoke. He had never considered silence as an event before. The deafening thunder of the stillness frightened him. From years of experience, Elizabeth knew of this effect and played it to her advantage, using it as a weapon to inspire awe and obedience – just as did now. Like many before him, Roman realized instinctively that she who could command such silence was surely to be feared. He kept his gaze resolutely focused on the paneled floor. After a moment, despite his best efforts, he began to quake.

"Rise."

The soldiers around him rose. After a moment's hesitation, Roman stood as well.

"Majesty," he began but was immediately shouted down.

"SILENCE! You do not speak to her Majesty unless given permission to do so. Are you so ignorant and naïve that you do not know this?"

Roman looked steadily at the man who spoke thus. Was this the 'Cecil' Alice had spoken of? He was older, and wore clothing more suited to the clergy than to the administrative class. His robes were black and floor length, while a small hat sat uncomfortably on his balding head. Only a deep burgundy, velvet sash around his waist provided color. Otherwise, the man would hardly draw attention from anyone. As he finished his barking command for silence, Roman bowed his head and waited. Another deep silence ensued.

"Tell us where you found this." Elizabeth spoke quietly, and dangled the ruby cross on its golden chain from her hand.

Roman was tongue-tied and Elizabeth looked round and laughed. Her courtiers followed her lead.

"What? No answer? First you speak when not asked, and now, when asked, you speak not. Are you from a foreign land where this is custom?"

Roman cleared his throat and spoke with as much confidence as he could muster.

"Majesty, it was given me by a young maid with flaming red hair. She begged me to see that it might be put before you at the earliest possible moment."

Elizabeth leaned forward in her great throne, sudden concern written across her face. She turned to the older man in the black robes.

"Dismiss everyone."

With a nod from the minister, the crowd which stood about her dissipated almost into thin air. A rustle of silk, the patter of hurried steps, the gentle clang of swords, then nothing. The great long gallery seemed to oscillate to an unheard chord of silent import. He waited. Elizabeth beckoned him forward. As he neared the throne, the minister put forth his hand to indicate Roman should come no closer. Elizabeth raised a brow and waited.

"Majesty, I serve you at the Tower, as a humble guard."

"I see your livery, man."

Roman took heart at the stern words, for they were spoken with an overlay of kindness.

"Majesty, last evening, a maid was captured during the dastardly events led by that traitor Essex. Many rebels were rounded up all were brought to the Tower. She was among those put in my charge."

Elizabeth waved her hand in exasperation.

"Where is this woman now?"

"Majesty, she is in the dungeon of the Tower, awaiting execution with the other rebels."

Elizabeth rose in a panic and turned to Cecil.

"GET HER NOW! Do you understand me? This is absurd! Get her now and bring her here!!"

For the second time that morning, Cecil dispatched guards to do Elizabeth's bidding. It was Elizabeth who now shook with fear. She slumped back upon her throne. As Cecil shouted orders to the guards, the queen looked directly at Roman.

She still held the cross in her hand. She said nothing and Roman felt a hand on his elbow.

"Bow now before your sovereign, and go with yonder guard. We shall call you back anon."

Roman did as he was told and shortly found himself back in the courtyard where the drama had begun. So the rebel girl had told the truth. But who was she? Roman was no closer to that answer than he had been before his unsettling audience with the queen. Strange the effect his words had had on her majesty. Clearly, she knew the rebel girl well, well enough to be anxious about her safety. His own safety now came to mind, and he rubbed his finger idly over the dress jacket of his guard's uniform as his thoughts continued to puddle amidst the events of the past twenty-four hours.

Word of his command performance before Elizabeth had spread throughout Whitehall, and he began to notice a pattern in the activity around the courtyard. No one spoke to him and no one walked directly past him. Nevertheless, small knots of ladies' maids, of guards, of noblemen in courtly attire were multiplying in the corners of the carefully laid out space and spilling onto the geometric walkways which defined it. And each time Roman looked at one of these groups, he found everyone in the group staring back. But no sooner did he take notice than everyone in the group would quickly look away, developing a sudden intense interest in this shrub, that bird, those flowers.

Whispers like wind through pines rose up all about him, and it was impossible for him not to feel conspicuous and afraid.

Two hours passed thus. He dared not move from the bench, yet he desperately wanted to know the turn of events which, at this point, he was fairly certain would influence his life for better, or for worse. He turned and looked behind him. The huge outer gates through which he had been dragged earlier in the morning stood closed, guarded and forbidding. He turned back and began to slump, but just as he did so a faint shout arose through the very same heavy oaken gates. He stood and turned in time to see them thrown open and a cadre of guards rushing towards him. They grasped him by the elbows and the back of his uniform, holding him tightly. All around the courtyard a silence as deep and cold as Yule snow fell upon the scene. As if on cue, all eyes turned once again to the gates – the minister who had stood by Elizabeth's side during Roman's audience was approaching, and Roman felt more than heard a quick and anxious intake of breath on the part of everyone present. The man was powerful. His manner of dress, which Roman had noted earlier, served to set him apart from all others in the courtyard. This was no noble courtier, no scheming wretch sniffing for the first opportunity which might come his way – this was authority personified. His dark robes and simple dress emphasized the man's utter lack of concern with foppery such as silks and feathers and pantaloons. He oozed power, his clothing and manner merely reinforcing the obvious. He had no need for trivial attempts to show status through clothing and posture – he had it coursing through his veins.

With a nod to the guards who held him fast, he stepped up to Roman.

"Young guard, what is your name?"

Roman bowed his head before speaking.

"Roman Collins, sir."

"I am Cecil, Lord Burghley, and we shall talk."

He waved his hand at the guards and they stepped away, out of earshot.

"Tell me again your story."

Roman repeated everything he could remember about the previous day's events. He described the girl as carefully as he could, knowing that Cecil was listening intently.

Cecil nodded.

"And you say you left this rebel maid in the dungeon, in a cell?"

"I did not see her put in the cell, but yes, she was taken back down the stairs and the guard was told to put her there." Roman paused. "Why?"

Cecil looked at him, calculating his honesty, his worth.

"Because there is no such woman there now. Nor, according to the guards we spoke with, has there ever been."

Roman stood up, flustered.

"That is ridiculous! Of course she was there! Why on earth would I make up such a story? Where would I have got such a fine piece of jewelry as the ruby cross? Answer me that, sir!"

Cecil stood, frowning.

"I do not like your tone, but that is hardly the point. Our Majesty is enraged at the situation. You are remanded to the Tower dungeon yourself, and sir . . ." he paused, ". . . pray God nothing has happened to the woman you have described, for 'tis your head in the balance."

Roman shouted protests at him but to no avail. This time, sensing his fate, he fought to escape the rough hands that held him tight but it was no use. He, Roman Collins, was to be taken through Traitor's Gate, incarcerated with the very wretches he was paid to watch. Impossible . . . but undeniable.

The vendor's wharf at Whitehall stretched far out upon the Thames. It was a sloping affair, built so that regardless of the ebbing and waxing of the tides, Whitehall remained accessible. Like a gallows plank way, he was led down to its end, his hands tied securely. He was shuffled into a small vessel with four oarsmen. No words were spoken, and in silence the tie was slipped and the boat turned northward. Roman carefully appraised the men guarding him and discerned that there could be no escape. The distance to the dank, watery entrance to the Tower was not far and the oarsmen pulled in a steady beat with the river's flow. Like a hundred times before, Roman passed under the gate. This time, however, he was hauled physically like a brute from the bow of the vessel, shoved down the spiral stairs, and thrown into the very cell the rebel girl had occupied. His hands were un-roped, and he was left alone.

"Mother of God and all that is holy," he muttered under his breath, "Who is the wench who hath put me here?"

Chapter Five

The Previous Evening

Henrietta's knees hurt from kneeling on the cold damp stone. She had prayed thus for more than an hour and so far God had not seen fit to respond. Where was He, she wondered? She was a good person and did not deserve such a measure of ill-fate as had befallen her. Surely He would come for her as He had done for Peter in the Bible, sending an angel to open up the prison door. She crossed herself and offered an explanation heavenward for her hubris.

"I am by no means as good as Saint Peter, obviously Father, but 'tis the same situation, would you not agree? Not that I would ever *ever* speak in your presence were not the occasion so dire since you are so great and I am only a woman and . . ."

She paused and mentally upbraided herself to prevent the prayer from becoming a mere babbling idiot's verbal wanderings. She prayed yet more.

But still nothing. After one more intense session, she shuddered with the cold and rose to her feet, groping in the dark for the bench she had noticed before the day's light had faded.

'So I must go it alone," she spoke the words aloud, though very softly, and felt their gravity. The enormity of her situation suddenly broke through the wall of denials she had carefully built and nurtured during her time in the cell. She began to shiver and tears began to flow.

"No! You will not give in!" Again, she spoke the words aloud as though strength was to be found in hearing them. "Are you not smarter than the troll who guards your door? Did you not escape his clutches once already?"

She paused, stood, and sat again.

Of course! She had escaped once before – and she must do so again! Henrietta's spirits revived as she set herself to plotting. She could not afford failure this time. Every part of her escape must be carefully and willfully executed, and should any one step miscarry, a default would need to be embedded in her scheme to ensure success. Had she not often heard that such careful planning was always the key? She must apply every ounce of her mental apparatus to the problem. No angle or possibility could be left to chance!

A shuffling outside her prison door, accompanied by a muffled conversation, interrupted her thoughts. Henrietta moved closer to hear it.

"Oh, aye, she is still in there."

An ugly laugh.

"She denied me earlier, but I am wiser now. We shall have our moment, me and that wench. Indeed."

His companion chuckled.

"Enjoy yourself, my friend, and use her well, for I understand she goes with the other traitors on the morrow to the executioner's block."

"Do not fear. There is sufficient time before she goes. In fact, I shall see to my pleasure now."

She heard the sound of a single set of footsteps moving away as she crossed herself and felt for the bench. She whispered ever so quietly to herself.

"Of course, I have also heard that a careful and willful plan is not always the best – indeed, 'tis frequently . . ." she grunted as she moved the bench closer to the door and stood upon it . . ." "over-rated. Perhaps 'tis better after all to grasp one's opportunities . . ."

The key turned in the rusty lock. The door swung inward. Using the massive iron handle as a foothold, Henrietta braced herself against the corner of the wall and stepped agilely onto the top of the door. Her weight was miniscule compared to that of the old oak, and had no effect on its opening. The guard below swung his lantern around the empty cell.

"What sorcery is this? "

In his confusion, he entered further, just far enough to give Henrietta the chance she needed. In a wink she dropped down behind him and flung herself outside of the cell. Instantly she slammed the door behind her, immuring her startled captor. A low light from a burning oil rag lit the filthy corridor. She ran to its end as the guard bellowed in full throat, screaming for his mate. This time, however, she did not immediately charge up the spiral stairs. Instead, she flattened herself in a dark corner behind a pillar. As the guard's companion screamed down the stairs toward her cell, Henrietta now raced up the massive staircase. Once at the top, she frantically searched her memory for the direction to the Traitor's Gate. Down the footpath she ran, avoiding the torches which lit the interior court. As she reached the water's edge, she heard the shouts growing louder as the alarm was sounded. A prisoner had escaped. They would be onto her in a flash. There would be no third escape for her.

With no time for thought, intuition and experience drove her actions. She pulled her dress over her head, slipped off her shoes and bundled them all together. Her chemise was light and would not weigh her down. She thought of her childhood at Coudenoure, on the banks of the Thames, when swimming in one's chemise was absolutely forbidden and therefore highly exciting. The water was very cold now, but she could manage it for a distance – if only she could clear the tower block, she could find a corner in which to dry out and pull herself together. She waded in. The shouts grew louder. She took a deep breath, and sank quietly beneath the gentle waves of the tide. On and on she swam through the freezing water, growing numb with the cold until finally she felt the great stone supports of the gate. Keeping her hand on the slimy stonework just beneath the surface, she swam on for another distance until she was certain her rise would be in the deep shadows of the gate. Gasping for air, she listened to the growing chaos and marked the scattering lights above as the search for her was now in full swing. Another deep breath, another freezing stretch put her just beyond the Tower's exterior. She kept close to the shore now and low as she could in the water, skirting the bank of the Thames and gradually putting distance between herself and danger. On and on she swam until the clatter of voices could no longer be heard, until the lights were completely hidden by the massive tower walls. Yes, she should be able to leave the river now and find her way on land.

Like an eerie, charmed river goddess in a fabled story, Henrietta rose from the still and icy waters.

No one noticed the small figure which crossed the road abutting the Thames. No one noticed the shaking, shivering figure that clung to the shadows of the night. Pausing only to put her filthy wet shoes on her freezing feet, she ran into the night, seeking she knew not what. Without warning, as she rounded the corner of a large, timbered structure, a glowing light pulsed forth from its back pasturage. What was it? She was numb with cold and moved cautiously towards it. At twenty feet out, she realized it was a rubbish heap, and that the scullery maid or yard boy from the house was in the final stages of burning waste. A small figure, swaddled within a cloak, a stick in hand, confirmed her estimation of the situation. Yes. She circled to the far side of the fire and cautiously crept forward. The cloak shifted slightly, indicating Henrietta had been seen, but no movement, no rise, no shout to be gone accompanied the slight acknowledgement of her presence. She moved closer, warming herself before the dying fire, laying her clothes out to dry.

An hour later, with damp clothes on her back, she huddled before the fire, uncertain as to her next move. She should move on, find sanctuary near Whitehall Palace, and from there make an attempt to see Elizabeth. But the warmth! Even as the embers began to die, she clung to the light and heat for comfort as to a mother's tender embrace. Still, the figure across from her neither moved nor spoke. Henrietta felt her eyes growing heavy – how long since she had slept? How long since she had eaten? She did not know. But if she could sleep, then perhaps she would be better able to think things through and advance her cause. In the final analysis, though, it did not matter what Henrietta wanted or thought. With the dying fire to keep her warm, her eyes closed involuntarily.

"Only for a moment," was her last thought before she felt the guards' hands upon her. The sun was well up into the sky, the silent watcher across the fire, her night-time companion, gone. As they led her away, back to the Tower with its moldering limestone blocks, she now longed only to be thrown back into her tiny cell, away from the glares, sneers and ogling of her captors. She would be alone again then and could try and puzzle out yet another way to alert the queen of the danger to her person from that traitor – and to her own plight as well. But her luck had turned sour. As the cell door swung inwards, she screamed out.

"You!" Henrietta cried.

"You!" came Roman's outraged response.

"If you had done as I asked we would not be here! God's liver, why did you not do as I demanded?" Henrietta cried.

Roman rose from the bench, tilted his head by way of a bow, and looked her up and down before speaking in a droll voice.

"Ah, and 'tis a pleasant to see you again as well, Madam. After all, what man does not like a woman who smells like river garbage, looks like river garbage, and spews river garbage from her mouth? And of course, let us not forget . . . a woman who puts you in the Tower dungeon. Oh, yes, indeed! Pray, continue so that my ecstasy be not unbroken here in our charming abode."

Henrietta gasped. She had never been spoken to thus.

"Sir, sir . . ." she spluttered, ". . . how dare you . . ."

"Oh do be quiet," Roman continued. "I am attempting to formulate a plan for escape, but your twittering nonsense is a hindrance . . ."

"A *plan*?" came Henrietta's caustic reply. "Sir, I have escaped from this place twice! Obviously, you have need of my talent in that area!"

"I shall pass on your "talent" in the area of escaping, for you madam you have also been caught twice – clearly your plans are not what one might call . . ."

"*Oh do be quiet.*" Henrietta mimicked his words from before. "Do as you like. As for me, I shall plan my own escape and I shall not be caught again, sir. Of that you may be sure."

Roman sat back down.

"Hmm, yes, I am certain you saved your *best* plan for your final attempt. All prisoners squander their first opportunities for escape on lesser plans, saving their best for their *least likely* chance of success."

"Are you always so rude?"

"Do you always think yourself superior?"

There the conversation paused. After some reflection, Henrietta began to stare at Roman as if in expectation. After a moment, he looked up at her from the bench – and raised a questioning eyebrow.

"I am in need of the bench, sir."

Roman roared with laughter.

"God in heaven. You are a fine piece of womanhood, madam." He rose, bowed deeply, and retired to the far side of the cell. Almost without thinking, he pulled from his pocket a stale crust of bread wrapped round a piece of ham – he had never met with Alice but that she did not supply him with food. Cooks were that way. As he raised it to his lips, he looked across at Henrietta. Her eyes never left the small morsel and he suddenly realized that she had likely not eaten since first incarcerated. Feeling a small twinge of shame, he reached over and offered Henrietta the stale tidbit. She downed it almost in a single bite. Leaning back against the wall, she burped loudly. Roman could not repress a satisfied laugh.

"Alright," she said waving her hand tiredly, "I am too fatigued and worried to fight with you."

"A truce, then?" Roman asked looking down at her. Despite her bedraggled appearance and their frightening situation, he felt his pulse quicken.

"A truce." Henrietta slid over to one end of the bench and patted the empty space beside her. "Sit, and let us consider what manner of trouble we face."

But no sooner had Henrietta spoken these words than a loud clanging was heard at the cell door. Once again, she heard the rusty key turning the ancient lock. She rose and instinctively stood close to Roman. An older guard, unknown to her but clearly familiar to Roman, entered slowly.

"Roman, my son."

"Clarence, my friend, thank God you are here. What is going on? Our Majesty will want to know that this young girl is safe – you must tell her!"

Before the elderly guard could answer, the burly man from the evening before shoved him aside and stepped into the cell. A small phalanx of soldiers filed in behind him.

"No, I think not," he said with a gleeful air, "For 'tis time to meet your maker."

Henrietta moved closer to Roman.

"You are mistaken, you oaf!" Roman's voice rose authoritatively. "I demand to see the captain!"

"Nay, the captain has no desire to see you. Or her." He gave a sharp look at Henrietta. "You see, Master Collins, the two of you have made him look foolish. Very foolish. This wench escaped and you apparently lied to Her Majesty the Queen herself! Mother in Heaven! Did you think the captain would not wear such shame hard? A rebel, escaped from his own prison, and a treasonous guard?"

Roman's eyes narrowed.

"Why are you here?"

"To escort you to the scaffold. The rebel girl's accomplices were taken care of this morning, and the captain wishes to finish the job before lunch."

"I demand a trial." Henrietta spoke with as much calm as her shaking body could muster. "I am entitled to one."

"Perhaps," came the gruff, sly reply. "But you will not receive one. We will make use of a scaffold inside the Tower, one hidden from the public, for our . . . special cases."

At his words, Henrietta felt her blood run cold. She clung tightly to Roman. But resistance was futile and escape impossible. Without further delay, the two were marched from their cell and up the spiral staircase one last time, towards their inevitable death.

Chapter Six

Those who knew the estate of Coudenoure seemed
never to forget it. Was it the charming symmetry of
the manor house itself which drew them back to it
time and again? Composed of two equal wings
astride a grand, central nave, its very simplicity
evoked a complex feeling of serene beauty, one at
peace with the natural world around it. Unlike
nearby Greenwich Palace or Whitehall in London or
even countless other countryside manors
throughout England, there was no sense of organic
growth to Coudenoure. It had never suffered the
vagaries of competing architectural styles preferred
by competing generations of owners. No one had
thought, or dared, to put his preferred stamp upon
the place. Rather, the estate was a law unto itself
and seemed to have arrived on the landscape fully
formed, as though set there by heaven one fine
afternoon and then forgotten. The giant limestone
blocks of which the manor house was made had
aged over the centuries to a soft, mellow hue, and its
diamond-paned windows, unusually and
unfashionably large, added a sense of warmth to
what might otherwise have been a cold and forlorn

remnant of an earlier age. So perhaps it was the manor house itself, after all, that settled in the heart and kept Coudenoure safe and warm in memory's embrace.

Then again, perhaps it was the sheer genius on display throughout the grounds. It seemed no element of thoughtful design had been overlooked in its layout. While many estates could boast of a measure of planning, with glass-house conservatories and outbuildings corralled into an organized and pleasing whole tucked just behind the main house, Coudenoure was unique. Near the manor house itself, precise, geometric gardens defined the grounds in a perhaps predictable way. But like ripples on a pond, those manmade gardens gave way to more complex forms of beauty in which nature held sway, not man. The grand yard of Coudenoure, which stretched from its doors to its perimeter wall, had long since been turned into a meadow. And like essence distilled, the meadow reflected an organized scheme. This was not evident in a first glance, or even a second. But as the seasons unfolded, the beauty inherent in each was reflected the meadow itself, and more intensely too than nature herself decreed. Whoever designed it had possessed a great understanding of place and of time. The crisp new colors of spring – fritillary and daffodils, peonies and roses, grasses and leaves – slowly gave way to the mature, vibrant colors of summer which in time let autumn have its raging, glorious browns, ambers, and reds until finally, the peace of winter enveloped all, and nothing but silent white beauty could be seen. So was it the grounds surrounding the manor house that tended to lodge so securely in one's heart?

Perhaps. But there was yet one further element of Coudenoure which made it so distinctive, and it was likely this from quality that the entire estate drew its irresistible charm, namely, the spirit of raw, independent, individualism it seemed to breath forth on every hand. It was evident in the meadow as front lawn with its skillful manipulation of nature, in the skeletal ruins of the grand chapel which had once graced Coudenoure's eastern portion and which had been left standing for beauty's sake alone, in its uncommonly large windows which bathed the main house's interior in light even on the darkest of winter days. It was as though Coudenoure's guiding principal was independent appreciation, creation and reverence for beauty, for nature, for organization as seen through the eyes of each and every creature who made its acquaintance. A sense of intelligent whimsy permeated its being.

Coudenoure had managed to escape the fashionable and the quick for two primary reasons: it was a small estate and for all its proximity to the seats of power was utterly lacking in ease of access. The far side of the manor abutted the main road to London from Greenwich Palace. A thick copse hid its fields from view, however, and there was no direct entry onto the grounds via that well-travelled artery. The arrangement was not intentional, but sprang from Coudenoure's original purpose – it had served for centuries as a monastery and was meant to be reached primarily by water, the Thames flowing along its southern boundary. The only overland means of approach was a small, unimproved road still employed by those from the nearby village, one which had doubtless begun life as a cow trail, had been upgraded to a road during the Roman occupation, and had then fallen into disuse in the many centuries following, slowly forgotten by all but the locals.

A forgotten jewel. A home for those who sought life away from the temporary and the profane. That was Coudenoure.

*****

Bess paced frantically before the great medieval hearth of Coudenoure's library. She had not slept, nor had she eaten. Where were they? What had happened?

Henrietta and Anne had left the previous evening. Anne was to ride to Greenwich Palace to warn the queen's supporters of Essex' uprising. His men had passed by Coudenoure on the Thames and been spied by the children of the estate as they played their games of pirates and princes.

Regardless of season, they insisted on pitching camp upon the high ridge which separated Coudenoure from the woods of Greenwich Palace. The old signal house, a remnant of the fire watch set at the time of the Spanish Armada, anchored their play.

Henrietta, in turn, had left for Whitehall to tell the queen directly of the danger she was in. Neither had returned, however, nor had she and Quinn heard any news about the rebellion or the safety of Elizabeth. In determined haste, Quinn had left for London. Anne was a poor horsewoman, but the journey to Greenwich Palace was short. Henrietta was the true worry. She was headstrong, determined, and like all youth, had precious little sense of her own mortality. The thought of what she might risk to achieve her ends made Bess and Quinn shudder. And so Quinn had ridden out in turn.

Dawn flowed sluggishly over a gray horizon, but as usual, the children of Coudenoure did not care. Indeed, such a swirling fog lent an air of sinister mystery to their pirate games. Prior to taking the ridge, they had conquered and pillaged the kitchen, making off with the slabs of bread, beef and cheese that Cook had thoughtfully left for them near the outer door. The long trek up the ridge was cold, and by the time they made the top dawn was giving way to a brighter, though frigid, winter's day. They set about their pre-assigned duties – scanning the Thames for signs of invasion, Coudenoure for signs of treachery, and the great field betwixt the ridge and Greenwich Wood for traitorous interlopers. Young Marshall, Cook's nephew who was recently apprenticed to the stableman, was the lookout over the field, and as every boy settled down to his business, Marshall spoke hesitantly. He was tiny even for his age, and only last month had the big boys allowed him to join in their games.

"Oye, I see trouble by the Wood," he declared uncertainly in his childish singsong voice. The others ignored him.

"I said I see *trouble*," came his insistent reply to their silence.

"If you do not stop, we will not allow you to play no more. The rule is you must wait until the signal that means *I* have spotted trouble. You do not get to spot it – that is *my* job because *I* am the leader. Me . . . William."

Marshall watched the older boy hesitantly. He was a full head taller and four years older than Marshall. He turned and looked again at what he had stated was trouble, then drew himself up as he spoke in the face of his own throbbing fear.

"I say, leader, I see *trouble*. By the Wood stands a horse with no rider, and beside the beast is a fallen figure."

That was all it took. The entire corps rushed to Marshall's side. Sure enough, on the far side of the meadow, very near the Wood, was the scene he had just described. But as they took it in, they also realized that such an event was not part of their game – it was very real.

"What do you think, eh?" A voice piped up from the back of the group. "'Tis not what we had planned – I thought trouble was to be spotted near the hedge at Coudenoure so we could all go get warm for a bit."

"Um," William said with growing concern, "You are right. But I believe that is the Lady Anne, for she has a red cloak and yon figure is covered in one."

Silence. Growing fear and concern. Suddenly, Marshall spoke.

"We cannot hesitate, for she is clearly hurt – she has not moved since I spotted her. I am going to her." He was surprised at his own bravery and decisiveness. The others heard his tone and fell into line behind him.

"I shall go tell Cook," said one.

William spoke up next.

"Marshall and I shall go and wait by the body for help from Coudenoure. You there, Janis, go quickly and tell the stableman, for we shall need a wagon.

You others, go and alert Cook. Quickly, now, for Lady Anne is in danger."

They scattered down the hill, running pell-mell on their various missions.

*****

"'Tis Lady Anne, alright, and I believe she is dead." William's voice was somber but clearly satisfied with the evolving drama. "She has not moved."

They had run breathlessly across the field. Upon seeing them the horse had trotted silently past them back towards Coudenoure as though his job were now done and he must needs see to his own breakfast of oats and hay.

"Yes, she is dead, poor woman." William continued in the same vein.

Marshall bent and clutched Anne's cold hand in both his own.

"Perhaps not. We must warm her, William."

"No, no, for she is dead."

"Do I *sound* dead?"

"BBBLLLaaaaaaaaggggghhhhh!!!" Both boys uttered a terrified shriek and rushed backwards, falling over themselves.

"She has risen from the dead!" screeched William. "She has come back to get us!"

"WWWaaaagggghhhh!!" Another primeval scream arose from the pair, but as they turned to run the not-so-dead voice spoke again.

"You there! Are you William, the smithy's boy?"

They turned, trembling like aspen. Anne's eyes were open now and the boys hesitantly approached her.

"You must help me up, for I cannot move my left arm, nor my right leg. I fear they are dreadful broken. Give me your cloaks for warmth."

They stood staring at the pale figure stretched out upon the frozen ground.

"Did you not hear me? *MOVE*, I say!"

They sat with her betwixt them, sharing their cloaks and body warmth with her. No more than five minutes passed before a rumble of wheels and shouting were heard on the Coudenoure side of the field.

"'Tis help come, my lady," said Marshall. "They shall get you home."

"What is your name, little one?"

"Marshall."

"Run ahead, Marshall, and let my mother Bess know that I am alive. Tell her how you found me and tell her to fetch a doctor."

Marshall was up and running before she could say anything else. He flew by the approaching wagon and ignored the cries for information from the adults who accompanied it. On and on he ran until finally he turned upon the long straight drive of the manor house. At its end, he saw Bess, mistress of Coudenoure, and Cook standing there and looking frantically towards the ridge. He was breathless by the time they grabbed him and helped him into the warm hall beyond. Quickly, and with a nervy calm seldom seen in one so young, he told his story. Cook said nothing but ran towards the kitchen barking orders. Bess too began commanding those who stood in the shadows waiting to help. She led Marshall into the library.

"My daughter is fine, she is fine." The words became a reassuring mantra for Bess. Two young boys built the fire higher until the blaze warmed even the farthest corners of the room. Bess continuously tucked blankets around Marshall as he sat in a chair three times too big for him. He found her fussing annoying and finally reached his skinny, tiny legs to the floor and stood, bowing as he did so.

"Madam Bess, I am not Lady Anne and so tucking me about will not help, if you do not mind."

Bess paused, looked at the child, and laughed.

"I did not even realize I was doing it," she said apologetically.

Marshall smoothed his worn and dirty clothes in an indignant manner. "Well, you *were*."

There was no time for more, for the crush of wheels upon gravel was heard. They were home.

Chapter Seven

She had had to leave Anne's side and take refuge in the kitchen, for she could not bear to hear her daughter's screams as the physician and his surgeons set her bones. The screams were intermittent, however – they were mixed with fainting spells which occurred when the torture became unbearable for the patient. Finally, they stopped altogether, and the doctor appeared in the kitchen where Bess and Cook were sobbing in each other's arms. They looked askance at him as he entered.

"The breaks will heal, for she is strong. But she is not young, Bess, and it will be some time before she can walk once more. Cook, take her some heavily laced broth, for she must sleep now. I will stay for some time to make certain she is tended correctly."

Anne took the broth almost cheerfully, even winking at her mother as she did so.

"I shall survive, mother, do not worry." She drank more. Cook had done a thorough job with the broth and alcohol and a great drowsiness soon settled upon the patient.

"Mother," she whispered before giving in to sleep, "You must see to Henrietta. She has no brains." Anne closed her eyes.

Bess smiled worriedly, knowing full well what Anne had meant. Henrietta had far too *much* intelligence for a young girl, but never let it rule her impulsive nature. They had not heard from her since her wild ride out the night before. She must be in trouble and needed her mother's help no doubt. And Quinn? Bess hurried from the room. Her husband was likely wherever Henrietta was and God knows the man would require her aid as well.

"Madam, I go with you."

"What?" Bess swirled the skirt of her gown around and found Marshall standing patiently behind her.

"You cannot ride alone. I go with you."

"But what can you do?" She wanted to laugh at the absurdity of the statement from the tiny boy but Marshall's gravity would not allow it. He ignored her question, grabbed her hand and tugged her from the room.

"Hurry. We must saddle and be off." Here he hesitated. "And bring coin, for we may have need of it."

*****

The streets of London were eerily quiet. Word of Essex' failed rebellion had spread even quicker than that of its inception. There was no need for the curfews set by Cecil and the queen's Privy Council, for no one desired to be caught abroad and questioned. Even the innocent might lose their heads under the circumstances, for the crown would brook no uncertainty in such uncertain times. Bess rode with Marshall beside her on a much smaller horse. As they cleared the diminutive and isolated hamlets which betokened coming into London proper, the child had known the way. He sometimes hesitated when streets became avenues or when intersections became webbed with myriad spokes, but always, he seemed finally to recognize whatever sign he looked for and led them on ever deeper into the city. At length, they came to an alley, dark even in the early morning sun as the buildings on either side of it were so close that one might almost touch them simultaneously. Marshall veered into the darkness and jumped from his mount while handing the reins up to Bess.

"Please, Madam, you must wait here. I have friends just over the road, and they will help me with information."

"You have friends? Over the road? Child, how old are you?"

Marshall tilted his head so that their eyes met.

"Ten," came the proud answer.

"How come you to know so much about London, or even have friends here?"

A calculated look appeared on the child's face.

"Madame, before I came to Coudenoure last year, I lived in London. I know these streets."

"Your parents allowed you to roam at will?" Bess harrumphed indignantly despite their situation.

Marshall smiled and disappeared. He had no wish to tell her that he had no parents, that Cook was not his auntie. Nor did he wish to divulge that Cook had taken him in after he had saved her brother from a rather inglorious affair at the end of a hangman's noose.

He pulled his cap low over his forehead and skulked quickly along the street they had just left. The London air, a mix of filth, fog, sweat and grub, filled his lungs and he unconsciously breathed deeply – it felt like home. Three streets and two sharp turns later, he entered a ratty storefront which advertised nothing and had only a small window onto the outside. A very young boy behind the counter saw him and squealed.

"Marshall! And where have you been?" He hugged him tightly despite the unmanliness of such an action. Marshall patted his arm and grinned.

"That can come later, Rouster, right now I am in a bit of a pickle."

Rouster's eyebrows shot up in happy anticipation. Marshall continued in a whisper.

"You heard about this uprising, did you?"

"Oh indeed," Rouster replied eagerly, "But they nabbed the traitor quick like. Over in front of Ben's place they did."

Marshall nodded.

"I am looking for a young girl and maybe an old man that were involved."

Rouster looked at Marshall with fear and concern.

"No, no, my friend, 'tis not what you think. They are innocent and had come to warn the queen. They may have been caught up in the roil."

Rouster shook his head slowly.

"Aye, Marshall, I know of this, for Ben saw a young maid being rowed down the Thames with the other traitors on yesterday."

"Where did they go?"

"To the Tower of course. I hear they will be executed within its walls today, for the Queen does not take kindly to traitors – and this man Essex was a friend of hers – can you imagine that, Marshall?"

"I must save that girl, and I will need your help. Can we do this?"

Rouster bowed deeply to his friend.

"I am here for you, as you have been for me. Why, I have a roof over my head now thanks to your . . ."

Marshall cut him off.

"No time. We must go."

Rouster pulled a key from a wall and they went quickly to the door. He turned and looked back only once. Once outside he locked the door behind them and placed the key beneath a rock on the windowsill. He would have no need of it now, for when they discovered he had left his post behind the counter, he would be turned out.

The two boys raced back to Bess. Marshall pulled his friend up behind him in the saddle of his horse and without a word the three of them rode out of the darkness. Five minutes later, they were outside the vendor gate of the Tower. Rouster slid from the saddle and tethered the reins to a nearby hitch while Bess and Marshall stood close behind. On silent cue, young man sauntered from the shadows and engaged the guard in casual conversation. Bess and Marshall strolled down the road in the opposite direction before crossing over and walking towards the pair. The guard was looking at something in Rouster's hand, something which clinked and tinkled pleasantly. The man tried to snatch it from the child's hand, but Rouster had made his living for years from situations like this – his reaction was a swift retreat. Threats could be heard. Rouster continued to clink and rub the coins together like a pleasant siren's song, carefully staying clear of the grasping hands until the bargain was made. After a moment, Bess and Marshall saw him shrug and turn back to the gate, passing the coins in his hand to the guard as he did so. A signal passed between the two boys and Marshall stepped up. The guard looked at them all with a nasty grin.

"But you will not get far, for this is the Tower, you understand?"

Bess' head wobbled in what she hoped would be taken as a confidant toss of her hair. Saints preserve us, she thought. She was trusting her fate and those of her husband and her granddaughter to the plan of two street urchins. She shuddered. The gate was unlocked, Rouster provided the guard with the other half of the agreed upon sum, and the three of them passed within. As soon as the gate was closed, Rouster took charge.

"We must hurry, for he tells me that the executions have been going on all morning, but that he knew the girl was to be saved for last. Hurry!"

They slipped along the shadowy walls, sometimes crawling behind hedges, sometimes running quickly through doors left unguarded because no one would ever dare penetrate so deeply into the Tower. At last, they passed under an ancient, arched portal and a small, interior courtyard was revealed. A handful of guards, servants, and ladies watched in horror as a head rolled from the elevated platform which took center stage. No one saw the threesome enter. No one heard Bess' sharp breath as she watched two figures make their way towards the scaffold. They were heavily guarded but as they reached the rickety, makeshift stairs which would lead them to their fates, the guards stepped away, revealing their prisoners.

They stood as one. From nowhere, a strong cold blast of air blew across the scene. Henrietta's flaming locks, now loose and hopelessly astray, blew across her alabaster face. Her gown, filthy and flimsy, pressed against her in the gust and revealed in every detail her girlish yet womanly form, and every eye in the courtyard took her in. But rather than shrinking into herself, hiding from the shame and blasphemy of her situation, she stared back defiantly. She locked her steady gray eyes upon those who would judge her, forcing them to look away in embarrassed confusion and guilt. One by one, she took them on.

Roman stood ramrod-straight as though at guard for Elizabeth herself. They would not break him. His livery, Tudor red and proud, still shouted his profession, screamed above the silent sneers of the crowd that here was a man who had served majesty itself, a man who would not be bowed by circumstance or the immoral acts of others. He ran his fingers through his dark and tangled lock, bringing a small semblance of respectability to their wayward swirls. He tugged sharply on the bottom of his coat, straightening its brass buttons until they formed a single bright line in the play in which he found himself.

He turned to his companion, the young girl who had started him on the bleak journey which had now brought them both to this moment. She faced him with shaking confidence, looking into his icy blue eyes with a trust and faith he had never seen. A faint smile played across her lips. As he looked down upon her innocent face, he knew an instant of happiness, for here was his woman. He knew not how it had come to pass, and he knew they would have no life together now, but in that moment she was his and he, hers. They were lost in one another's eyes, oblivious to the swordsman atop the scaffolding who called out his readiness to the guards.

"What the hell." Roman spoke the words low and slow as he stared at Henrietta and bent towards her.

"What the hell." Came her response.

He took her face in his hands and kissed her lips. She placed her freezing hands on his head, feeling his curls and his warmth, pulling him closer. His arms wrapped round her waist and their kiss became electric. Those who had come for the thrill and entertainment of an execution found themselves engulfed in the fire of a tragic love. The wind blew hard and brought an echo of youth and passion to each of those who watched. Even the guards stood in awe of the power which flowed out from the helpless figures of the doomed lovers.

Roman pulled his lips away, whispering in Henrietta's ear. She looked at him and nodded. Together, hand in hand, they mounted the scaffold.

Chapter Eight

Quinn opened his eyes and winced. Where was he? The ground beneath him was cold, hardened with the first frost of the season, and yet he himself was warm. With a groan, he sat up and looked about. A small fire, barely enough to light the immediate area, burned bravely against the night – it was this sliver of warmth which had kept him from freezing.

"Old man, you must be careful." The voice came from the shadows. A young street boy, no more than seven or eight Quinn judged, moved towards him, a small cup in his hand.

"Drink this."

Quinn did as he was told. It was little more than boiled water with a bit of broth, but it revived him, and he began to come to his senses. The boy sat beside him and they shared the cup.

"Where am I?" Quinn asked, looking around.

"You are in my place," he said with simple pride.

Quinn looked about. The child's *place* was nothing more than a niche created by an oversized pillar which supported a small bridge across a narrow rill of water. Thick scrub surrounded the area, creating a sanctuary against the outer world. The boy let him take it in before continuing.

"You were trying to rescue some maid and you were spectacularly unsuccessful."

A wry smile played across Quinn's wrinkled countenance. He remembered now what had happened. Seeing Henrietta, calling out to her, trying to save her, then . . . darkness.

"Yes, I remember now, and you are correct." Quinn ran his fingers lightly over the back of his head, examining the enormous knot which had now made itself at home there. After a moment, he turned to the boy.

"Who are you?"

"Ben."

"Ben, what is your full name?"

The child smiled.

"Ben." He let it sink in. "I saw you were a gentleman and it is my opinion that such men as you might be thankful to men like me when you are rescued from a scrape – a scrape you were definitely losing. And you might share a coin or two with me to indicate your thankfulness. So I saved you."

"You saved me for money? Not for morality and justice?"

"No, I cannot say that I did," the boy adopted a slow drawl. "For morality – 'tis a luxury when one is starving on the streets. Would you not agree? As to how I saved you, well, I pulled you away from the guards and the traitors, I did. I slapped you, made you open your eyes, and I fairly carried you to this place, my home. 'Tis getting on for dawn now. I was beginning to wonder if you would pass on or tarry here longer yet."

Quinn looked the lad over. His clothes were filthy and ragged. He was not certain the child had ever bathed. But his language – it had a peculiar, lyrical quality to it. He said as much.

"Oh, I see. You are one of those that believe men in my situation can have no poetry in their bones?"

"No," Quinn rubbed the back of his head as he spoke, "that is not the case. But you a boy of the streets – where would you have learned such craft? You do not even read."

It was the urchin's turn to give a wry smile. He disappeared into the shadow only to return with a package bundled carefully in dark wool, tied with a hefty strap of rope. He sat it in front of Quinn and nodded.

"Go ahead, old man. Open it."

Quinn carefully untied the double knot and wool which protected whatever lay within. Clearly, it meant a great deal to the child, for while his own clothes would barely warm a person on a summer's day, he had used wool not to insulate himself but to protect his package. Quinn carefully removed the woolen cover. After a moment, he picked up the one on top.

"'Tis a fine book you have here."

The boy said nothing.

"*The Discovery of Guiana*".

The package held two more books and as Quinn pulled them forth he read the titles aloud.

"*Historia Animalium* and *Divine Comedy*."

Still silence.

"You have good taste, young man. Where did you get these?"

"I bought them fair and right, old man."

Quinn snorted. "If you would not mind, my name is Quinn."

"I learned to read at the workhouse for young men, St. John's as it is known. One of the older boys taught me. Marshall. He was a fine friend to me."

Quinn looked at the youth. A sense of yearning had crept into his voice.

"What happened to your friend Marshall?"

The urchin looked at him like a sage upon a novitiate.

"What happens to all of us street boys, eh? We do our best, and some of us get lucky and some of us, well, when we can take the workhouse no more, we move to places like my place here. Marshall, I know he must have moved from London, for he would not abandon me. No, he would not. I am certain when he is settled he will come for me. Just the other day, I saw Rouster, and he said the same."

A small sigh escaped the child's lips, and he held his hands nearer the fire. Quinn studied him carefully. He wondered what kind of life might have informed such a philosophy. And someone who loved books so much that he spent all he had on them, even in the face of extreme privation! He felt suddenly lightheaded.

"What were you doing with the rebels, old man," the boy seemed to prefer his original name for Quinn, "And who was the maid?"

Quinn closed his eyes as he spoke.

"She is my granddaughter. She had come to London from Coudenoure to warn the queen of the uprising."

"I do not know this name, Coudenoure. Where is it?"

"That is not important."

Silence.

"Tell me, where did they take Henrietta, my granddaughter – do you know?"

"To the Tower."

Quinn drained the cup and stood uncertainly. He looked down at the child who had saved him, who read philosophy and poetry and spoke like a man. He sent a prayer heavenward that he was indeed just that, at least on this day.

"If my granddaughter is to be saved, you must go to Whitehall," Quinn commanded. "Do not ask for the queen. You are to seek out a certain man, one Robert Cecil, Lord Burghley, and tell him our tale, making certain to tell him where Henrietta is."

The child stood and pulled his ragged cloak about his thin shoulders.

"Now," Quinn began, "I shall tell you how to reach Cecil . . ."

He was waved into silence.

"I am a man of the London streets, old man. Do not attempt to school me in such things, nor should you think you know best to whom I should reach out. 'Tis impertinent on your part. Not to mention foolish."

Quinn smiled. The boy's confidence was infectious.

"And you must tell me how to get to the Tower."

A long discussion ensued complete with finger tracings on the outer cover of the top book. Finally, the boy fell quiet. Quinn tousled his hair and smiled at him.

"I had a boy once like you." He caught himself before his voice broke. "Let us hope we meet again."

The child quickly bundled and retied his precious books, placing them once more into their secret abode against the pillar. The sun was fully up now as they stepped out together into the street. With a mutual nod, they took their leave.

*****

Elizabeth was unhappy, and so those surrounding her were unhappy. Regardless of the room she was in – the Great Public Hall, her private library, the Long Gallery – she paced fretfully. The uprising of the previous day seemed a distant memory, one replaced by a more urgent and deeply emotional event.

Henrietta had been captured and thrown in the Tower, and yet, impossibly, she was not there. Those new to the queen's court wondered about the strong reaction to such a trivial matter. They gossiped in the murky background as the aged queen shouted and hurled insults at those whose job it was to get her what she wanted. They could not produce Henrietta, and so they suffered. But who was this child that meant so much to the queen? Neither Elizabeth nor Cecil, her shadow, offered any explanation.

"Majesty, you must let this go. The men of the Tower have their orders to bring the girl here. In the interim, you must ride about and be seen. Do not think that there are not others who would take up Essex' evil scheme and run with it? Your people must see you." Cecil's voice was politely adamant.

"Where could she be?" was the fussy imperious reply.

"I insist, Majesty." Cecil knew he was plying uncertain waters and so accompanied the words with a deep, obsequious bow. His words seemed finally to reach the queen. She rose and indicated she would like her mount. A worried look crossed Cecil's face.

"Majesty, your carriage is safer, and for a queen your age . . ."

The look he received in response lowered temperatures across all of London. Cecil bowed again, even deeper this time, and a commotion arose as it was announced that the queen would ride about the streets to assure her subjects of her safety.

Whitehall lay upon the banks of the Thames with only a wide avenue separating it from the muddy waters. While there were other, grander doors and gates, Elizabeth preferred to exit the grand building onto the Thames Road. The wharves and docks which floated all along the opposite quay were always busy, full of people and transport, goods and gossip. There was no quicker way for her egress to be announced and told abroad than by those on the water as well as on the street. She exited now, robed in regal purple and ermine. Her stiff, gossamer ruff rose behind her head, creating a tableau of her pearl and ruby laced hair and face. Onlookers were kept far from her, for the uprising was still fresh and possibly still potent. Only her own guard was allowed near her. Trumpets sounded, guards lined the way, and she slowly paraded towards her horse. From nowhere, she felt a hard, sharp tug on her outermost cloak. But even as she turned to see what might be causing such an annoyance, her guards raced forward with grabbing motions.

"Catch him! Seize him!" A scuffle ensued. Elizabeth could not see the perpetrator, surrounded as he was by a dozen guards. She was preparing to move on, to forget the moment, when a shrill, childish cry pierced the air.

"Hennnrrriiiiieetttaaaa!! Henrietttaaaaa!!"

The man-child had succeeded.

*****

Quinn kept his face in the shadow of his cloak. The child had been right, and the guard at the small outer door was only too happy to supplement his income. He expressed no interest in Quinn's business, only warning him that once inside the walled fortress, there was no easy exit, for this was the Tower. As Quinn nodded his understanding, the man pocketed the proffered money and unlocked the door. Wait.

What was that? He turned his head quickly, looking across the narrow, cobbled way. Something

familiar had caught his peripheral vision and
lodged momentarily in his mind – but what was it?
He scanned the far side of the road. A child with its
mother, both heavily robed and veiled against the
sharp winter air, were strolling slowly past. A
market basket hung from the woman's arm, and she
clutched the child's hand firmly in her own. They
moved slowly, almost deliberately. He scrutinized
the pair closely, but there was nothing familiar
about them, nor was there anyone else in that area.
Quinn then shifted his gaze to the street which
stretched out behind the guard – an urchin was
ambling towards them but Quinn saw nothing
untoward or familiar in the child's movements. He
did wonder, momentarily, what such a small child
might be about on such a cold morning, but even as
his thoughts turned towards the great epidemic that
was London's homeless and unloved population of
street urchins, he quickly pulled them back. The
pair across the street continued on their way. No,
he did not know what had caused the sudden sense
of familiarity. Perhaps it was only the recent
damage to his head. Pulling his hood closer, he
entered the gate. A clanging, turning sound behind
him told him there was now no going back. His
heart was racing as he blindly followed the
instructions given him by the man-child. Sure
enough, ten minutes later, he found himself in an
interior courtyard where a temporary scaffolding
had been raised. A crowd of several hundreds or
more stood about, relishing the horror provided by
a good morning's worth of proper executions.
Traitors deserved such fates and each time the blood

ran and a head rolled, the same shocked, satisfied gasp swept across the otherwise silent albeit well-dressed mob. The executioner had just finished and his assistants were preparing for whomever might come next. Quinn quickly assessed the area.

The only entrance into the courtyard was through the arch under which he had just passed. Each side of the quadrangle was composed of ancient stonework reaching on high, seemingly unto heaven. If he were to be successful in rescuing Henrietta, they would then have to escape through the arch under which he had just passed. Beyond that, he had no plan. The raised platform of the scaffold was situated not in the middle of the courtyard, but almost against one corner. One had to walk a hundred feet diagonally across the yard to be near enough to fully enjoy the spectacle.

Suddenly, a hush fell over the crowd. Quinn edged closer to the stairs leading onto the scaffold. Another cloaked and hooded figure had entered the courtyard and this person, too, was edging closer to the executioner. For anyone who cared to notice, a street urchin casually disappeared behind the scaffolding while another, cap pulled low, seemed to be focused not on the drama being played out on the wooden stage, but on his own cloak tied round his waist with a sturdy leather belt. He was fussing with its knot and seemed oblivious to all else. The sound of boots approaching through the archway now rose on the morning air, and a phalanx of Tower guards appeared. Even without a drum to beat their march, they moved in locked step as though on parade. Their formation had no troops in its center and Quinn knew what, or rather who, was sandwiched securely within, but he was shocked when the red uniforms parted and revealed not one, but two people – a young couple. Oh Henrietta! He almost spoke the words aloud, for it was indeed his granddaughter and an equally disheveled young man in a guard's uniform. Like all others in the courtyard, he absolutely could not look away as the man bent slowly over the flame-haired maid, pulled her to him, and kissed her slowly. She pulled him closer and a great sigh went round the crowd. Not only would they be able to report on the horror of the executions to friends, families and public house mates, but now they would have this tale of heartbreaking young love to relate as well. How tragic! It was positively delicious and as the pair clasped hands and stepped onto the rickety stairs, a solemn, giddy hush fell across the courtyard. One by one, the maid and her lover took the steps. One by one, they moved closer to their fate. The crowd crushed towards the platform, leaning in to catch every detail of the young pair – did she hang back on that step? Did he clutch her hand more tightly just then? Did she pale? Would she faint? So intense was the moment that when the scream came, the crowd, en masse, jumped and squealed in surprise and terror. The couple paused and looked out over the crowd. The swordsman took a step backward.

It was the street urchin. Only he no longer wore a low cap and his leather belt now served as a whip with steel tipped ends. He screamed again, keeping the crowd focused on himself.

"Now, Rouster, now!" He yelled the words as the guards moved towards him.

"Do I know that boy? *Marshall*?" Quinn was speaking the words when he realized that it wasn't just the boy who was familiar. The muffled figure who had entered the courtyard behind him threw off her cloak and shoved towards the steps.

"Bess!" His wife turned as he roared her name.

"Quinn!"

There was no need for explanation, for they had always thought as one.

Another scream rose on the wind but it was from the executioner. When the burly bearded man had stepped back in response to Marshall's initial scream, he had blundered into a leather noose placed carefully, quietly and strategically on the floor of the platform just behind where he stood. As he now moved forward, Rouster, secreted behind the scaffolding, jerked the loose end of the noose with all his might. It was enough to bring down the executioner, and he fell forward onto the crowd below, bellowing in rage.

Bess and Quinn reached the stairs just as Roman and Henrietta raced down them.

"Put this on, dear, pull the hood closely so none may recognize you and *run*!"

Roman stared in amazement at the old couple – who were these people that they would give their lives for his companion? There was no time to think, only to grasp Quinn's shoulder for a split second and look him in the eye with grateful silence before sprinting across the courtyard hand in hand with Henrietta. But they stood no chance, for the guards had sprung to life and were in hot pursuit. Yet it seemed not to matter to them – their steps were lyrical and light – the eternal steps of love and youth. The guards closed in.

And then, the strangest thing of all occurred.

The crowd which only moments earlier had fed on the impending spectacle of Henrietta and Roman being executed and had lusted for their blood had a change of heart. Whether it was the pathos of young love or the plight of Henrietta and Roman, whether it was the passion of their kiss and their stalwart march together up the stairs – something had triggered pity in the masses and like a tide suddenly turned, they took up the cause of the young lovers. As much as they had relished the certain doom about to befall the pair, so much more did they now relish hope and their role in seeing it was not disappointed.

Instinct born of a thousand generations, deeper and far more meaningful than thought, guided the mob as they moved forward and spoke as one.

"Help them! We must help them! Quickly!"

From all quarters the cry went up. A great swarm of bodies and screams and kicks and jabs engulfed the guards. Even as they fell upon Roman and Henrietta, they too felt in turn the tight grip of hands clutching at them from all sides, the press of bodies thrown against them. The cries and screams rose louder, the melee grew larger. Bess and Quinn joined the fray, desperately attempting to make their way to the middle of what had become a jumbled mass of humanity occupying the middle of the courtyard in a raucous melee. Even the executioner himself joined the fight. Of all that were present in the courtyard at that moment, only two declined to participate in the battle which now was joined. No one noticed the two small street urchins as they pocketed their leather strap. All were too occupied with the struggle at hand to perceive them sidling past the undulating crush of bodies and furious uproar towards the arched entryway. And certainly, no one paid any mind to them as they hugged the wall and dashed without the gate, finally ducking behind a hedge on the other side. No. No one at all. By the time the trumpets sounded, they had cleared the grounds completely and were headed for the safety of London's tangled, inner streets, where only the impoverished entered, where only the desperate resided. They were home.

*****

Elizabeth had barely heard the child's message at Whitehall Palace before she leapt on her horse, screaming for her guard to engage with her. The distance between Whitehall and the Tower was not great, and those who saw her that morning on her frantic ride, ermine robes billowing out behind her, stared and shouted with pride. Their virgin mistress could still, even after all these years, give vent and ride like a knight into battle.

She was at the Tower before her horse guards could manage to out pace her. With trumpets blaring and horse hoofs clattering on the cobblestone ways, they finally passed her by and galloped towards the courtyard. The archway entry magnified the sound, and as they sidestepped their mounts so that she might make her way through, silence fell. The scene which met her eyes was surreal.

Like her father, Elizabeth had always loved tapestries. The great Flemish masters of the art were able to capture a moment in time and weave it into permanence with their almost magical skill. The tableau set out before her now in the courtyard that morning reminded her of such a moment. As the trumpets had blared forth the news of her approach, the combatants had immediately ceased their struggle. And yet they all remained frozen in the positions they had occupied upon hearing the tattoo as though Judgment Day had arrived and they now awaited their fates. Women with hats in hands raised and ready to beat down their adversaries, guards with coats and jackets torn asunder, noblemen with ripped sleeves and noblewomen with hoops flying, piled one and all into a huge mass like kindling and wood awaiting a martyr, suddenly froze, each and every one, then turned expectantly towards the sound of her horse.

The queen's presence rained down heavily upon them, and the jumbled throng quickly began to sort themselves out. Like layers of onion they peeled themselves off the pile and rose from the debris, collected their accoutrement and bowed as gracefully as the circumstances allowed. Near the bottom of the pile, Elizabeth heard familiar voices. She nodded to a nearby guard to assist. As Bess and Quinn were helped to their feet, she addressed a single word to them.

"Henrietta."

From beneath the remaining bodies, a muffled voice cried forth.

"I am here, Majesty, and I have come to warn you!"

"Well," came her Majesty's reply with a small twitch of her lips, "My morning began rather slowly, but I anticipate a fine afternoon."

She turned to Cecil, gave quiet instructions, and rode silently back through the archway. She bowed her head, not in prayer, but to hide the grin which she could no longer suppress as a chuckle escaped her lips. Indeed.

Chapter Nine

Two lots.

Sir Robert Cecil was tired of this day. This week. And why could no one understand his orders? For the third time, he repeated himself. Once more, he thought, and my head shall pop off in a fury.

"TWO! Can you not count, you slobbering nuts? Hmm? Two! One . . . TWO!" His scathing tone was quickly deteriorating into a raging growl.

"But Lord Burghley, to whom shall we look for guidance, for all these before us shall want to be in the 'good' pile. No one, sir, shall admit to perfidy and therefore consign themselves to the knaves' and traitors' pile."

"Pile? I do not want a 'pile'," Cecil said deliberately as though speaking to a child. "I want two groups – those who aided the maid Henrietta shall be in one, and those who did not shall be placed in the other."

"Well, sir," came the slow reply, "Into which pile shall I put the maid Henrietta herself? A separate pile? For then, you see, one cannot be a pile if one is only one, *and*, that would make three piles, now would it not sir?"

Cecil sat at his large, dark desk, the same one his father had used before him, his girth comfortably supported against its edge. Six inches from that edge was a well-worn spot, so well-worn in fact that the wood was slightly concave at that point. He stared at the guard before him for a full minute without responding. Then, with a soul-wrenching sigh, he placed his forehead on the well-worn spot. This man guarded the kingdom, he thought dolefully – surely 'tis God's grace that England survived still yet.

"Do you see the maid before you, man? Eh? God's toes, were you dropped when a wee babe?" Cecil noted the hurt look on the guard's face and tried to moderate the despair in his voice. "Send in your superior Owen." Pause. "And Owen, you do not need to return with him."

Owen bowed and crept from the room.

But even as Owen backed respectfully out of sight, Cecil had to admit to the quandary. The maid, Henrietta, had declined to return to Coudenoure with the older couple whom Elizabeth had sent home immediately – the queen had refused to have them questioned or guarded, waving away the concerns of her privy council and guard. She had sent one of her own carriages to transport them back to their beloved estate. In light of Quinn's head wound, a physician was directed to Coudenoure as well. But the granddaughter . . . Cecil smiled in spite of himself. If I were younger, he thought, there would be a woman who might take my heart. What courage! Henrietta stayed with Roman. What bond had arisen so quickly? No, Cecil, he thought to himself, for some love is eternal and only waits to be found – it has always existed and always will.

He picked up the parchment which sat on one side of his desk, grunted, and scribbled a note in its margin. His clerk had provided him a hurried, written synopsis of the morning's events and he began re-reading it slowly. It seemed that some young soldier . . . Cecil hesitated and looked down the page, skimming the cramped lines until he found that for which he searched. Yes, there it was – the name Roman Collins. He looked up, staring at nothing in particular and tapping his quill on the desk. After a moment he returned to the page.

One Roman Collins had placed the ruby cross on the Queen's breakfast tray – here, Cecil paused and wrote in the margin once again, noting that the queen's security must needs be checked since total strangers were currently able to place items on her breakfast tray. Mister Collins' story about having received it from a young maid being held had not proven true and so he had earned himself a place in the Tower dungeon. And yet, Cecil stroked his beard – the queen had recognized the jeweled piece and clearly knew the maid to whom Collins referred.

At that point, the story set out by his clerk became murky indeed. Somehow, the maid Henrietta had escaped but when re-captured was thrown in with young Collins. Why they were slated to be executed was treasonous indeed but not on their part, and that particular bit of perfidy bore no relation to Essex. The Captain of the Tower Guard had not wished to see his reputation sullied before the queen. On the sly, he was taking care of the problem. Without the girl and without the boy there would be no one to contradict his story. Henrietta had never been in the Tower – how could she have been? No one had ever escaped his careful and loyal watch upon Her Majesty's own jail. But the Captain had not foreseen Bess and Quinn, he had not shown himself prescient concerning the passion between the two young people, and never did he guess the effect their fire would have upon the crowd.

It was one for the ages, Cecil thought to himself. There was one part of the tale, however, he felt was missing, and so he called for his clerk, continuing to glance over the manuscript while he waited.

"Tell me," he called out as the door to his chamber finally opened, "One of the ladies present at this morning's debacle mentioned two young street urchins. She believed they played a significant role in this couple's averting of the executioner's axe."

The clerk nodded in agreement.

"Aye, Lord Burghley, several bystanders said as much – I am writing witness statements now. But when the courtyard was sealed that no one might escape and all must tell their tale, no such lads were found. Indeed, there no children present at all. 'Tis strange."

Burghley agreed.

"They must have slipped away during the chaos and before her Majesty arrived. What would cause young boys to risk such a thing, eh? 'Tis passably strange, as you have said. I can make no sense of it at all. And how came they to know the Tower?"

The clerk, having no answer, left without reply, and Burghley was once again left alone.

After a long moment, he spoke softly to himself.

"Strange indeed."

*****

As the great royal carriage rumbled along, Quinn chatted brightly with Bess. At first, she watched him closely, her beloved partner, but finally felt ease returning when there seemed to be no sign of lasting trauma from the ugly looking blow Quinn had received to the back of his head.

As they turned and entered upon the familiar, long and straight gravel drive, Quinn had eagerly anticipated returning to his home. He looked at it now with pride and pleasure. The events of London rendered it with a different palette. The winter browns seemed more intense, the small green nubs of new growth more vibrant. The house itself looked different – smaller, perhaps? Or was it that the stones had aged and Quinn had never noticed it before. He thought of his early days on the estate, when his own father, the esteemed royal architect Robert Janyns, had been gifted with land abutting the western side of Coudenoure. Henry the VIII had signed the deed himself, and Quinn closed his eyes as they bumped along, remembering the great man and sovereign. So much time gone by and so quickly.

Coudenoure had come to the de Greys from Henry the VII, the result of Bosworth Field, generations earlier. Quinn had eventually married Bess, his childhood playmate and now mistress of Coudenoure and the love of his life. Where had all those years gone?

As he gingerly exited the carriage, he looked at the front doors of the manor house as though seeing them for the first time.

The queen's physician had chosen not to ride with them and as a result had arrived earlier. He greeted them and helped Quinn into the library. He bundled his patient beneath warm blankets in a deep, comfortable chair, the one in which Quinn always sat.

As he settled beneath the warmth, a fatigue like no other washed over him. He closed his eyes and saw the water of an ocean tide edging closer. Bess spoke his name and he took her hand and smiled. They had always been together and always would be.

The tide of fatigue washed higher. Bess held his hand tightly. And then, with no further warning, a final, eternal wave washed him away in its warm embrace.

*****

"But he was fine! He was talking to me and laughing in the carriage! This cannot be!"

Weeks later, this same refrain continued to bubble forth seemingly involuntarily from Bess. She was unable to move beyond her grief, and, indeed, did not even recognize it for what it was. She seemed to be expecting to see Quinn come rolling out of his workroom any moment with some new idea, or ambling through the front door with an insect in his pocket or a wildflower in his hand.

Nothing eased the pain, and she constantly looked for her mate to appear, wandering the rooms of Coudenoure like a haunt on its ramblings.

Those around Bess grew ever more concerned but she threw off their ministrations. Henrietta, her beloved granddaughter, returned from London, but who was the young man with her? One Roman Collins? Who was he? At Anne's request, the queen's physician had stayed on, but as the days turned into weeks and Bess withdrew further into a reality of her own making, he began to brace the family for the possibility that she preferred that make-believe world to the one in which Quinn was no more.

She had lost her anchor, why could they not see that? And where was the queen, the one person who might understand. Why had she not come? Bess had no way of knowing the crises which demanded the aging queen's attention. If she had, she would not have cared, for she had been there for Elizabeth in her hour of need. So why now was the kindness not returned? By the time the lone, gilded carriage rolled in somber state down Coudenoure's drive, Quinn had been gone a month. A guardsman opened the door and Elizabeth stepped out. There was no Bess to greet her and she climbed the stairs to her friend's bedchamber.

No one answered her quiet knock and she entered anyway. Bess sat before the fire, quiet and still like a mouse waiting for the cat's paw. The queen took off her cloak and sat down opposite. Bess neither rose nor spoke.

"I remember another time you and I gathered here," Elizabeth began. She had been told by Anne of Bess' refusal to engage with anything or anyone since Quinn's death. She saw it now firsthand, for Bess continued to say nothing.

"It was when Dudley married. Do you remember?"

Silence.

"Do you remember?" Elizabeth repeated the question gently. "How you comforted me? What was it you called him – a tart monger?"

A slight smile crossed Bess' lips. Elizabeth took heart and went on.

"Yes, and what about that time I was ill with the scourge of small pox? You! Looking out the window of Hampton Palace, commenting on the undignified exodus of all my lords and ladies lest they be caught by the arm of that dreadful plague."

Bess chuckled now and looked into the eyes of her friend. She did not see the richly adorned gown, nor did she see the jewels cast and spun into her majesty's caul. She saw a woman, a comrade with whom she had lived her life. A witness to her being. Elizabeth smiled back at her. As queen, she was renowned for insisting that rank and privilege be evident in one's clothing – she had even changed the sumptuary laws to include language precluding this class from wearing purple, that class from being about without a cap. But at Coudenoure none of that mattered to her. It was as if the long drive from the pitted road to the heavy wych elm doors of the estate served as a buffer between the reality of England and the reality of Coudenoure. A thousand times she had felt the world and its troubles drop away as she neared the manor house, and a thousand times she had felt the rush of family and home as she passed under its great mantel.

Where but here was she truly at home, loved for herself, known through and through as Elizabeth, not as queen? Bess sensed her mood and nodded.

"Yes, my sovereign and friend, we have been through a lot together, have we not?"

"You *are* my friend, Bess, but you are my family first. Are you not the offspring of my own sister? Born of my own dear father?"

Bess turned her gray, sunken eyes upon her.

"Where have you been? I have needed you these weeks."

"I am sorry. I was delayed." Only to Bess would the queen ever apologize; only to her would she acknowledge her own humanity. She reached out now and held Bess' hand firmly in her own.

"You must move on, Bess. Quinn is gone."

Tears welled up in Bess' eyes.

"And how, pray tell, would you recommend that I do *that*? Hmm? Shall I command my spirit to forget him with whom I spent my life? When I wake in the morning, shall I demand of myself that I not miss his warmth, his touch? Or perhaps I shall forbid my mind to dwell upon him when I walk the estate – the meadow he planted, the glass houses he built, his strange and glorious workshop. Tell me, how do I forget him?"

Elizabeth leaned back and shook her head.

"I do not know. When Dudley married, I was angry beyond words. When he died, I became an empty vessel with no capacity to feel. And then Essex came into my life and I thought I should live again, if only for a day."

A rueful laugh escaped Bess.

"When they write the words that define us all, of Essex it shall be written . . ."

Elizabeth interrupted.

". . . shall be written that he was a peacock . . ."

". . . who fanned his tail . . ." Bess supplied.

". . . and called and squawked until . . ."

Here, Bess used her best imitation of the Earl of Devereux.

"Oh, Majesty, do you not see how pretty I am? And would you not like to live your life under my thumb? Come, let us marry!"

They both laughed at the nonsense of their words and Elizabeth used the moment to focus Bess' thoughts elsewhere.

"Tell me about Henrietta's young man." She paused and giggled. "They met in a dungeon cell, proceeded together to the executioner's block, committed treason by escaping and now gallop about the estate like wild rabbits."

Bess waved her hand.

"I know not – but if you say a cross word to him or about him, you must be prepared to endure Henrietta's wrath. They have become inseparable and if this were not Coudenoure, their behavior would be a disgrace to us all."

"They are not . . ."

"No, no of course not. But the kiss they shared as they mounted the scaffold seems to have sealed their love."

"*Love?*"

Again, Bess waved her hand tiredly.

"My auntie, try and suggest to Henrietta that it is not love, would you, and let me know how accepting she is of your interpretation of her feelings."

Elizabeth sighed.

"You can tell them nothing, young people. They do as they please."

"Indeed, and I believe the same was said of us." They both giggled.

"Come," Bess rose and reached out to help Elizabeth, "Let us go meet the young man, and you may tell me your opinion of him based upon knowledge rather than hearsay. I ask only one thing of you."

"Yes?" said the queen.

"Do not, I beg you, make any mention of sheep."

*****

Roman shifted uneasily on his feet, cap in hand. Elizabeth sat side by side with Bess in the library and stared at him without speaking. He and Henrietta had been summoned from the glass house which they were inspecting 'to give an account of himself', so he was told, to the queen.

"What does that mean?" he had asked Henrietta as they hurried towards the library.

"Answer her questions and do not ramble. You will be fine." But her answer had been terse and worried, for if Elizabeth did not approve of Roman, Roman would not be long at Coudenoure.

"Tell me, young Roman Collins, what you think of Coudenoure?"

It was not what Roman had been expecting. He had prepared a small statement of himself and his family, but now frantically considered how best to answer a question for which he was unprepared.

"Well, Majesty, the place is falling down."

Dead silence from the room. It was not the usual description given of the estate.

"The stables need rebuilding, the orchard could be expanded and the fences along the western side should be mended."

Pause.

"The stonework on the south corner of the manor house needs attention, and the roof of the Lady Bess' workshop sags – it should be replaced. None of this, however, rises to the level of need that I see in the fields."

Henrietta saw where her beau was going and tried to head him off.

"Roman, the fields are fine." Her words had a decided finality about them. But he blithely ignored the veiled message she was sending and continued.

"I believe there is a more profitable use of Coudenoure's lands."

Elizabeth felt the consternation of Henrietta and found it amusing – what was the young man going to say that made her so nervous?

Elizabeth nodded for him to continue. Bess smiled.

"I believe that the lands could support sheep, but not just any sheep. The fields could be rotated – used for feed some years and for grazing others. There is a fine variety of sheep I believe would do quite well in this region – the Ryeland."

Elizabeth began to smile – so this was what Bess had warned her of – the man loved wool. Henrietta stared out the window and sighed.

"Now, of course, Majesty" fifteen minutes later, "We would have to take into account the summer humidity, for as everyone knows . . ."

Elizabeth had had enough and brutally, but with amusement, cut him off mid-sentence.

"I understand you are a tower guard?"

Roman stopped abruptly and then launched into his prepared speech of his family and their connection to the woolen industry.

"Young man, I asked about your work as a guard, not for a history of English wool."

Roman hesitated – the tone in Elizabeth's voice was unnerving. With a deep breath, he broke off his ruminations on sheep-raising in Surrey and told her of his parents' ambition for him and his station at the Tower. But for Roman, all things started and ended with wool.

". . . but the Tudor livery, the uniforms, Majesty. Do you notice how they pull to the left when they are buttoned? I believe that if a worsted material were to be used instead, spun here at home in England . . ."

Elizabeth shot a glance at Bess and they both exploded with laughter. Roman looked shocked and slightly embarrassed.

The queen waved Henrietta and him from the room.

"Well? Your opinion, Auntie?" asked Bess.

Elizabeth touched her head and pretended to confusion.

"I do not know, Bess. My thoughts are . . . woolly."

They both roared.

"Yes, my feelings exactly. I believe there may be sheep in Coudenoure's future."

"Yes," Elizabeth could not stop laughing, "But what kind of sheep? Shall we go with the upland with the shorter, coarser wool? Or perhaps the Lincolnshire?"

For the first time since Quinn's death, Bess felt a lessening of her grief, and a small measure of comfort. Elizabeth saw a bit of color return to her friend's face, and sighed secretly with relief.

"I must leave you now, dearest," she told Bess, ". . . for I have a most interesting audience in the morning."

Bess cocked her head inquiringly, but Elizabeth only smiled in response.

*****

Henrietta and Roman stopped just long enough in the grand entryway to don cloaks and hats before easing quietly out through the heavy front doors. In the weeks since the events surrounding Essex' uprising Roman's presence at Coudenoure had become commonplace. He and Henrietta were frequently seen wandering the estate, discussing various aspects of its operations and grounds. They were a melody unto themselves, she with her flaming locks escaping from this caul or that, he with his flowing black hair billowing out behind him in the blustery spring air until it seemed to intertwine with Henrietta's. Their passion was not of a quiet nature, but produced sparks that even the servants and craftsmen who passed them in their perambulations understood. And no one who saw them could help but smile, for they were the quintessential expression of what all hoped for but so few ever found: love, deep and true.

Henrietta steered their course towards the west side of the estate where lay the skeletal remains of the old monastery church and the stone-fenced graveyard. Roman had never seen this side of the Coudenoure before and remarked as much to Henrietta. She nodded.

"Yes, 'tis not a place to be taken lightly."

"What do you mean?"

She said nothing but walked on pulling her cloak closer against the sharp spring breeze. Eventually, she made her way to the stone bench which sat within the small cemetery's confines. She settled herself comfortably and as Roman sat beside her she finally spoke.

"Those ruins yonder have been here since the Lord's year 1213," she began. "You see, Coudenoure was originally a monastery. The manor house was the friars' dwelling place, and the church was their spiritual home."

"What happened?"

"They were removed to Cambridge, where they joined with another such order. Because it sits upon Greenwich Wood, and because the land fell to the crown, Coudenoure became a hunting lodge for the royal family."

"How then did it pass into the hands of your family?"

Henrietta turned and smiled at her beloved. He sat slightly slouched, fingers laced easily across his middle. He looked at her with a doting smile and she felt her breath arrest. Was it possible his eyes were bluer today, or his hands stronger, more well-proportioned than yesterday?

"That is why I brought you hear today, Roman. You see, your father is not the only self-made man in the kingdom."

"To hear him tell it, he is." Roman laughed. "He was a tenant farmer. You are marrying the son of a tenant farmer." There was a lightness in Roman's voice. It was freeing to talk about his humble beginnings to Henrietta – it was clear she did not care.

"You have not mentioned marriage before." Henrietta looked down and blushed in spite of herself.

Roman realized that he had spoken his thoughts aloud. He too blushed and looked down, wondering what to say next.

"Henrietta, since I saw you on the prisoners' barge when I took you to the Tower, I have not stopped thinking of you, even for a moment. I hope you know how much I love you, and how ardently, and I hope you feel the same."

Henrietta continued to look down, as still as stone.

"I hope you will consent to marry me and be my wife . . ."

"Yes, Roman, YES!" Henrietta interrupted him. Holding his hands tightly in hers, she felt a deep need as his eyes traveled slowly from her hair, to her forehead, then to her eyes. The look was steady and soon passed to her lips, where it rested with an intensity Henrietta had never felt before. Yet she remained as she had been and did not turn away. She was unafraid of their passion. Unable to bear the moment, Roman smiled.

"So 'tis settled, then. We shall marry."

And just like that, it was done.

They enjoyed the sun and the bright, warm feeling which enveloped them. Finally, Henrietta resumed her narrative as though the monumental declarations had never occurred.

"In 1487 my ancestor Thomas de Grey defended Henry the VII and saved the great man's life at Bosworth."

"I know of that battle – it set the Tudors upon the throne of England."

Henrietta nodded.

"In thankful repayment, Henry raised Thomas to a baron, and gave him Coudenoure and the grounds which comprise this estate. Since that time, it has been in my family, for I am of Thomas de Grey's lineage."

"Ah," Roman said with understanding, "Another self-made man."

"Yes, Roman, I too come from those who would work their way to a better life."

"And how comes it to you? You said your mother, Catherine, died in childbirth."

"My father was a minor nobleman of the deep north, along the Scottish boundaries. He was a second son, and was given the choice of priesthood or the sea. He chose the sea and through that decision came to Coudenoure where he and mother married."

"And do you have lands, estates, in the north through his lineage?"

Henrietta shrugged.

"I do not know, but I rather doubt it. My father's elder brother, his only sibling, married a Scottish noble woman, but that is all I know for certain. Likely they had children and all such worth would pass to their line."

They sat in comfortable silence, as though they had known each other their entire lives. It was a feeling of home such as neither had ever experienced. The day drew on, and finally they rose.

"You must speak to Bess about our decision forthwith, and of course the banns must be read. There is much planning to be done."

"I am sorry your father is not here."

"'Tis fine, Roman. Coudenoure is my home, and my grandmother is its matriarch. It is all I have ever known and all I have ever wanted." She paused before adding, "And of course, you must ask the queen, for nobles may not marry without her blessing and consent."

Roman stopped and a panicked look spread across his face.

"She believes me to be a nit. Each time she has met me I have been in less than favorable circumstances. Why, just today, just now, I believe I may have babbled on a bit about wool."

Henrietta started laughing.

"Yes, and I believe that being met for the first time at the bottom of a pile of bodies in the executioner's courtyard at the Tower may have influenced her as well. And trying to escape at that." She could not stop laughing. "Yes, Roman, we shall see how much you love me for I am certain she will remember your first meeting." Another pause. "And I believe you might consider leaving wool out of the next conversation."

But Roman's happiness would not be pierced. He grabbed Henrietta's hand in a bold gesture and they tripped together back to the manor laughing the entire way.

The great ebony horses of Elizabeth's carriage, together with her mounted guardsmen, were moving sedately down the drive as Henrietta and Roman flew happily through the orchard towards the front doors of the house. Elizabeth saw them, smiled, and leaned back in her coach, enjoying the spectacle and mystery of young love. Her smile was short-lived however, for a carriage wheel hit hard upon a small rut in the drive. She grabbed the stick she kept exclusively at hand for such occasions and pounded on ceiling until the carriage stopped. A worried face appeared in her window.

"Majesty?" A deep bow was met with a deep scowl.

"Can you not drive a carriage, man?"

The worried face now became chagrined. Another deep bow was met with yet another deep scowl. Then a sigh.

"Oh, never mind. Tell the guardsmen to ready my barge at Coudenoure's wharf. I shall take the river back to Whitehall."

"Majesty." The face disappeared.

"*Majesty*, indeed," Elizabeth harrumphed. "One rut in the *entire* drive and he manages to find it. God's liver, where have our standards gone?" The entourage moved on.

Chapter Ten

Three small figures huddled against the cold. The kindling fire, made with damp wood lifted from a rich man's timber stack, sputtered and belched. Its heat was minimal. Rouster had managed to secure an apple and a bit of fat from a street vendor and Ben stirred them in his cooking pan, keeping a watchful eye on what would be their only meal.

"So you believe we should go." He spoke the words without looking up.

Rouster, huddled between the two bigger boys, looked from Ben to Marshall, waiting for his response.

Marshall nodded.

"I believe so. If we do not we may miss an opportunity."

"But Marshall, what if they mean us harm?" Rouster's eyes were large and frightened. "I have already lost my work at the shop!"

"'Tis bad luck that. The old woman should not have turned you out. After all, you did lock up the store before you left and you did return. The queen's own had need of your services – you could not refuse!"

Rouster nodded.

"Aye, Marshall, and I will always be at your service. And the service of my queen. But 'tis misfortune that is all."

Marshall patted the boy's tiny hand, signaling his empathy.

"They mean us no harm. We saved the guard and the girl from the executioner. I believe they mean to reward us."

Ben carefully poured the thin broth into the one cup he possessed and they began passing it between them, sipping the warm gruel. After a moment, he spoke again.

"Tell me, Marshall, about these people – the old man and woman, the maid, and this place . . . Caldenud?"

"Coudenoure," Marshall corrected him. "'Tis a quiet estate with no pretensions and no appreciation of class and circumstance. The only thing I have noted that matters to those who live there is talent and hard work. 'Tis a strange place indeed. The cook is friends with the lady of the manor who is friends with the queen who visits occasionally. There is a grand library – you would faint away, Ben, should you ever see it – glass houses where all manner of vegetables are grown, and a strange workshop belonging to Quinn, the master of the house. The mistress has her own building behind the main house. It is filled with stone which she beats into the most marvelous shapes and figures." He paused, remembering. "Yes, a strange, magical place indeed."

Ben poured the last of the broth into the cup and reverentially took a sip before passing it on.

"But Marshall," Rouster's voice trembled with fear and tears welled in his eyes, "Should the queen speak to me, what would I do?"

"I shall do the talking, Rouster, so do not worry."

Sensing Rouster's fear, Ben chimed in.

"Yes, do not worry, Rouster. If things should go badly, I shall see that you escape."

Marshall stood, warming his hands in front of Ben's little fire by the bridge.

"We are together?"

"As men," said Ben.

"As men," echoed Rouster.

"Then let us sleep, for the morn shall come upon us soon enough."

*****

Elizabeth turned first this way, then that, taking in her appearance in the looking glass held by her maid. Her gown was of the deepest black velvet, and the gold lacing and finish on its bodice shimmered when it caught the morning light. Slashes of silver cut the sleeves, accentuating the richness of her costume. Great loops of pearls were placed around her neck, their creamy white textures echoing that of her face, made up now as the public expected to see her – white, unsmiling, with yet more pearls adorning the wig of tightly curled red hair she habitually wore.

She was looking forward to the morning's audience, for children were seldom in her presence. Only ever at Coudenoure was she exposed to their antics, their brutal truths, their innocence. But this morning three were being brought in. Urchins. What would they have to say to her, she wondered? She allowed herself a smile as she left her room and walked towards the Long Gallery with Lord Burghley.

"Majesty, the three of them refused baths and clothing."

Elizabeth grinned.

"Why?"

"The youngest, smallest one, Rouster I believe is his name, was terrified of being separated from his comrades. Additionally, he seemed to think that if he parted with his clothing he could not escape if the moment dictated such action." Burghley shrugged before finishing, "And the other two would not leave him, so, Majesty, they come into your presence filthy and stinking of the street."

A chuckle was the only response.

"I like such loyalty – 'tis a rare trait, do you not agree?"

"Majesty, I do, but in this case our noses shall pay its price."

They entered the Long Gallery through a side door, and Elizabeth arranged herself carefully on her throne. Guards lined the wall behind her and Cecil stood to her right. Again, the smile.

"Bring them in."

At the far end of the hall, the high, heavy double doors were opened to the sound of trumpets. Guards, three deep on either side, banged their spikes on the floor. Then . . . silence. Elizabeth looked at Cecil. He shrugged.

A kerfuffle arose at the open doors and as Elizabeth watched three tiny boys were shoved into line and pushed into view. They stood frozen until a swift hand on their backs shoved them forward. Once in motion, they seemed unable to stop and glided on until a few feet from the queen on her dais. She looked down at them. Two of them bowed while the third stood, mouth agape, horror written across his tiny, pale features.

Elizabeth had intended to find her fun in frightening them with majesty, spectacle and ceremony. But it had been too easy and she realized that given their fear it was nothing but mean to continue. She leaned forward and smiled. The tiny one screamed. Had it not been for Marshall stepping on his foot, grounding him to the spot, Rouster would have run full tilt down the gallery. After a moment, he gathered himself. Elizabeth eyed them speculatively – so thin, when had they last eaten? She let her glance stray to the side of the gallery where windows looked out upon the great orchard. On a long table there stood a platter of fruits, candies and gingered bread. Rouster's eyes followed hers. She looked back at him and finally spoke.

"Child, my servants have provided me with yon treats, but I cannot eat them all. It would be a pity to waste them, do you not agree?" Her voice was kind and gentle. Rouster nodded.

"But what can I do?" Elizabeth continued. "Cecil does not like treats," she pointed at her minister. "I wonder if anyone else could help me eat them all?"

Rouster was mesmerized. He looked – three times – at the queen, then the plate, the queen . . . then the plate. Finally he spoke.

"Well, missus, I can help you if you like."

Elizabeth stifled a laugh and indicated agreement. Before anyone could stop him, Rouster ran to the platter, picked it up and ran back to the dais. Balancing it carefully, he stepped up until he was beside Elizabeth. Finally, some sense of decorum seemed to return to his mind.

"You first!" He piped.

"And your friends? Shall we invite them?"

Rouster nodded and spoke as he stuffed an entire candied fig in his mouth.

"Ben has a gift for you!"

"Indeed!" Elizabeth said. "Which one of you is Ben?"

Ben's white-blond hair flopped over his face as he bowed and approached the dais. Elizabeth had never seen such pale blue eyes before. They were serious, and the child's entire demeanor demanded respect. He bowed again and from within his blouse pulled a grubby package, tied with coarse string. Stepping forward, he spoke.

"Majesty, I present you with this fine book. 'Tis my belief that it is the finest in all of England."

Elizabeth made a show of carefully unwrapping the package, but there was no need for artifice when she saw the volume. A silent gasp escaped her lips and tears came to her eyes.

"Where did you get this?" She found herself staring at a copy of *The Divine Comedy.*

"I traded a flitch of bacon I had acquired. 'Twas very dear but as you can see, Queen, Majesty, 'twas worth the price. Notice the stitching on the binding – is it not quality?"

"You gave up your food to purchase a book?"

"Would not you?"

Elizabeth smiled at the young bibliophile in kindly gratitude. Her gaze finally shifted to Marshall, who remained where he had come to rest originally. She crooked her finger for him to come forward. Rouster stuffed two figs in his mouth, smacking happily. Marshall bowed deeply and moved to the dais.

"I believe you know Coudenoure."

"Majesty, I make my home there – I am an apprentice in the stables."

"Ah, I see. And do they have many horses?"

Marshall hesitated.

"No, three riders and the plough animals. Those are the only ones. But 'tis enough for me to learn the trade and then I shall have a future. Do you not agree?"

Elizabeth looked at the three faces, filthy and street-wise beyond their years. She brushed them aside and back into their lineup. Rouster grabbed three scones on his way off the dais.

"Gentlemen, your loyalty to the crown and to me personally has touched my heart. "'Tis rare that I see such bravery, even amongst my own guard."

The three little faces shone with pride.

"I believe, as my father did before me, that such loyalty should be rewarded. Lord Burghley, do you not agree?"

Cecil stepped solemnly forward.

"I believe, Majesty, that the paths for these loyal men are clear."

"I agree," she opined. "For example, Rouster, I believe you might enjoy working in a kitchen, surrounded by food and learning to cook food. Would you like that?"

Rouster dropped the scone he was mid-way through and flew into Elizabeth's lap but then suddenly pulled back with a serious mien.

"Tell me, missus, would I be allowed to eat the scraps?"

She stroked his filthy hair and kissed him lightly on the forehead.

"Cecil, write a note to Lady Bess, and tell her the crown wishes to apprentice a young cook at Coudenoure. We shall pay, of course, for his room, his board and his education."

She turned to Ben.

"Did you know, sir, that Coudenoure has one of the finest libraries in all of England?"

"No, Majesty, I did not. They are very fortunate, then."

"Oh, aye, but recently, Lady Anne, the keeper of the library, took a bad fall and will be laid up for many months. And after that, she will no longer be able to move about freely, such as is required by a large, important collection."

Ben's mouth opened slightly.

"Tell me, young Ben, would you like to apprentice with her, and then return to me as a librarian scholar? Cambridge has great need of bright minds to fill its halls, and England too."

Ben bowed deeply, too overcome for words.

"And finally, we come to Marshall."

"Majesty?"

"I was told of your role in saving my Henrietta. You, child, have a rare quality. You can inspire men to follow and more than that, you can lead them. I shall apprentice you directly to my Master of the Horse, and in due time and with due education, you will rise to my guard. Will that please you?"

"Majesty, I will serve you and your house all my days."

Elizabeth sent them from her and leaned back into her throne.

"Cecil! Why cannot all my audiences be so satisfying? Why cannot all my subjects be as these three men-children? Eh?"

She rose and turned.

"I shall ride out now so that my people may see me. Fetch my horse. 'Tis a fine day, is it not?"

She patted her wig and hummed an old melody as she walked lightly from the room.

*****

Roman knew the conversation he must have with his parents that evening would not be an easy one. Usually, blame for difficulties lay in many quarters but this time the fault was entirely his. He had caught a wherry as it passed along the Thames at Coudenoure, and the other passenger was only too happy to share the cost of the remaining distance into London. He had no desire for conversation and spent the ride immersed in his own thoughts. Where to begin?

First, he must tell them that he was a Tower Guard no more. He had not in fact been one since his near-execution. Perhaps he should begin his story with that? Garner sympathy before proceeding? Somehow, he could not see Matthew and Elinor Collins being sympathetic to him being nearly executed and them knowing nothing of it. And still knowing nothing of it some weeks later. No, he should not begin there.

Perhaps he should open the tale with Henrietta and the ruby cross. He knew that they were deeply curious as to the outcome of that episode, but he had been oddly reluctant to share the tale with them. He knew that a maid once imprisoned in the Tower was not their hoped-for bride for their only son. No, best not to start there either.

But there would be questions regardless of where he started. For example, why did he rise each morning, don his Tower livery, and leave the house as though nothing were amiss? And he had not done this one day, but for several weeks. The pain he would cause his parents when he told them the truth – that he was in love with the rebel girl and each day traveled to her home – was too great to bear. And so, every morning he dressed for work and left the house as if nothing had changed.

He wanted them to love Henrietta as he did – desperately. He wanted them to know that he was leaving everything else behind in order to follow in his father's footsteps, that he would become a sheep farmer at Coudenoure, and that he and his father, together, could continue in the world they both knew best. Let the 'better life' go! The better life for Roman and his father was not to be found in abandoning their craft, their trade, but in passing it on with pride.

Henrietta understood this and supported him in the decision. Indeed, she had no intention of leaving her estate nor of her future husband risking life and limb each day at the Tower. She was headstrong and passionate, but more than that she was practical. And if he wanted to raise sheep and sell wool, his bride to be saw nothing wrong with his scheme, particularly since it meshed perfectly with her own. But how to tell them? They would be dreadfully upset at so many things – his engagement, his work, his lying – the list was almost endless. How did it come to this pass, he wondered? A wry smile crossed his dark and handsome face, for he knew damned well that it had come to pass because of his reluctance to disappoint his parents. What a mess! Tonight, he must set it all straight.

As the wherry pulled close to shore, he paid the oarsmen and leapt out, dreading what lay before him but glad that he had determined to get it over with at last. He walked on in the gloom, intent on nothing but his opening words. As usual, he slipped into the house quietly and began his dance of locating the silent wood planks on the floor. He would wash and prepare an opening before seeing them. He got no further than the second step.

"Roman Ainsworth Collins?" His father seldom used his full name. Roman turned.

"Why the full name, father? Have I committed some crime?" Roman gave what he hoped was a jocular laugh as he sauntered into the parlor. He felt draped in guilt, tripping over its heavy folds in fact. The moment he saw his mother's ashen face, he felt his knees weaken – strange how he could face down an executioner with Henrietta at his side, but could not so much as stand when his mother and father confronted him. Could they possibly know? Of course not! He had told no one among the household staff.

"Cook made a special dinner today, your favorite – mutton stew." His mother's voice trailed off into sobs. Matthew took up the story.

"It was *so* good that we had a servant boy run some to you at the Tower. After all, we know how you love it, and we always try to do everything we can for you because you are our only son and we love you beyond measure."

Roman stood head down.

"Imagine our surprise . . ." even his father, his giant, commanding, stern, and always in-control father, was unable to maintain his steely facade – a sob rent his voice.

A great silence engulfed the room. Roman was not certain but that it had set the entire world aflame in silent protestation of his trickery. He swallowed hard.

"Mother, father, I am engaged!"

Oh dear God no, I should not have opened with that, Roman decided frantically. Too late. He coughed.

"I have met the most wonderful girl, and I know you will love her even as I do."

"Where did you meet her?"

Oh no, no, no. He should start over, otherwise, what???: "I met her as we were marching to be executed?" Another cough. His mother rose, a horrified look on her face.

"Is it her? *It is!* That rebel whore you spoke of? The one in the Tower dungeon? You have lost your livelihood and are marrying a *tart*?" She finished on a shriek, wig askew, fanning herself mightily.

It was a fast downhill roll on a slick wooden sled after that. On and on they went until their voices drowned out reason, overtook love, shut out kinship.

"And we will raise sheep, father, yes, you heard me – *sheep* – on her estate, and I shall be a wool man like my father and his father before him! 'Tis in my blood and how you could deny me such is a mystery!"

"*Sheep? After all we have sacrificed for you?*"

"Sheep! Yes! Great flocks of them!"

"Get out! And do not come back!"

"Never!" Roman screamed the word and stormed out into the silky fog which now enveloped London.

He spent a cold night in the stables and left before the servants arrived at dawn.

*****

Sometimes, regret is not enough. Roman wandered the streets of London, endlessly reliving the ugly, terrifying scene of the night before. He was angry, ashamed, embarrassed, hurt – almost no negative emotion escaped him as he walked blindly along the narrow dirt and cobbled ways. His mother's heartbreak burned like fire upon his conscience. Where had such words come from? What was he thinking? The two people who loved him the most and he had single-handedly, almost cavalierly, broken their hearts. Oh God, what kind of son am I? What type of man?

Surely I must return to my work at the Tower, for 'tis an unholy sin to crush the hearts of one's parents in such a way. They would be happy once again, then, if he should do so. And further, he ruminated, Henrietta and I are foolish to think of raising sheep, of steeping our children in such a tradition. But of all the many conversations in which he and Henrietta had shared their secrets and their dreams, her only hesitation had come precisely with him being so employed. She had not wanted him doing such dangerous work. She preferred the model she had always known at Coudenoure – a husband and wife who managed the estate and its interests together. If he returned to the Tower, how could he tell *her*? What would he say?

His thoughts wound tighter and tighter about his soul until he wanted to cry out to God on high for an answer. But he knew well enough that he himself would have to face the consequences of his own actions. By late day, hungry and tired, Roman had made a decision. The Thames was ebbing, giving him time to complete the mechanics of his hastily sketched plan. By nightfall, he was westerly bound.

Chapter Eleven

Anne lay back on the pillows arranged for her in a deep library chair. Her right leg was carefully stretched forth on a wide, pillowed bench hastily constructed for just that purpose. A wood splint encased it from the upper thigh to the ankle, its pieces kept in rigid alignment by the application of leather laces pre-soaked in salt water to ensure maximum shrinkage when applied to the splint. Her left arm was subject to the same arrangement.

Her dark black hair seemed even more raven against the pale hue of her now sallow complexion. The recovery had not been easy, and an already pale countenance had been rendered wan by continuous pain and suffering. Today was the first day she had felt human since the accident and the freezing night spent out on the meadow waiting for aid. This morning, she had insisted on being dressed in her brightest blue linen frock, the one embroidered with spring bouquets across its skirt, and then to be brought down to the library and placed near its huge front window. From such a vantage point, she watched the meadow warm beneath the spring sun and smiled as the yard boys began their annual ritual of breaking Coudenoure out of its wintry cocoon. They swept, raked and generally ran about, enjoying the day as much as she was. She heard the familiar creak of the library door opening, and a maid appeared with two folded pieces of parchment set upon a silver tray. She took them silently, and the woman disappeared as she had come.

Anne turned the two epistles over and over in her hand, studying them carefully, enjoying the little mystery they presented. She recognized the writing on one of them, and turning it over saw the waxen imprint of the queen's own seal. Setting the other aside, she opened it carefully and began reading.

Anne Dearest,

I know it will be you who reads this first, for your mother is not much given to it, and Henrietta is too consumed by Roman to bother with small treats such as letters. Are you well? I pray daily for your release from those ghastly splints they have you in. If it is true, as they say, that you will always be unable to walk without assistance, well, we shall have made for you the finest cane in all the land. Get well, my great niece, so that we may once again see joy in your eyes.

Lord Burghley, at my direction, has been looking into the Collins' family, and I am glad to report that they are acceptable for marriage into Coudenoure. The eldest, one Matthew, rose from a tenant farmer and is now a quite wealthy merchant in London. Apparently, Roman comes by his love of wool quite honestly. There was a sister who married an earl, but she died in childbirth, leaving the family with only one heir, Roman.

A commission was purchased for him in my guard, but since the debacle at the Tower, he has not returned. I understand from Henrietta and from him that he intends to raise sheep at Coudenoure – this shall be interesting, do you not think?

By the by, you shall have a helper in your library shortly. A young urchin named Ben was pivotal in saving Henrietta from the executioner's axe. I was deeply surprised and touched to learn that he is a true bibliophile! Imagine: living under a bridge and spending all of his pennies on books rather than food or shelter. He reads quite well and is eloquent in his speech. In return for his good deed at the Tower, I wish him to apprentice at Coudenoure. You are, of course, to teach him Latin, Greek, French, and the care of Coudenoure's precious tomes and manuscripts. Another child, Rouster, will apprentice in the kitchen as his reward for his part in the imbroglio.

I bid you fond love, my child, and will visit Coudenoure when my appointments allow me a little freedom.

Elizabeth Rex

Anne re-read the letter, delighting in news from the outside world, but also curious as to one of the bits of information. Roman Collins had not been back to the Tower. That in itself was not remarkable, for he had become an endearing presence at Coudenoure. But for almost a week now, he had also been absent from their estate. She leaned back in the chair and let her gaze rest on the great wide meadow beyond the window. If Roman was not at Coudenoure nor at the Tower either, then where was the young man? His absence had not been quite long enough to create alarm, yet had already been sufficient to create worry and fretting in Henrietta. Each day, she was up with the sun and down to Coudenoure's small dock on the Thames where she patiently waited for Roman. But day after day the wherries and rowboats passed her by, delivering no one to Coudenoure. Where was he?

Realizing that she was fiddling with the papers in her hands, Anne now remembered the second letter. She carefully broke the seal and opened the parchment, glancing at the bottom of the page first to ascertain who else might be sending a note to Coudenoure. Lines of perplexity appeared on her face as soon as she began reading:

My dearest sister Anne (if I may be so bold as to call you thus),

Since Henrietta does not deign to look at letters and your mother prefers hammering in her workshop, I know it will be you who is reading this.

Anne laughed at the observation, so similar to the queen's. Was Coudenoure as predictable as that?

I write to you because my heart is breaking, and no matter what I do, I shall break another's heart as well. Some days ago, I told my parents of my engagement to my fairest Henrietta. Anne, they know nothing of her save for her supposed involvement with Essex' rebellion and the resultant time that she was imprisoned in the Tower dungeon. And yet they judge her! They allowed me no breath to sing her praises but forbade the marriage and demanded I return to my commission at the Tower!

"God's liver," Anne said softly, "You tell your parents you intend to marry a traitor, imprisoned and condemned to execution, and then blame them for their lack of understanding. You are young, Roman, so so young." She continued reading.

My father and I could not agree and my mother sobbed.

Anne closed her eyes, imagining the awful scene.

*I am thrown out, and assured them I will never
return. Please do not think that I intend to marry
Henrietta as a penniless, homeless man with no
prospects. Indeed not.*

*On that dreadful day with my parents, I arranged
my affairs. I had a considerable amount of coin I had
been putting aside. I retrieved it, and set out for the
west country. My intent is to buy at least three rams
and as many ewes as possible of the Ryeland variety.
Anne, I have studied the terrain and climate at
Coudenoure and am familiar with what wool does best
in what pasturage. I believe firmly that these sheep
will thrive at Coudenoure. The fleece is fine and as
just the other day . . .*

Despite the seriousness of the circumstances,
Anne could not help but laugh – Roman was once
again on about sheep and wool. She skipped
several lines.

*. . . but the rams, from the north, would not benefit
from the clime . . .*

More lines skipped.

*I shall employ a drover and he shall see them safely
home to Coudenuore. I shall return upon their
purchase, and set about the necessary construction for
their good health and upkeep.*

*My mother breaks my heart, but Anne, what could
I do? Everything I am I owe to Matthew and Elinor
Collins, my parents who sacrificed so that I might*

have a better life. I love them beyond the eternal pale, but I cannot live without Henrietta, and sheep, well, sheep are sheep!

I have not shared this news with Henrietta, for I wanted to talk to you about it first. You are wise, Anne, and impartial, and I am certain the advice you will give me shall guide me in this most terrible situation.

Anon, my dear sister to be,

Roman

"*Sheep are sheep?* Trenchant." Anne closed her eyes and thought. Roman's love for his parents was evident throughout his letter, but his stubbornness was as well. Yet it would be wrong for the boy and Henrietta to marry without the Collins' approval, and to deny them a presence at their only child's wedding would be a stain upon the union of the two families. No, it would not pass.

A small bell sat near her on the table by the chair. She rang it now, and when the servant appeared, prepared to tackle the issue head-on.

*****

Two days later, in the early afternoon, an unknown carriage appeared at Coudenoure. A sharp wind blew, bending the new growth in Quinn's Meadow to its own purpose, and the traveler who disembarked pulled various cloaks and stoles more closely to ward off the cold it brought with it. The ancient iron knocker upon the door was employed, and the guest was promptly shown into the library where Anne awaited with tea and a light repast.

"Forgive me for not rising, Madame, but as you can see, I have recently had an accident from which I am still recovering. I am honored that you have come in response to my letter. Please, sit, for we have much to discuss."

The hood from the outermost cloak was slowly pushed back and the woolen garment removed. Elinor Collins bowed, and advanced.

*****

It had been years since Roman had left London and travelled in the countryside. His now routine trips to Coudenoure represented the farthest afield he had ventured since the days when he had travelled with his father on business. Even yet, however, he remembered those journeys with the greatest fondness, recollecting them more as father and son adventures than as business trips. Once he had collected his small funds and written to Coudenoure, he had ceremoniously rid himself of all clothing he was accustomed to wearing in London – both his queen's livery and the breeches, hose, doublet and cap of a well-to-do gentleman – and dressed himself instead in the garb of a country man. He would travel as such, and indeed, would become such upon his return. His upcoming nuptials might brand him a baron, but nothing could change his love of simplicity or his passion for the quiet countryside.

His recent expeditions to Coudenoure had only confirmed this native passion. The estate was small, isolated and rocked along to a rhythm independent of fashion, and as with Henrietta, he loved it from the moment he saw it. He was not a religious man, but Henrietta and Coudenoure seemed eerily, almost mystically to have come his way, as though God had pre-determined that indeed, he would lead the life that generations of his ancestors had through the ages as serfs and tenant farmers of wealthy noblemen. But with this difference: he now worked for no one save Henrietta and their soon-to-come family. There was no landlord to take his wool as payment for the land, no tithe to be paid to the great master of the estate, no longing for a better life – it was there already. He would breed sheep that would produce the finest wool England had ever seen – he could hardly bear the time between now and that blessed future.

He bought passage on a feed barge, one which brought food and supplies from the counties to London, and returned there with nonesuch as its secondary cargo. They left at dawn and floated lazily upon a misty, quiet Thames. This was the same journey he and his father had embarked upon many times before in the past, and the sights and sounds of the river flooded his memory with a nostalgic, fleeting sense of things gone by. Yes – he remembered that bend in the river – there should be a public house just beyond it – yes! It was still there! Farther on, a broad meadow in early bloom – he had seen it before, he knew for certain. He sat by himself, well away from the other travelers who had sought passage on the old, rickety transport up river. He wanted to drink it all in and remember everything – it felt like going home and he thought his heart would burst with happiness. But as they reached an ancient elm which hung out over the wide water, he saw a rope with a loop in the end swaying from a low-hanging branch. Children were gathered on the bank, taking turns in the swing, daring each other not to fall into the chilly water of the Thames. And he remembered. Yes. His father had once paid the owner of whatever small transport they were on to stop, so that he, Roman, might join in and experience such wild excitement. His father had done that for him, wanting him to know and experience the life he himself had never known.

His father. Roman was surprised to find that the emotion which accompanied the vivid memory was regret, not anger. He pushed it from his mind and once again turned to the future.

He was going to Leominster, or more accurately the countryside which surrounded it where the small, Ryeland sheep, those prized for producing the finest wool in England, could be found. His father routinely traded the commodity at the Wool Exchange on behalf of a dozen or more farms and common land crofts spread across the region which drained the River.

Here, in the marches between Wales and England, history was written on the land itself. Offa's Dyck, the mysterious earthen work which traversed the entire border, stretched and writhed its way across the land, snaking to the west of hills, raising up its mighty walls in the low river valleys, skirting rivers and villages. It was said that in deep history, the Anglo Saxon King Offa, chief among the lords of Mercia, had constructed it using corvée owed him by his feudal lords. Comprised of a deep ditch with an earthen wall abutting it, it was meant to ward against hostilities emanating from the Welsh kingdom, Powys. Even now the ditch on the Powys side, scooped out to build the high earthen wall on the Mercia side, reminded all who saw it of the power of statehood, and the power of England.

For Roman, breathing in the county air, feeling the slow pulse of the river beneath the barge, watching the timeless activity of farmers in their fields and leas as the transport floated past, the moment was as near perfect as he could remember. Henrietta, Coudenoure, childhood memories, upriver in search of wool . . . home. Everything somehow spoke to him of home.

Several stops along the way seemed to hasten the day's departure, and as night fell Roman hunkered down on the barge. He lay in the cool night air listening to the quiet lapping of the river against the timbers upon which he lay and dreamt of Henrietta.

*****

Roman's intent was to visit one of the crofts which his father represented. It was owned by Kirk Williams, a man his father had known from his early years as a tenant farmer. They had bonded on market days, at regional fairs, and on rare trips to London where all woolsmen congregated in the wool district. Over time, as Matthew Collins rose, so too had Kirk Williams defined his own path. He had not had the opportunity to move to London and join the exchange, but even if it had presented itself, he would have declined, for he was a man for whom family and farm were all that mattered. Through years of careful trading, he had slowly changed his herd from predominantly Cotswolds – a heavy breed of sheep known for its long, straight wool – to Ryelands. The land seemed to suit them better, and in the event the weight of the fleece had confirmed for him the soundness of his reasoning.

On the fifth day of his travel, Roman found himself crossing the vast track of common land shared by Kirk Williams and other farmers in the area. He had not thought of what he would say when he finally reached the modest, thatch-roofed home of the man. Would he still be there? If he were out in the fields, would his wife remember Roman? Try as he might, he could not remember her name. Would they hear him out and understand his purpose? Or would they perhaps turn him away as one might a beggar?

The pasture trail slowly became a rutted mud road wide enough for a wagon. All was as Roman had remembered it. One final turn beyond a small hill of glaciated moraine and yes, there it was. He advanced haltingly and was still a hundred feet out when the door of the house opened and a large woman appeared, dressed in frilly pink cap, men's britches, and a loose fitting blouse with a woolen over-vest. Her hair, streaked with gray, was pulled tightly beneath the cap. Arms akimbo, she watched his approach warily through a squinty frown. Without warning, a broad grin split her sun-burned, wrinkled face and she rushed towards him.

"Oh aye, it would be Roman, now, would it not? I will know when I see your eyes, for they were ever the bluest I have seen."

He remembered the name.

"Mistress Molly Williams! It *is* me, Roman!"

She hugged him as a mother would, then stood back and took him in with a fussy grin.

"My word, child, you are now a man. And where is Matthew, eh?"

Without waiting for an answer, she tugged him to the house all the while bubbling out directions.

"Lil'Kirk, there is a lamb on the outer ridge with no ewe. See to it! And Rose, girl, fetch some tea and biscuits for we have a traveler!"

She took him into the main room of the house, a hall and kitchen combined. Rushes mixed with lavender and thyme were strewn across the ancient floor. To one side were two rough-hewn wooden chairs, and it was here that they sat. Molly poured the tea and offered him a rock hard scone. They were quiet for some time, allowing the situation to settle. Finally, Molly spoke.

"I have to wear this cap, you see, lest they forget I am a woman." She laughed delightedly.

"And your husband? Kirk? How is he?"

Molly gave him a perplexed look.

"Son, do you not know? Big Kirk was taken by the plague three years ago, he was. Your father did not tell you?" Her face softened but showed no regret, only the lines of a life lived within the strict boundaries of a harsh and unmitigated reality. Roman stared at her, not quite taking it in.

"Gone, you say? My father never said a thing!"

Molly sipped her tea.

"Oh aye, 'tis because he would not want to worry you or make you sad. He always had a keen eye out for your future he did. He wants only the best for his only son. And tell me, how is Matthew? Still the great man of the Exchange?"

Roman stared at her.

"Molly, we are estranged now."

"What?! And for how long, Master Roman?"

"Almost a week."

Molly threw back her head and roared with laughter.

"A whole week, eh? Big Kirk and I had fights that lasted longer than that."

"Madame, I assure you there is no humor in the situation. 'Tis terrible, indeed."

She sipped her tea as Roman poured out what he considered to be his sad tale. When he had finished, she poured him another cup and remained silent. Slightly annoyed at her lack of sympathy but deeply appreciative of the tea and company, he finally managed a polite cough, followed by a long sigh.

"So you see, Molly, my life is now that of an independent, honest countryman."

"Yes," Molly said drily, "An independent, honest countryman with considerable resources."

Again, Roman stared.

"Tell me, young Roman, are you not educated?"

"I am."

"Does your family not have a fine house and money?"

"Yeessss." Roman did not like the direction she was heading.

"And are you to marry the woman – a noblewoman at that – who is the woman of your dreams?"

He nodded.

"And do you suppose your father, a mere tenant farmer, got where he is by being open to suggestion or perhaps do you think he got there by being pigheaded?"

Silence.

Molly smiled gently at the confusion in Roman's eyes.

"Lil'Kirk and his father were not speaking when the plague carried the old one away, and many's the time he has come to me with tears in his eyes, distraught. 'If only I had not argued with him, if only I had been able to tell him how much I love him and appreciate what he has accomplished. If only . . .'. Why, sometimes it makes me sob, so great is his remorse. A mere argument became an eternal estrangement. 'Tis too, too sad."

A sinking feeling set in for Roman.

She stood up.

"Why are you here, young Roman?"

He stood.

"I have brought all the money I have with me. I wish to buy two rams and as many ewes as possible for I will use them to start my own flock."

"We have Ryelands. Why not Cotswolds?"

Roman was now on familiar ground. Molly knew the value of her Ryeland fleece.

"I considered them," he said honestly, "But Coudenoure is a small estate, and as you know, the flocking habit of Cotswolds is wide and ranging. I need sheep who do not mind a tighter pasturage."

Molly nodded and moved towards the front door.

"Well, we shall see. In the meantime, you shall visit for two days. We will talk old times and consider drovers. There are many tariffs and usage taxes upon the lands and roads now – 'tis not as it was before. No, it now costs a fair penny to move a flock any distance, and Coudenoure is far. You will need someone who knows the backways."

"Backways?"

She laughed.

"Boy, you have much to learn. Now go and help Lil'Kirk. He is off in yon field. The north flock must be brought in and mind the pass, for the lambs were being picked off there. When that is done, you must get the cows in and milked. Ask the maid there about turning the cheese. "

Roman grinned.

"So a full day I shall have! I shall be hungry for my supper at the end of it all!"

Molly smiled sweetly.

"That should hold you until the noon hour. After that, the shearing stable must be cleaned and the plough horses' brought in, groomed, fed and bedded."

With that, she turned away. Roman smiled weakly and went in search of Lil'Kirk.

The next two days were the most educational of his entire life.

On the third morning they discussed business.

"Two rams, my finest, and four ewes. I do not want your cash, Roman, but the return in good time of *three rams* and *six* ewes. And mind my wish for young ones."

"'Tis a high price."

"Indeed," came the sardonic reply.

The sun lit the sky a rosy pink, and as the drover they had hired began herding his small flock eastward, Roman bowed deeply to Lil'Kirk and Molly.

"And Lil'Kirk, do not feel sad about your estrangement from your father upon his death. I am sure in heaven he knows of your deep regret and forgives you."

Roman turned and began making his way down the rutted wagon track.

"What in God's name is the man talking about?" Lil'Kirk asked his mother quietly. "Father and I never had a fight, not even a small one!"

Molly chuckled, adjusted her pink, frilly cap, and grinned.

"Aye, but Roman does not know that."

They turned to their day's work.

*****

Nightfall. Matthew and Elinor sat in their customary chairs. Matthew had not gone to the Exchange that day, deciding instead to stay in bed until noon and then, once dressed, to remain in the sitting room staring at nothing all afternoon. Elinor had dressed in what she referred to as her house clothes – an old, stained dress with several neat, although obvious, repairs. She had then proceeded to the kitchen where she ate an entire platter of sweetened, dried fruit, four scones and a plate of ham. Before noon. By late afternoon, she had pulled herself together somewhat and put on shoes and had her hair done up by her maid. It had been thus for days.

Normally, the old couple had a routine which never varied. Late afternoon, Elinor would dress in her finest, sit patiently in the sitting room doing needlework or tatting and wait for Matthew to return home from his day at the Wool Exchange. As soon as he did, a servant would bring tea and a light repast while a full discussion ensued between Elinor and her husband. Usually, the conversation revolved around the day's events and they took turns filling one another in on this happening or that circumstance. Elinor might speak first, telling of her decision about this scullery maid or that groomsman, about her bargaining at the milliner's for a fair price on ribbon, or about the increasing scarcity of beef in the marketplace. In turn, Matthew might rail about the increasing price of fleece due to the increase of taxes across the land, or perhaps he would turn to the conversation he had had with a friend from the north in which they discussed their domestic situations. This habitual ending to the day, calcified and codified through the years, had suddenly been undone by the disappearance of Roman. And it was that vanishing which caused the near palpable gloom in which they now lived.

Some days earlier, they had received a note from one Lady Anne of Coudenoure. She hesitated to intrude upon their lives, but had received a letter from their dear son, who was betrothed to her niece, the tart from the Tower who was apparently named Henrietta. She enclosed his letter with her own. As Matthew read it aloud to Elinor, they both wept. Their boy loved them after all. He had not forsaken them nor did he despise them.

Elinor had immediately gone to Coudenoure. Upon her return to London, she had described the situation to Matthew who had already come to the conclusion that 'twas better to have a son who loved his family's trade than no son at all. If Roman was to marry some wild child rebel, one whom he had met while in prison, well, there must surely be worse things in life.

Letters and visits had ensued between the two families, and all had settled down to wait upon Roman's return. But as the days stretched ever longer, despair set in. Perhaps he had been set upon by brigands, or was wandering the west country with no money, begging for his very existence and unable to return to London and Coudenoure. His parents gave into their despair. Each evening, they still sat together in the sitting room, but their conversation was nothing but one long confession of their many mistakes over the years and what, if they had been good parents, they would have done for their boy. It was not productive.

Two more weeks passed, bringing them to this point, to this evening. They both knew that they simply could not continue in stasis while the world swirled about them. They must engage, find a way through the quagmire in which they were now trapped. They sat in the twilight, not bothering with the candles, the room lit only by the glow from the fire. A silence had fallen between them as they considered their options.

Without warning, they heard the front door fly open and bang loudly against the wall. No sooner had they risen than a filthy ragged stranger ran into the sitting room – a beggar with raven dark hair, a scruff of jet black beard and piercing blue eyes.

"Roman!" Elinor screamed and threw herself into her son's arms. He hugged her then gently moved her aside to face his father. Matthew and he spoke in tandem, both choking on emotion.

"Roman."

"Father."

"I was wrong."

"I was wrong."

"Can you ever forgive me?"

"Can you ever forgive me?"

"You are everything."

"I owe you everything."

It was a good night for the Collins family.

*****

Two days later, in a quiet and small ceremony in the library at Coudenoure, Henrietta Hill and Roman Collins became man and wife. The good father had barely time for his last words before Henrietta threw herself into Roman's arms. Their kiss at first initiated beaming smiles and quiet 'ahs'. As it went on, however, the smiles turned to embarrassed squirms. Finally, and with a blush on his cheeks, the father intervened with a blessing. They were married at last.

Elizabeth, as always, did not attend, for her presence would have distracted from the bride's moment. In her place she sent Lord Burghley. He was as ever dressed in his dark woolen habit but in accord with the day's festivities, a jaunty blue scarf wrapped his waist, matching his small ecclesiastical cap. As he exited the carriage, the groomsman made to close its door.

"Oye! I am here, man, and I do not wish to climb out the window!"

From within the carriage a small, simply dressed boy appeared. His breeches were slightly large for his tiny frame, but they were clean and well-made. A dark hat fit snugly about his head.

Waiting for them on the steps of Coudenoure were Bess and Anne, both dressed in finery seldom worn. The Collins' were there as well. But Marshall paid no heed to any of them as he ran to the small child holding Anne's hand.

"Ben! Ben!" He suddenly remembered himself and slowed his pell-mell run to a more adult pace. Ben stepped forward and hugged him.

"I remember you, young man!" Anne exclaimed.

"I am Marshall St. John. Before our kind Majesty provided me a home and an apprenticeship, I was here."

"Yes, you went for help on the day of my accident," Anne said. "Tell me, young Ben's last name is St. John as well – are you related?"

Both boys laughed delightedly. In a droll voice, Marshall responded.

"You have a St. John in your kitchen as well – Rouster St. John. We were all three left on the workhouse stoop, the Work House of St. John's Friars, and so we all took it as our name. 'Tis a fine idea, do you not agree? Three brothers we!"

Before she could respond, the front door slammed open and a lightning fast figure threw himself into Marshall's arms. Marshall grinned from ear to ear.

"Rouster? I almost cannot recognize you!"

Rouster sighed happily. Gone was the rail-thin urchin of London. In his place was a well-fed child of Coudenoure.

Bess related the day to Elizabeth as they sat one evening before the massive, medieval fireplace in the library at Coudenoure.

"So it ended well, I see," the queen ventured. "And are they happy yet?"

Bess waved her hand airily.

"How would we know, auntie, for they are seldom seen. They are either out and about at Coudenoure, building fences, inspecting pastures . . ."

Elizabeth interrupted her sharply.

"You mean they are supervising the people who do that, do you not?"

"Oh nooooo," Bess replied. "They participate in the actual labor! I tell them not to, that it is unbecoming a baron and his wife, but do they listen?"

Both women sighed and spoke their favorite phrase, "What is this kingdom coming to?"

"Henrietta is a traditional woman as far as a house, a home, and a husband go," Bess continued. "She has never wanted more than that. She is bright, bright indeed, but seems to have missed the wanderlust so apparent in her forebears." She paused and coughed. "But that is where her tradition ends, for she is a very physical young woman, and enjoys the rigors of actually running Coudenoure with Roman."

She coughed again and again Elizabeth spoke sharply.

"My last two visits have found you with the same cough. Shall I send a physician?"

Bess shook her head, with yet more coughing.

"No, 'tis a seasonal illness. It will pass with the coming of the autumn. Now, we will play at cards."

But it did not pass.

Chapter Twelve

December 1602

On a cold, snowy day, gray with shades and shadow, Elizabeth sat on the old stone bench in the graveyard at Coudenoure. She looked out across the landscape, barren and bleak, and saw no evidence of life. Quinn's meadow lay as still and silent as a corpse. No gray partridges scratched for seeds upon the frozen earth, no colorful partridges, their plumes asail, skated merrily on the breeze. A deep and silent pall had gathered the place in its folds, and no signs of life escaped its velvet embrace.

Elizabeth swung her cane free of the heavy winter cloak which swaddled her thin form. Her ladies had taken to dressing her with heavy woolen undergarments to keep her warm and ward off the chill. Her dress was woolen as well, but no matter the manner of dress, she was frequently cold.

She brought her gaze and her wandering thoughts back to the gravestone before her, and tapped her cane gently on its wide marble edge.

"How could you leave me, Bess?"

She sat in silent repose tapping slowly upon the stone.

"We were the last, you know. And now, well, 'tis only me."

She closed her eyes and thought upon those who had gone before.

"No one among my present court knew my father, no one among my courtiers and ladies remember my mother."

She thought of Essex and farther away still Dudley, the love of her life. The sudden memory of him brought a gentle smile and the tapping quickened.

"You rascal," she said softly aloud, "You were always out for my kingdom. And yet you loved me I am certain. And you knew me. Who but you were part of my childhood, yes?"

Tap tap tap.

"Bess, your great grandchildren are fine. They have named them Thomas and Elizabeth, is that not grand? And twins they are!"

Tap tap tap.

"Honestly, we are all surprised that there have been no more. They can barely keep their hands to themselves, Roman and Henrietta, and Bess, I promise you, they eye one another like a tart and her client, I promise you. But they are happy. They never leave Coudenoure, but go endlessly about the place together. It would be charming except I have come to wonder what they do when they are over yon hill alone, I certainly have." Pause. "But it barely interests me now."

Tap tap tap.

"The first time I came to Coudenoure, there was an old woman sitting where I sit now, Agnes, tapping her cane upon a gravestone. 'Tis symmetry, is it not?"

She rose and began walking away. After a moment, she turned and bowed deeply.

"To all who have gone before, do not close the door quite yet I pray, for I shall join you anon, and leave this cold and sodden place for those who would come after."

*****

On March 24, 1603, Elizabeth I, daughter of the great King Henry VIII, granddaughter of Henry VII, died. Her passing severed the Tudor line of kingship, and that of the Stuarts would rise now in its place. But it did not sever the Tudor bloodline, for at a quiet estate on the western side of the great palace of Greenwich, it lived on.

Chapter Thirteen

The Stuarts

The Scottish marches were tribal, terrible in their primal beauty and isolation. Great streaks of raw color – purples, oranges, rusts and greens – swathed the low lying hills that rose above the barren scape, etching in stark relief the boundary between sky and earth. There, on that great and endless horizon, in the hills and vales and rivers and streams, God had painted the world in a pure and deliberate fashion. And it sang a siren's song to the souls of all who saw it, speaking a language so deep, so primordial that it needed no words and no sounds. It called out to the unwary with its lingering melancholy, and was carried on the whistling song of the cold north winds which blew from climes unimaginable. Its notes, like the land itself, seemed not of this earth.

Those who passed this way frequently gasped in wonder at the scenery laid out before them. Even to those who had lived and ruled this world for centuries, the lonely heaths were fierce and formidable and so achingly beautiful as to cause those who traversed them to meditate in quiet reverence on the majesty of God. The clans ruling this land seldom showed mercy and knew no authority save their own, reflecting in their character the gray winds that blew down from the north across the bleak and barren landscape some 96 miles wide. It was a lawless place, this boundary world, caught between Scotland and England like a hare in a net. This was the belt which girdled James' kingdom of Scotland.

*****

Henrietta sat on a huge, glaciated rock which looked out over a deep and rambling valley. Beside her Roman slept undisturbed. Their horses were tethered to a low hanging branch near the rutted road on which they travelled. She glanced at them, then at Roman before running her hand lightly across his tumbling locks, smiling as she did so. Absently, she twisted her flaming curls beneath the caul from which they had escaped. All the while she breathed in the vast and lonely landscape before her. So this was her father's land, his home country.

She had known little of her mother Catherine, and less of her father, one Joshua Edward Hill. Bess, Quinn and Anne had told her stories in her youth of how the beauty of her mother had captured the northerner's heart, and of Catherine's passion for the highlander. Her parents had loved deeply, if only for a brief moment – Joshua had been killed in battle in the New World and Catherine had died giving Henrietta life.

Early on, Henrietta had not realized that the stories painted for her with their almost mythical heroine and hero were meant to normalize her childhood. She had not fully appreciated the absence of her parents for the simple reason that she came to adulthood at Coudenoure deep in the warm embrace of her family. It was what she knew, what she had always known. As an adult, she had wondered more about them, but only in an abstract way, for her life was lovingly embedded in the very fabric of the estate.

On the day the stranger rode slowly up the straight and graveled drive of Coudenoure, she and Roman had been taking tea in front of the manor house. Like generations before them, they watched their children – Thomas and Elizabeth – romp through what was now known as Quinn's Meadow, named after her grandfather who had torn up the lovely sodded lawn and replaced it with perhaps the finest meadowland in England. It wore its spring gown now, and the children ran and laughed through its welcoming blossoms before settling down to their intended purpose.

Thomas, ever the willing servant of his twin sister Elizabeth, had been charged with keeping at the ready the paraphernalia they had hauled along with them: two tiny wooden boxes with sliding lids, a makeshift butterfly net, and a coil of string. He walked slowly behind her, casting searching glances now to the right, now to the left. Elizabeth did the same. They were in search of the hedgehog they had seen two days previously in the nearby yew hedge. That they would find it, capture it and domesticate it seemed highly improbable to everyone except them. Should they come across any interesting anything while they hunted, the two boxes should suffice.

Henrietta was the first to see the horseman. Dressed in dreary black and with a large brimmed hat, so thin as to be vulnerable to a high wind, he plodded slowly up the drive.

"What do you think?" She asked Roman, shading her eyes with her hand.

He studied the man carefully as he came closer.

"I do not know," he replied nonchalantly. "But I suppose we shall see."

At that moment, the great front doors of house creaked open, and Ben ran out, followed by Anne. She walked slowly now, with a crutch, but her face was serene, calm and happy. No one had realized the profound joy she would find in raising Ben St.

John, including her. When the urchin had first come
to Coudenoure, sent there by the queen, they had
wondered what to do with the small boy. Despite
Elizabeth insisting he should apprentice in the
library, it seemed strange even by Coudenoure
standards that a small child could want such a life.
He had resolved the problem for them.

Day after day, they found him in among the
books in the library, perched in this quiet corner or
that, reading. It was necessary to remind him to eat.
One afternoon, barely a week after he had come to
Coudenoure, he had finally emerged from his self-
imposed cocoon and spoken to Anne.

"Tell me, kind lady," he had said softly, eyes
shining, "Would this be Greek?"

Anne had been sitting nearby trying, once again,
to enjoy the tediousness of needlepoint. She gladly
put her hoop aside and took the book the boy
proffered.

"Why, so it is!" she exclaimed. "And how did
you come to that conclusion?"

He ignored her question, intent on his own
inquiry.

"Might you teach me?"

Their bond was sealed. From that moment on as
Elizabeth had foreseen, Ben became Anne's shadow.

They read together, catalogued books and papyri together, dusted, discussed, and mapped out the collection's inadequacies and its strengths together. Then they started over again. The boy was the child Anne had never had. As for Ben – he had never been religious, but each evening, before going to sleep in the small room given to him as his on the second floor, he dropped to his knees and thanked God in his bright heaven for bringing him here.

The two of them joined Roman and Henrietta on the front drive now, watching with lazy curiosity as the rider dismounted, tethered his horse, bowed, and finally approached. Roman stood. He was still in his youth, but had filled out his previously slim torso. The work in the fields as he learned the craft of farming and sheep had replaced the lean muscle of youth with the strength of an adult man.

"Good day, sir."

The stranger held his hat in his hand and bowed again. Henrietta noticed a slight trembling in the man's hand. As he bowed, the same shaking crossed his entire frame. She felt pity for the stranger and rose.

"And to you sire. I am Old John Taberman and I bring news from his Lordship."

The man's deep voice was laden with fatigue and Henrietta spoke quickly.

"Kind sir, you have obviously come some distance. Pray, sit here with us and have a small repast while you tell us of your mission."

Her kindness seemed to fortify the old man, and he shuffled to the chair offered and did a slow fall into it.

Henrietta stood, beckoned to a nearby servant, and after a moment, tea and a small plate of food were brought out. The fine spring weather was discussed, the children and their games admired, the chance of rain later in the day calculated. Only then, when the tired rider had settled and revived himself with a sip or two of tea and a bite of scone did Roman direct the conversation to what was on each of their minds.

"What brings you to Coudenoure, sir?"

For the first time, Henrietta noticed an old leather satchel secured by a strap across their guest's bony chest. He patted it lightly as he spoke.

I come today with a message from my master, the legal authority for Castle Donoway and the great family thereof."

Henrietta and Anne looked at him sharply. The lethargy of the sunny spring afternoon was gone in an instant. The stranger continued.

"May I?"

Roman nodded. He was not certain why both women had suddenly become rigid and alert at the mention of a faraway castle, but he saw the fun in the old man's deliberate movements and Henrietta's predictable and accustomed reaction of impatience.

The messenger slowly unwound the leather string of the satchel's flap from a button of leather on its front. Henrietta tapped her foot pleasantly on the gravel, watching him. Deliberately, he continued.

"How long is that leather strip?" she thought to herself. The pace of the tapping picked up and she shifted in her seat. Roman smiled brightly at her and chuckled. His wife noted his idea of amusement and stored it up for later adjudication. After an eternity, the man reached within his bag and produced a slim, rectangular wooden box which now he solemnly passed to Roman.

Roman carefully inspected the curiosity, feeling its weight and observing the odd, runic lines with which it was decorated, then turned to Henrietta with laughing eyes.

"Hmm." was all he said.

She could have beaten him with Anne's cane. After a moment, Roman slowly opened the lid and peered within. Henrietta was almost on the verge of shrieking.

"Dear?" She stopped short for fear of letting out what she really wanted to say.

Undeterred, Roman now drew forth a scrolled and sealed parchment from within, scrutinized it – and then with glee turned to Anne. Henrietta smiled icily at her husband. He continued to chuckle under his breath.

"Anne, pray look at the seal – what does it say?"

Ben leapt from his seat and almost tripped in his haste to get to Anne's side. Henrietta gripped the side of her chair and bit her tongue.

Together, Anne and Ben examined the seal.

"I believe, Lady Anne, that seal belongs to a clan on England's border. Do you remember last week, when we were enjoying the book on heraldry and symbolism left to Coudenoure by the good Sir William Cecil? That pattern . . ." he rubbed his finger gently over the wax, ". . . is indeed the arms for the Donoway Clan, I am certain."

Anne placed her hand gently, protectively, on Ben's back and leaned closer to the seal.

"I believe you are correct!"

Ben smiled happily. Henrietta spoke in a squeaky voice.

"Shall we *OPEN IT*?"

Ben's little fingers carefully broke the wax seal and pealed it away as Anne watched on. Finally, she passed the scroll the Henrietta.

"Perhaps you will read it aloud for us, dear niece?"

After shooting her laughing husband a look so hot it might have ignited it might have set the cook fire alight, Henrietta began to read.

"To the Baroness of Coudenoure

It is with great urgency that I post this missive to you, madame.

If you are the daughter of Sir Joshua Edward Hill, the brother of the Earl of Langdon, then I entreat you to read further.

The earl and his wife had no offspring, and two weeks prior to my writing, the good man died. Lady Helen, his wife, has been gone ten years. She was the last of her line and there are no known relatives on her side. 'Tis true she represented the Donoway 'Clan', but truth be told such Donoways as there were are long gone, and 'twas just the master and her in the Castle Donoway.

Before he died, the earl dictated his wishes to me. They are as follows:

He directed me to seek out his brother, the aforementioned man, and to inform him that circumstances have decreed that he is now the Earl of Langdon. Should the brother have preceded him in death, as we believe he did, the Earl wished me to seek out any issue born to the man. Many years ago, a letter arrived from this place to which I have sent my missive, one Coudenoure, telling of a daughter born to Sir Hill and of his death in the New World. It is that information which has precipitated this document.

Should that child be alive, I humbly request that he or she ride north to claim the inheritance. Should no such issue have arisen from the dead man, I should be grateful for that knowledge.

My messenger has been paid well for his service. He shall wait upon your actions and directions before returning to me.

I am, your humble servant,

Ian Hurlbert.

"A castle!" Ben squeaked excitedly.

"Tell us about this place, Castle Donoway," Anne said quietly.

The messenger reached for a second scone and spoke laconically.

"'Tis on the northern side of the Scottish marches, not so far from the western coast. Many years ago, 'twas a fine castle with perhaps 20,000 acres. Some crops were grown, but most of the land was given over to the raising of sheep . . ."

"Sheep?" Roman cut in.

The old man nodded assent and continued.

". . . but the family's fortunes dwindled and they sold some of the land to satisfy debt. 'Tis a rather small place now with only sheep."

"What breed of sheep?"

Well, sir, I believe the Earl had experimented with two northern types – he mixed the Orkney, known for its ability to withstand cold, with the Romney Marsh, known for its excellent, lustrous wool.

"Hmm, yes, indeed. And what was the result?"

"*NO.*" Henrietta was constantly amazed at Roman's ability to insert sheep into any conversation. Granted, he did not begin this particular aside, but he clearly intended to pursue it. She glared a warning at him.

"Kind sir," she turned to the messenger, "Pray continue about the castle itself."

"Well, Madame, 'tis much grander than it sounds. Again, in its day it was very fine. But the Earl and his mistress did not keep the place up. I am told they lived in one wing only, and all the rest is now home to bats and other vermin."

"And the land?" Anne inquired.

"'Tis fine land it is. The Donegals are masters of the heath all about Donoway, and they are a fair lot – I believe the Earl would give you a fair price should you wish to sell."

He finished off his tea and started in on a third scone.

"There is naught much in the old place, save for the sheep and some musty old books. I am told they are so old they are falling apart, so they would not be much use to anyone, m'lady."

"BOOKS?"

Roman threw back his head and laughed as Henrietta assumed a worn and patient look – her life's burden had been distilled down to its essence now, consisting of sheep and books. It promised to be an interesting day.

On the next morning hence, with saddle pouches chocked full with bacon, bread, ale and cheese, Old John had ridden north. On the third day, Roman and Henrietta had followed.

*****

As she sat on the rock looking out over the highlands, Roman stirred. At the same time, a great rumbling arose behind them. It quickly sorted itself into the thunder of a mighty horse, and Henrietta and Roman rose and moved towards the road. The great warhorse pounded towards them, its rider draped in Tudor livery. He saw the young couple and reined in the sweating beast.

"I see you wear our good queen's livery," Roman said.

The man on the horse had a haggard appearance. His face was lean and weather-beaten with three days shadow upon its hollow cheeks and chin. He crossed himself before speaking.

"The queen is dead, two days now."

Henrietta and Roman crossed themselves in turn.

"We knew that she was ill, but not quite so ill as that."

"Aye, it comes to us all. And she had a good reign. She kept the peace, she did."

He jerked the reins of his horse.

"I must needs be off, for I am from her court and I ride to bear the news to our new sovereign."

He lifted his voice as he again crossed himself.

"The queen is dead!"

Henrietta and Roman spoke the lines with him.

"The queen is dead! Long live the king!"

He spurred his mount on and disappeared onto the rising moor.

Roman and Henrietta watched him in silence, each lost in what the queen's death might mean for England. Who was this new sovereign? Would he rule justly? Known as James VI in Scotland, he would take the name James I when once on the English throne.

"We should be off," Roman said finally, glancing at the sun. "We ought to try and make Donoway by dusk."

As he spoke, another rider thundered into view from the south. He, too, rode alone. His horse, deepest ebony and sweating profusely, matched the rider's own heavy breathing. Garbed in the non-descript clothing of a poor man, he nevertheless exuded the authority usually associated with nobility. Just as the rider before him had done, he reined in his mount as he approached the young couple.

"And who would you be?" he asked boldly.

"I am Roman Collins, a sheep merchant from the south. And you?" Roman gave a curt and curious bow.

"Lord Darneagle, lad."

A pleasant, though brief, silence ensued.

"You ride hard, I see," Roman eventually ventured.

"Aye, for I bring news to the marches. The queen is dead."

"Indeed, we heard such news not one hour ago, from another rider."

The older man jerked his head in attention.

"I am sorry, what words did you just speak?"

Roman repeated the words.

"The man rode from the queen's court to inform James himself."

The stranger yanked hard on his mount's reins, causing the animal to rear despite its obvious exhaustion.

"To James himself, you say."

"Yes. The signal torches from London to Scotland were most assuredly lit, so undoubtedly it is known. I believe the gentleman rode ahead of the official delegation which is sure to arrive. Indeed, I thought you might be part of it as well."

A vigorous nod of dissent came his way.

Roman finished by intoning the familiar chorus.

"The queen is dead. Long live the king."

Again, the rider looked sharply at him.

"You are too hasty. The queen is dead, oh aye, but long live the king?" He gave a wicked laugh. "Let us wait before we pronounce such a thing, shall we?"

He spurred his mount was gone in an instant, astonishment at his chilling declaration still written on Henrietta and Roman's faces.

"What does that mean, husband?"

Roman began untying their own mounts.

"Trouble. That is what it means."

He passed the reins of Henrietta's horse over to her.

"Let us finish our business here, my love, and leave quickly and quietly, for I do not like what I see upon the horizon."

Chapter Fourteen

The Stuart Court

The courtiers were gone, his wife asleep in her own bedchamber. At moments like this, James VI's thoughts roamed free. Tonight, they took a familiar path.

Witches were forever upon his mind. He knew them to be everywhere – in the dank and forbidding folds of the Scottish glens where the whispering firs confirmed their presence; in the fog which settled in preternaturally on warm summer days; in the foul smelling waters and estuaries of the coastal lands as dusk settled in and the seabirds quietened. Sometimes, should he be riding alone, he could feel their hands upon his body, hear their inviting entreaties. Sirens they were. Scotland was such a land as to give aid and comfort to the wretched and evil creatures. With its bogs and marshes, with its wild highlands and deep winter nights, it provided a haven for all manner of devils. But witches, aye, they were a special breed apart.

Why, witches could hide in plain sight. Had he himself not seen white witches – those truly clever ones, hard to uncover, known for their healing powers, always stirring their brews and potions and broths, claiming health benefits for those who might drink deeply of them. "Come hither", they might coax, "and take this herbal brew I have made – it will help your chest cough; here, lad, partake of this potion, for it will heal your ulcers and wounds." Oh aye, clever they were, practicing their dark art upon the hapless, the sick and the dying. They abided even in unexpected places. Yes. They were everywhere. Always waiting for him, casting their bird-like eyes in hooded glances this way, that way, ever calculating.

From whence did they get their dark power? If they contracted with Satan for it, had they actually met that fearsome and evil beast? It was well known that where there was one witch there were surely others, for they could not exist without a coven – like an army upon a battlefield, their strength was enhanced and magnified through numbers. They gathered upon the vast empty plains of the land, in the howling winds and the winter's black night, calling forth the darkness of their souls, bewitching and entrapping all innocents who dared cross them.

He thought back to the day when he brought his new wife, Queen Anne, home from Denmark, and the roiling, blistering storm that had taken one ship from the Scottish flotilla whilst his own had barely survived, limping into port, ragged and damaged. 'Twas the work of a witch, that storm, he well knew.

A sudden banging outside his chamber door caused him to jump and twitch.

"What is it?" he called out in an imperious tone. A small knock upon the door.

"Sire, I am sorry, Majesty, for I dropped a tray. Beg pardon, Majesty."

He nodded at the shaking servant and as she pulled the door behind her he returned to his own thoughts. After a moment, he picked up the small looking-glass which lay on the table near him and held it to his face.

It was a long, pale face, with deep set and light brown eyes flecked with gold. He stroked the thin, auburn beard, feeling its coarseness and noticed, not for the first time, how wispy his moustache had become.

"Oh, aye," he said softly to himself with a wry, crooked smile, ". . . but you yet have your hair." He moved his hand up and stroked his pale auburn locks. After a moment, he put the looking glass aside and moved to the window, continuing the conversation with himself.

"So, King James, how does it feel? Eh? You will be king of all now, of Scotland, of Ireland. Of England."

How many years had such a union been sought? Did not his own mother try to claim by force what was now being offered to him in peace?

"'Twas what your mother wanted, was it not? Hmm? But it was not hers to have."

His thoughts shifted briefly to the mother he had never known, Mary, Queen of Scotland before his reign began. Mary, whom in her hour of need he had denied. For as long as he could remember, he had been warned against her, for she had been known to have strange powers over men. Charming, flighty, French. Scots needed a man to rule them, not a scheming shrew – they would have none but the strongest upon the throne.

The English, well, they were a different matter. They had accepted a woman in a man's position – what a foppish lot they were. What would they think of him, he wondered? He knew the prejudice which infused English thought against those from the North Country: the Scots were felt to be rustic at best – ignorant, uncultured and argumentative; they were thought ill-mannered and suspicious, clinging to the pagan ways of the deep past. The English would have to move past that now that he would be their sovereign. He found their notion of a strong parliament which assisted in the rule of the kingdom ludicrous. They would find that an absolute monarch with absolute power was a far better model for a Greater Britain. They would have to, for he did not intend to give them a choice.

He sighed. So much to do now that he had been proclaimed King of England. Where to begin? Perhaps with the progress south so that his new subjects might see their new king? He did not care for humanity up close – the reeking masses, the sick, those near starvation from the constant famines and the plagues which swept the land. But it would be kind of him to allow them a glimpse of himself as he moved south in state. In state . . . indeed – the clothes and accolades! The pageantry! He called out for his dresser and clerk – it would be a busy few weeks.

Chapter Fifteen

"Yonder?" Roman pointed to a hulking pile of a castle which rose in the far distance. Its crenellated ramparts spoke of an aged Scottish lineage and its mossy walls did not deny the tale. It seemed to rise fully formed out of the earth as though its ancient towers had been there since creation.

The yeoman mumbled affirmatively to the question and continued leaning upon his makeshift plough. It was hard work moving it through the boggy soil, and both the sway-backed mule who pulled and the middle-aged man who pushed were more than happy to take a small break from their toils, clearly enough. The laborer wiped the sweat from his brow and took a drink from the ale jug offered him by Roman.

"So you have business there?"

"Yes," came the reply, "Tell me, is anyone about now?"

A gruff laugh.

"I expect so. The old earl died some weeks afore, but the estate's caretaker lives on there. I heard he was waiting for the new Earl."

The man took another drink and eyed Roman speculatively.

"Yes, I am he."

Roman considered asking the withered, tired man upon whose land did he toil, but decided quickly that such intrusive questions were not necessary. Henrietta and he had already come to an agreement about the castle and its lands – there was no need to share their plans just yet.

Henrietta had not dismounted but waited impatiently for Roman to finish his conversation. The yeoman looked at her and smiled.

"You may be the earl, sire, but your missus, well, she could be the old man's daughter she could. There is something about the chin . . ." he rubbed his own to emphasize his words, "Aye, a close resemblance."

Henrietta smiled but said nothing.

"And tell me, good sir," Roman asked casually, "Are there sheep upon these lands?"

"Good day, kind sir." Henrietta's words were sweet but the look she gave Roman was not. He sprang back up into his saddle, tipped his woolen cap at the man and they rode on.

"Sheep?" Henrietta said under her breath. "We are about to behold our very own castle and you ask about sheep?"

Roman grinned, brushed his horse against hers and leaning in gave her a glancing kiss on the check.

She smiled and they trotted on in peace.

*****

Castle Donoway was every bit the wreck they had been promised. What had once been a commanding and fortified clan stronghold now stood as a bleak outpost upon the Scottish marches, lonely, untended, and almost forgotten. Only one wing stood complete. Like a carcass in a lonely field, the local vultures had picked away at the very fabric of the old building and its contents – its bricks and stones had been pilfered for other uses. As the walls had sagged and the roof caved in, its curtains and tapestries had rotted and had been picked away at by avian thieves. The fences had been tumbled by time and were almost completely covered by the vegetation that crept about the place like visitors to a dying man's chamber.

The drive, whose faint lines could still be seen from a distance, was barely discernable as such as they descended the last rolling hill and approached their treasure. It did not help that a deep and cold gloom, the Scottish harbinger of nightfall, begin to rise all about. Henrietta shivered as she spoke.

"'Tis terrible gloomy, Roman, and I do not care for it. Let us knock quickly, for if there is no one here we shall have to make other plans for the night – we are mostly without food and water."

Roman laughed.

"We shall make no other plans, my love, for if no one answers we shall enter our castle – upon my word, it is ours and we shall find something to eat and drink within, I am certain."

But there was no need for such contingencies. As they made their final approach across the last one hundred feet of yard, long gone to seed, the door opened and a solitary man stepped out.

He was of that age when a man is no longer young but not yet into middle-age. His clothes gave no hint as to his station or purpose in life. They were dark, multi-layered and hung loosely about his tall frame. Henrietta thought fleetingly of Coudenoure, and the eccentric manner of dress of its inhabitants – fashion was not for them and the clothes worn by this tall Scotsman were likewise simple in the extreme. He was neither thin nor stooped, as some men of such build frequently became, but rather pleasantly proportional – enough youth mixed with an elegant amount of sober age. His hair was graying at his temples, fading to a deep chestnut overall. His demeanor was one of polite questioning, and he bowed tentatively to Roman and Henrietta as they dismounted.

"I am Roman Collins, Baron of Coudenoure, and this is my wife, the Lady Henrietta."

A smile crossed the man's entire face.

"Welcome! I must say, I suspected that the strangers I saw approaching were from that now fabled place." He paused. "Well, not actually fabled you understand. But fabled since we sent the messenger southward to London."

Roman smiled. Despite the slightly off-kilter explanation of 'fabled', he liked the man immediately. He exuded a warm and twinkling disposition while his baritone voice gave away his Scottish ancestry. It was an altogether pleasing combination and he glanced at Henrietta and saw that she, too, was smiling.

"I am Ian Hurlbert, the lawyer who sent the inquiry and also the caretaker of Donoway for the past two years. Come in, my Lord and Lady, and welcome. I received news of your journey yesterday and have been burning a bright fire ever since so that the tired and ancient bones of the castle might be seen in their best light when you arrived. Old John returned with your letter only yesterday. Had he been a bit slower or you faster, you might have passed your own post!"

He beckoned them in and they found themselves in a medieval and dark fortress, with barely more warmth than the chill that was setting in outdoors. The waning light from the high slit windows barely touched the floor, but Ian had lit stout candles which sat squarely upon iron sconces embedded in the walls. The effect of their flickering illumination bid the cold shadows welcome the visitors, if only grudgingly. As Henrietta took in the scene a glint of metal from high in the shadows caught her attention and she discovered – far up upon the walls – great plinths protruding from the ancient stones. Upon each one was a suit of armor. Some bore the family crest, some did not; some had a strange chain-like metal mesh she had never seen before; between several of the martial displays hung huge pennants, white with a stark red central cross as their only symbol. She nudged Roman and he, too, turned his glance skyward, dumbfounded by the spectacle above them. Once seen, the armor's presence could not be erased. The empty suits seemed to stand guard, soberly, solemnly and with a purpose long since become a mystery. They had been prepared for the wrack and ruin indicated by the façade of Castle Donoway, but not for the ethereal sense of time long lost which pervaded the interior of this fortress, now breached by disuse yet still standing lonely guard upon the Scottish marches. Roman shivered; Henrietta embraced it and felt the tug of a family she had never known; Ian remained quietly respectful, allowing the couple time to take in the faded grandeur. After a space, he beckoned them further into the recesses of the castle.

They entered a short passageway and realized they were simply moving through the depth of the old, colossal stone walls. On the other side, they came to what had been used as living quarters by the old earl, and now by Ian. A single massive room had been neatly subdivided by a bed, two chairs, several small tables and a plethora of wooden crates and boxes. Each 'room' had a side near to the huge granite fireplace, ensuring an equal distribution of its warmth and light on the heavy winter eves. Enormous iron candelabras, positioned round about the hearth and the room's artificial divisions, provided the antidote to the creeping sadness of decay that hung about the place. It was almost cheerful. Ian nodded to a small child, previously unseen by Henrietta and Roman, and the boy scurried off to do his master's bidding.

"Those great red crosses . . ." Henrietta motioned towards the outer room, ". . . tell me. I believe they were carried by the knights who besieged the holy city of Jerusalem in ancient times."

Ian looked at the woman sharply. For the first time he caught a sense of her resemblance to the old earl. Clearly, she was educated.

"Aye, m'lady. 'Tis the Donoway family story. Many generations past, the patriarch of this great and storied family participated in the fight to free Jerusalem. They marched under the very pennants which you see before you. I am not certain of the age of the armor but believe it to be of that time as well. 'Tis remarkable, really, to have an artifact linked with Jerusalem that one can touch with one's own hand."

"Indeed." Henrietta barely breathed the word.

The child returned carrying a small tray of bread, dried apples and meat. A woman followed on his heels with a jug of ale. They bowed, left, and the three attacked the meal with vigor.

"There are many wood boxes." Roman observed, pointing about the room as he ate.

"Ah, well, sire, I hope you will not mind. When I arrived here at the bidding of the old earl, he demanded that I perform an inventory of what might still have value amid the ruin of the family's estate. I did as he wished, and discovered upon the second floor a small library."

Roman shot a long, knowing grin at Henrietta.

A long pause ensued and a shadow of guilt settled on Ian's intelligent face.

"There is something I believe I must share with you."

All trace of humor disappeared. Roman and Henrietta leaned forward.

"I fear you may be unhappy with what I am about to disclose."

Silence. Henrietta's eyes were growing wider by the second; Roman's, more wary.

"You see, I discovered a substantial number of valuable and *relatively* valuable items. There are tapestries, some even Flemish, I believe. One or two are yet in fine condition – the damp and the moths have not had their way entirely. There are several valuable paintings and some of whose value I am uncertain."

Henrietta raised an eyebrow as an invitation for detail.

"For instance, there is a Holbein. Two fine portraits of the Lady Helen and the old earl, both by Arnold Bronckhorst, hang in an upstairs gallery; there are rugs of Saracen origin, brought back from Jerusalem, and a bust of someone I know not, by Donatello, the great Italian."

"I do not see your dilemma, Ian," Roman said bluntly.

"Well, sire, just before the earl's death, I suggested to him that we protect these treasures from further decay by placing them carefully in wooden storage crates. Once he was gone, I would have no right to do so unless he had directed me thus. I was deeply concerned that without proper care, these items would in the not distant future be given to rot and ruin."

Roman had had enough.

"Get to your point, man."

"The earl agreed and left the work to me. It was necessary to begin the commissioning of a great many crates and I have done so. But sire, rather than beginning with the treasures in greatest need of conservation, I began with the books, for you see, sire, I am afflicted with bibliomania."

Roman howled with laughter. Henrietta sighed.

"I do not understand. There are many works of art here that desperately need protecting from the elements. I have been concerned that you would not agree with my decision to save the books first."

Roman was still laughing. Henrietta explained the reason, but her mind was elsewhere. For many years, she had wondered why her aunt, the Lady Anne, had never taken a husband. She knew the tale of the false Marlowe who had broken her heart, but Anne was so beautiful even now, so educated and bright and kind, she resisted the belief held by all of Coudenoure that Anne would rather spend her life alone with her books and her languages. Indeed, since her marriage to Roman, and since little Ben had come to stay, Henrietta had seen longing looks from the older woman, as though she had come to realize what she had missed out on, something that would have fulfilled her perhaps even more so than her library. There was a sadness that clung to those looks and Henrietta had searched long and hard for a way to bring happiness to the woman who had raised her as her own.

And now here, seated in front of her, was the answer! She was certain. Here was a fine scholar, intelligent and educated and in his prime – just what her Anne needed. Ian was warm, funny and would fit well at Coudenoure with his love of books and odd, fashion-less manner of dressing. And he and Roman seemed to have already forged a budding friendship. But how to manage it? That was the trick. As Roman and Ian continued their conversation, Henrietta smiled and occasionally pulled tidbits of personal information from the man she was quickly moving towards being her uncle.

He was a bachelor. Henrietta had already guessed as much, for no wife would let a husband disappear into the marches for an indeterminate period of time. He had been schooled at home by his father (excellent), a baron. Ian himself was a second son and so had chosen law as his career (fine, fine), and he confessed to being a man who chose intellectual pursuits over those of sport or gamesmanship (how much better could it get?).

By the end of the conversation, Henrietta had made her plans.

"We cannot stay long, Ian, but you are right, these family heirlooms must not be allowed to return to dust. I would ask that you intensify (for she could not WAIT for him to meet Auntie Anne) your efforts in this area. We shall pay generously for your work and time – and as soon as is feasible you shall begin a progress south, overseeing the train safely to Coudenoure."

She glanced at Roman and found him eyeing her brazenness with suspicious speculation. He knew she had settled upon some scheme, but he could not discern what it might. Normally, he was able to predict his dear wife's purposes and machinations – because she immediately set to blabbing forth her plan for all the world to hear. But this time she had concealed that accustomed tell and merely smiled at him. Innocently. Ian watched the interplay with interest, realizing that these two loved one another very much, knew each other even as only true lovers do – and that master Roman was having an unusual problem in not being able to read his wife. Well, all relationships need a little mystery, he decided.

He enthusiastically agreed to the proposal Henrietta had outlined.

"Indeed, I have always wanted to see London, so this will be a boon to me, as to you. We shall work quickly over the coming weeks to set your plans for Castle Donoway upon legal ground and ensure that your title is as it should be. After that, I shall continue storing and packing your valuables for the trip south, and then see you safely on your way while I follow anon."

They all smiled in agreement. Roman knew there would be interesting pillow talk that night.

*****

The morning dawned bright and Henrietta wondered why she had felt such unease the previous evening. Wrapped in her heavy cloak with an additional scarf pulled and knotted about her face, she had stepped out early, leaving Roman alone in their bed. She had always been an early riser and this morning she was particularly motivated. A strong urge to see the land of which her father had been an inseparable part swept over her in waves. But there was a more practical reason for her perambulations this morning as well.

Roman and she had ridden hard to reach the marches. Despite knowing that Elizabeth and Thomas were well cared for in their absence, her maternal instincts had dictated a quick trip – she had never been apart from the twins and the situation, despite being benign, made her deeply anxious. The resulting ride, hard and fast over rutted and treacherous roads, had bruised her considerably. Like all noblewomen, she rode side-saddle, and the back of her right knee – the point at which the saddle horn made contact with her leg – was chaffed and red, and ached considerably. Hours in the saddle had stiffened her joints and she knew if she did not take deliberate care to exercise them before the ride home, it would prove even more difficult than the ride north. And so she walked.

As the morning mist curled and slipped away, Ian joined her.

"I see you are up and about early this morning, m'lady." They fell into an easy gait along an overgrown path.

"Yes, I must be, for I am unaccustomed to such long rides."

A pleasant pause ensued.

"After you and the earl retired last evening, I looked over the documents you brought with you."

"We received legal counsel from Lord Burghley before coming north," Henrietta explained. "He advised that the parish records of my parents' wedding, my birth, and my own marriage, would be necessary to establish the claim beyond all doubt."

"Ah, well, he is a wise fellow, this Burghley. Tell me, what is your intent for the future of Castle Donoway?"

Henrietta laughed.

"Such as it is? Roman believes a caretaker should be established and allowed to manage the lands. In lieu of payment, the man may count as his own any proceeds from the flocks or the fields."

Ian seemed to consider this proposal.

"Yes, 'tis a good plan, particularly since the Doneagle clan is anxious to purchase the Donoway properties in their entirety. This will signal them that the estate will not be given away – a decent price must be offered."

"Do you know anyone hereabout who could be trusted in such a position?"

"Aye, I do. Look yonder – do you see that man with his tired old mule?"

Henrietta smiled.

"Indeed. We spoke with him on our way to Donoway."

"He is the last tenant farmer on the estate. He is honest and knows the land. And, I believe the earl will be impressed with his knowledge of sheep."

"The earl is impressed by sheep alone, my good Ian, and anyone who knows anything about them is halfway to winning his respect."

Ian laughed.

"Also, Lady Henrietta . . ."

"Please, at Coudenoure, we do not use titles. 'Tis unusual I know but it works well."

"Also . . . Henrietta . . . the groundsman is married with two young boys. I believe the entire family would benefit from the arrangement."

"We must speak with Roman but it sounds fine to me. Now, talk to me about how you will accomplish your southbound progress."

There ensued detailed conversation of moving works of art such a long distance, a seldom-undertaken event.

*****

It was finally done, and Ian stood as he had upon their arrival, alone at the mighty door of Castle Donoway. The tired ramparts raised themselves against the gray mist of the early morning and Ian looked skyward. He well knew that the marches were at the mercy of sudden wintry blasts this time of year – winds which began their rise far out over the cold and brooding sea, arriving suddenly and without warning, and wreaking havoc on those who earned their living or plied their trade in the elements. If he were to avoid such situations he would need to follow the earl and his wife shortly. And yet the notion of hurrying, particularly in such a large undertaking as moving a wagon train south, was not one he relished. He was a lawyer, a man who delighted in a deliberative approach to life. Even the smallest matter had been known to catch and hold his attention for inordinate amounts of time. His mother had said he procrastinated; his professors at university (for he had been schooled at Edinburgh, one of their very first students) had found him methodical to the point of madness; his fellow lawyers knew that in a battle of detail and logic, he was the last lawyer one should take sides against. He would slay you with minutiae and in the end be proven right as well.

As Henrietta and Roman mounted their rested horses and rode away, Ian returned to the great room and warm fire within Donoway. He sat, alone, as he had done before they came. A small pile of books lay beside him on the floor. That, too, had been there before. He wore his customary garments and sat slumped in his usual chair, resting his head against the tips of the fingers on his right hand. The boy had gone to fetch tea for him. All was as it was before. But it was not.

The visit by the young couple, their enthusiasm and zest for, well, just about anything, had blown through his being like a hard wind. His soul had long been shuttered and closed tight against what he termed the vagaries of emotion, but they had teased them open, and he sat now feeling oddly empty, and, for the first time in his life, alone. Had he ever been that young? And those two fit one another in ways he had never seen before. It was not that they spoke the same sentences or thought the same way about this dilemma or that situation. No. They were opposite in many ways – she tempestuous and impatient, him, steady yet with a deep and burning passion for the few things he seemed to truly care about. They were not alike and yet belonged together like dawn and dusk – one could not exist without the other.

The boy placed the tea on the table beside him and disappeared. He rose, stirred the fire, and returned again to his habitual chair. Ian smiled wryly as he poured some tea and thought on Roman Collins.

The young man had seen fit to warn him of Henrietta's plans for himself and her beloved aunt. He had assured Ian that he was not only free to ignore her machinations, but in doing so might save everyone a great deal of trouble. He knew for a fact that the lady in question, Anne, had no knowledge of her niece's well-meant intentions, and so the only one to be disappointed would be Henrietta. And in Roman's opinion, such a disappointment might well cure his wife of her infernal meddling with other people's hearts and lives. Ian had laughed out loud as Roman had provided several examples of Henrietta's attempted matchmaking with various men and women at Coudenoure. The best had gone bad, the worst were just hysterically funny for all involved – except the principles. And yet she persisted.

Ian sipped his tea and closed his eyes. He had not bothered to tell Roman how terribly flattered he was. The notion that someone as accomplished and bright as Henrietta might view him, the tattered and old Ian Hurlbert, as matchmaking material had warmed his heart. Each evening, as the threesome had sat together, he had dutifully answered the artfully careless questions about himself and his background posed by Henrietta. Usually, Roman sat smiling at such times.

He could not say why he had never married. There had been school, and of course the care of his aging parents, and also lack of money and situation. Really, so many things. And then, in the wink of an eye, he was old. Too old to be putting himself forward with embarrassing and emotional declarations of love. Writing poetry of a flaming desire he did not feel. It had all passed him by.

Initially, when he discovered this about himself, he had felt empty, vacant. But as more years had piled on the heap already before him, that sense of loss had quietened and finally left him until his books and his lawyering were all he really wanted. Henrietta's vision of him as eligible either spoke volumes about her inability to see matters as they truly were, or, volumes about the aunt on whose behalf she was knitting up her plan. Either way, it was charming and he was certain that after the flutter of emotion created by her scheming, by the young couple's visit and by his upcoming trip to the environs of London had passed, his life would return to what it had become. He finished his tea and rose to check on the building of crates and containers going on behind the estate in the tenant quarters.

Chapter Sixteen

"And what if the good Ian Hurlbert is not interested in the good Lady Anne? Henrietta, have you considered that possibility?"

They were leaving Castle Donoway and walked their horses along the dirt path beyond the drive of the estate proper. The groundsman had assembled his entire family and they stood along the way, smiling and wishing Henrietta and Roman a safe trip. His wife passed a small bundle to Henrietta.

"'Tis food for your journey, m'lady."

Henrietta bent and thanked the old girl, not mentioning that their saddle pouches were already full.

"And 'tis a bit of something else."

The woman stood on tiptoe and whispered in Henrietta's ear.

"Oh! My! That is wonderful! Thank you, mistress, for I am sure I shall need it!"

The old woman continued whispering in Henrietta's ear.

"No, you may rest easy, old one, for no such words will cross my lips."

They passed on, and Roman again asked the question.

"And what if the good Ian Hurlbert is not interested in the good Lady Anne? Henrietta, have you considered that possibility?"

"Roman, where is your faith?"

"My faith in what, wife? Your ability to predict love between two people who have never even met?"

"Well, yes."

They both laughed.

"If Ian is blind and completely useless, and does not see the opportunity for a fulfilling and loving life with my aunt, then he may leave and go the way he came."

"I see."

"But that will not happen."

They mounted and set their horses into an easy trot. Roman shifted topics as castle Donoway began to disappear behind them.

"What was the whispering between you and that woman before?"

"I had spoken with her of the chafing behind my right knee – 'tis in danger of becoming inflamed. She made a poultice for me to place against it at night and said it would help heal the rawness."

"Why did she whisper?"

"Oh, Scotland is a backwards land, and there are those – out in the hills, along the marches – who still believe in witchcraft. She did not want anyone to know for fear she would be labeled and persecuted thus."

Roman laughed.

"Good Lord in heaven! What a strange place!"

Henrietta agreed, flicked her crop against her mount and galloped on. But no sooner had the heather fields and low rolling hills fallen away than her mount came to an unexpected stop. She leaned forward and patted its neck.

"What is it, Biscuit?" She gave the horse a gentle nudge with her heels, but still it stood immobile. Roman pulled alongside her.

"Why are you stopping?"

"'Tis not me, but Biscuit – I believe something has happened to her leg."

She quickly dismounted and threw the reins to Roman. From a small pocket inside her cloak she pulled a slice of apple – she knew Biscuit had a soft spot for the fruit and so she almost always rode with a bit tucked up in her riding gear as a treat for the animal. She gently patted the horse's nose and offered it to the sweaty beast. Biscuit took it happily, but when Henrietta tried to pull her forward, she snorted and refused. Roman jumped down from his own mount and began checking the hooves of Henrietta's favorite horse. After a moment, he completed the task and patted the rump of the beast.

"No, it must be a pull or tear of some sort. We shall have to walk until we can get help – will Biscuit move at all?"

Again, Henrietta reached within her cloak. Talking gently to Biscuit, she coaxed her a few steps forward.

"I think we can do it, but it will be slow progress indeed. T'would be better if we could send to Coudenoure for a stable boy who could bring a decent mount and who in turn could walk Biscuit on home."

"On *home*! Henrietta, 'tis the length of England! The animal must be sold and another bought for the trip!"

Henrietta looked at her husband with an expression he knew all too well. She was not one to forsake beast or man just because they were lame or incapacitated – if she loved them, they would always find safe haven with her. Roman could either engage in a fight he was sure to lose, or, he could oblige his wife and help her get Biscuit home. There was the added benefit of Henrietta's gratitude to him, which in most situations was well worth the loss of a silly argument. She smiled at him and he conceded. 'Twas usually thus.

"My love, here is what we must do . . ."

Chapter Seventeen

James was stunned at how quickly they appeared, those Englishmen who wished to curry favor with the new King from the heathen lands of the north. And he was open to such flattery, preening himself in the blinding light of their attentions. Indeed, when it was all said and done, some 300 knighthoods were handed out to those who had troubled themselves to come hither unto him. But even as he wallowed in their obsequious and likely shallow loyalty, he began to worry about the kingdom they had left behind.

With so many trekking to Scotland, who was minding his most royal business in London? Day after day they arrived seeking his grace. What initially he had deemed novel and right he now began to consider slightly alarming. His first letter to his southern court had done nothing to stem the tide of supplicants upon the road north, and he had amused himself by wondering if his English subjects understood their own language. Now stronger words were required.

A misty rain had begun to fall, and shadows crossed the great lawn outside his window. He lit the thick and heavy candle that stood upon his desk and began to write.

"Right trusty and well-beloved cousins and councilors, we greet you heartily well."

He sat back in his chair, considering the tone he should adopt. The rain had picked up and now beat against the pane. His thoughts began to wander – what would he find in this new kingdom of his? Would it please him? The rain tapped on. He had always liked the sound and the sight of a heavy fog rolling in. It took considerable effort to regain his train of thought and continue the letter.

He decided a few sentences of polite blather should be put upon the page before he gave his new subjects his imperial directive.

". . . it be very agreeable to us and we receive no small contentment by the dutiful disposition of so many noble gentlemen, our subjects, daily coming to meet us . . ."

Pause. Now to the heart of the matter. He dipped his quill.

". . . yet it is no less acceptable to us to have a sufficient number of you together attending at London with your accustomed care upon our affairs, and the rest to be waiting upon their particular charges lest, by your absence from them, anything should fall out

which might breed disorder, or be omitted which might any way tend to the settling of the estate."

Well, surely they could understand that. Now, perhaps a polite but authoritative closing.

"And, at our approaching nearer unto you, you shall be further advertised of our pleasure.

Thus we bid you all heartily farewell. From our palace of Holyrood house, in the first year of our reign.

James R.

The rain stopped and the fog settled. Instinctively, James reached for a nearby shawl. He continued staring out the window for some time, contemplating what was yet to come and what had recently passed. Of all the noblemen who now sought him out, almost none knew of the secret correspondence of the past two years between himself and Cecil, so secret that numbers were used rather than names.

This had been a necessary feint, for had the queen known that they were laying plans for a post-Elizabeth world, a peaceful transition of power would have been all but impossible – she would surely have cried conspiracy and followed that with action against him. Maybe even against her favorite, Cecil. But she had never discovered the correspondence and if she had, well, James giggled to himself, she would not have understood the code. James was referred to in the letters as '30', Elizabeth

– '24', Cecil – '10'. Important characters in the coming transition to a Great Britain (as he had taken to calling his new kingdom) were all assigned a number. The intrigue was delicious and fed his suspicious mind. Aye, as he acknowledged even to his courtiers, he was indeed mistrustful by nature, and they would do well to have a care for all works that might rouse such spirits within him.

But they had gone undetected in their treasonous activity, he and Elizabeth's great minister, and now his accession was unimpeded and almost guaranteed to be tranquil.

James had determined that his progress south should be slow, allowing many stops at English estates along the way. He had heard much of English wealth during his reign in Scotland, but still it caught him off guard as he moved through his new land: Belvoir Castle, the near mythic seat of the Dukes of Rutland; Worksop, situated grandly on the edge of the mighty Sherwood Forest, home of the legendary Robin Hood, the great estates of Doncaster – all beguiling him with a civilized opulence that Scotland had never possessed.

The market road connecting the north to the midlands and on to London had seldom seen such traffic. In addition to the carts and wagons carrying his household and belongings, courtiers and ministers hastened from one estate to the next, jockeying for a few minutes with the new king. Those unconnected with the great progress were swept from the thoroughfare by his bodyguard and looked on with confusion and awe as their new sovereign passed by. James was in his element, feeling the adoration of the masses yet not having to engage with them.

*****

Henrietta's attention was caught by a growing clatter emanating from behind them.

"Roman, there is much more traffic upon this road than previously when we rode north. Do you notice?"

"I do. I believe it must be connected with the ascension and progress of our good King James – do you not agree?"

But Henrietta had no chance to respond. Two horsemen in unfamiliar livery thundered over the ridge they had just crossed, coming to a halt beside them before revealing themselves as whifflers.

"Clear the road! The King cometh!"

"I am the Earl of Donoway," Roman informed them, "And I shall be pleased to see the King pass this way."

Within a few moments, six more liveried men, two abreast, appeared over the crest. As they neared, Henrietta stared, but not at the man on the prancing black beast who rode before the six, for he was clearly King James. She stared at the man closest to his right side, nearest she and Roman. Immediately, she noted his sword, unsheathed and at the ready.

It was the same man who had passed them before on their way north, the one who had laughed and promised death to the king. And she knew. Beyond doubt she knew. Without thinking, she stepped before the king, forcing the entire entourage to a halt. Roman, not understanding her motivation, moved closer.

The group made to pass when she stepped forward again, forcing them to a halt. She bowed deeply to James before turning quickly to the man beside him wedging herself between the king and his mounts.

"Lady, step back! You have no right to move thus!" The guard she recognized called out sharply.

Henrietta's eyes were flaming blue steel.

"Sir, I know you, do I not?"

"Step aside! You delay the king!" His voice was a low growl. His eyes moved to the king's face and nervousness seemed to set in. His hand moved slightly towards the hasp of his sword.

"No, sir, I shall not, for I believe you mean our good King James no good!"

Before the words were completely free, Henrietta grabbed the exposed hilt of the sword. But quicker was he and as he pulled the great weapon free a thick red line appeared across her hand.

"Sir, step away from my wife! I know you now!"

But even as Roman spoke the traitor raised his sword and lunged towards James. Henrietta was quicker – wrapping her hand in her skirt she lifted it and hit the sword with all her might, shifting its trajectory away from the king. In a flash, Roman had pounced upon him from the farther side and pulled him from his saddle even as the other guards finally sprang into action. A great curse sprang from his lips.

"To James death! Son of that whore Mary he is nothing but an ill-formed bastard!"

He lay back on the ground, his neck surrounded by sword tips. James, pale and shaken, moved his steed to one side, hesitantly watching the proceedings. As though on invisible signal, more horsemen appeared and surrounded the king, all facing outwards and assuming a defensive posture. No one moved.

When it eventually became clear that the man had no confederates present and had acted alone, James spoke quietly, calling Roman and Henrietta to him and patting his chest – he had worn thick, enforced underclothing since childhood. He had heard the whispers of paranoia but ignored them. And now, his suspicions were proven true.

"How came you to know this man and his treacherous plans?"

Roman explained their previous encounter with the perfidious Scotsman, still prone before them.

After a moment, the king turned to Henrietta.

"And you recognized him, even with the change in livery and upon a different horse?"

"Majesty, I did."

James smiled a smile that was almost skin-deep.

"It seems I owe you, child, and your husband. Tell me who you are."

Again, Roman provided the requested background.

"Donoway," James stroked his beard upon hearing the familiar clan name, "Yes, I am familiar with that clan, but this Coudenoure, I do not know."

"'Tis a small baronetcy adjacent to your great palace at Greenwich, Majesty." Another bow.

The king nodded and looked keenly at Henrietta.

"You are young to be so sure of yourself, Madam."

Henrietta smiled in acknowledgement but remained silent.

"Your hand, is the cut serious? Shall I send my physician to assist you?"

Henrietta glanced at the cut. Deep but manageable. A thought occurred and she pulled the poultice the old lady had given her from her saddlebag.

"Majesty, 'tis a gracious offer, but I have here a poultice which should speed the healing. 'Twas given me by a woman I am sure knows the art of healing well. I shall be fine."

The king's glance hardened and both Henrietta and Roman noted it. After a moment and with no further words he rode on. The traitor was taken away bound to be questioned, leaving Henrietta and Roman standing in place.

"So even in this bright land, witches abound," James spoke softly to himself under his breath. "How else could she know of the treachery against my life and position herself to prevent it?"

Much later in the day, the same thoughts continued to rise in his anxious mind.

"A white witch, but a witch just the same. We must see this Coudenoure, for where there is one, there are sure to be others."

Chapter Eighteen

The cool spring air had given way to the ripe heat of summer. Anne sat on the front drive, sipping tea and watching the twins, Thomas and Elizabeth, at play in the great meadow. Elizabeth had also convinced Ben to join their games, and the three of them were engaging in a wild game of tag. Anne thoroughly approved, for it meant they would sleep well that night. It was the children who first saw them.

"Papa! Mamma!" Thomas was a tow-headed child with bright dark eyes, an unusual combination which never failed to captivate all who met him. He had a shy, toothy smile and was quick with his hugs, another trait which endeared him to all of Coudenoure. He ran pell-mell across the meadow towards the horses which had turned onto the long, straight drive. Henrietta leapt from her saddle and ran to him, gathering him in her arms. Two seconds later, Elizabeth threw herself into her mother's arms and the three tumbled together into the soft meadow grass, laughing, screaming and hugging.

Roman paused, smiled, and gathered the reins of Henrietta's new mount before continuing on. They had left Biscuit and a stableman long ago on the road south – they would likely be some time.

Anne stood, leaning upon her cane. A wide grin accompanied her outstretched hand.

"I wondered if I should send Ben out after you!"

"Ben?"

Anne nodded.

"He and his fellows seem to know all manner of things not just about London, but about travel as well."

She looked across the field where Henrietta, Ben, Thomas and Elizabeth were slowly making their way to the manor house.

"Roman, I must tell you quickly, for the children intend to surprise you and my niece with their discovery."

Roman listened intently, grinning. As Anne finished her whispered message, Roman was tackled and fell to the ground in mock surrender. A tussle ensued and after long hugs and kisses, the party moved indoors. As they called for tea and food and settled in, Elizabeth assumed an air of tremendous importance. Thomas lined up beside her.

"We have made a mousentous disyervery."

"Indeed," came Roman's dry reply. "I doubt that very much."

"Papa, no! It is true – we have made a, a . . ." Thomas looked wide-eyed at Elizabeth.

"As I said, Papa," Elizabeth sounded as impatient as her mother frequently did, ". . . a motentious di-dovery."

Henrietta smiled, getting into the spirit.

"Um, Roman, my love, I understood there were no more of those to be found – was that not your understanding as well?"

Roman shook his head in vigorous affirmation as he folded a piece of roast beef between the halves of a sweet-buttered biscuit.

Elizabeth stomped her tiny foot. Thomas looked at her and she pointed to his foot, which he promptly stomped as well.

"Close your eyes!"

"Cose you eyes!" echoed Thomas.

Henrietta and Roman dutifully closed their eyes.

"You, too!" came the near hysterical directive to Ben and Anne. They all did as they were told, despite being well aware of the game being enacted – it had filled their days since the discovery by Elizabeth and Thomas.

As they did so, the patter of feet running across the library sounded clearly.

"Now, push Thomas, like before!"

A grating sound was heard, followed momentarily by another one. The room became still.

"Open your eyes, you two. You must now try and find them."

"Where are they?" Henrietta asked in a low and amused tone.

"They have discovered a small cellar of some sort behind the fireplace."

"What?"

"Yes. Now, they can hear you but only if you shout, so you must move about, shouting thus . . ."

Anne stood and began shouting.

"Where are Elizabeth and Thomas? Roman, have you seen Elizabeth and Thomas?"

Laughing, he responded.

"NO! What about you, Mamma? Have you seen our children?"

"NO! 'Tis so sad! Where have they gone?"

They could hear muted screams and giggles coming from the secret room. After a moment, Roman moved close to the great hearth, grinned at Henrietta and Anne, and shouted again.

"Aye, Momma, 'tis sad indeed! They are gone! We shall have to replace them!"

The giggling stopped.

"Yes, Papa, you are right – we must find new children!"

Silent pause. Screaming. No giggling.

They opened the small, secret door and pulled the children out, then Ben carefully reset the hidden entryway. Roman watched him intently. Seeing his interest, Ben obligingly moved through the steps necessary to trigger the opening.

"You see, sir, you must first push against the seam of the underside of the stone near the end of the mantel, like this."

He positioned his small hand beneath the massive carved limestone and Roman bent to observe. After a moment, he nodded. Ben continued.

"You must have an accomplice sir, for the next step requires that you continue pressing while another pushes against the pillar, the support, for the mantel. It is impossible to exert enough forward pressure unless you are standing directly in front of it."

Roman quickly moved to the side of the mantel and pressed. Almost instantly, the giant slab glided sideways, revealing the entrance to the room below.

"How on earth . . ." Roman gasped.

"The bottom of the mantel piece is a different stone, and when you press, it releases the hinge upon the other. It is offset, and so slides naturally. But there must be yet another part, one that I have not been able to discover, for I believe the process too simple otherwise."

They went through the steps several times, each time learning more about the ancient, hidden mechanism. The children, coddled and reassured, ran to the kitchen for sweets while Henrietta and Anne set to observing the opening and closing of the secret door as well.

"Did you know about this place?" Henrietta asked Anne.

"No, and I do not believe Quinn and Bess did either, nor, I believe, did my grandmother, Constance."

"What is down there?"

"Let us find out!" Roman lifted a fat candle from a nearby sconce and led the way.

"I shall stay out in case you need rescue," Anne remarked slyly.

A few small stairs led directly into a low-ceilinged room, no more than five or six feet wide and deep. In the corner, several old burlap and linen bags were piled helter-skelter. Two large, heavy, identical crucifixes lay opposite. A dull luster shone from the four ends of each of the golden crosses. The dust of a thousand ages lay over the place like a shroud.

"Saints protect us," Henrietta muttered quietly, "What is this place?"

Ben spoke up.

"I believe it to be a priest hole." He spoke the words with a solemn voice while the others continued to inspect the newfound place. Roman picked up the crucifixes and turned to the others.

"I cannot see these well in this dimness. Let us return to the library."

*****

"They were playing one day, and Elizabeth was trying to reach the great sword." Anne explained as they continued their tea and ale back in the library, the food long since having been devoured. "As she climbed so did Thomas from the side and the result was the discovery."

"I tell you, it is a priest hole." Ben reiterated his belief before disappearing into the kitchen where he knew Rouster would have tidbits of sweets and meats he would share with his friend.

Henrietta shook her head.

"I do not believe it is – think about it. The great Catholic wars were fought during the lives of our remembered ancestors – Thomas and Elizabeth de Gray, Constance, Bess. If they had known of such a place or needed such, they would surely have passed that secret on to us."

Anne agreed. Roman had said nothing, sitting to one side, using his shirt sleeve to dust and polish the two crucifixes. He stood now and joined the group.

"These are not just crucifixes. Have a look, for unless I am mistaken, those stones on the four ends of each of the crosses are jewel stones. Look."

He passed them around. A silence fell over the threesome as they rubbed the gems haphazardly polished by Roman. On each end, set securely within the gold of the cross, were three stones: one glowed red with a deep blood color, the next breathed an amber fire and the last reflected from within its faceted and icy depths the blue of an ocean on a bright and cloudless day. The pattern was repeated on each end and the jewels were identical.

"You are right, my love, but why are they in a hidden space, thrown into a corner, discarded?"

"I do not know, Henrietta."

"Before Coudenoure became the baronetcy of Thomas de Grey," Anne said slowly, "It belonged to an order of Catholic friars. It was they who built this place."

"Why did they leave?" Roman asked her.

"All I know is that they joined with their brethren at a another friary at Cambridge in the far distant past, so distant in fact that before our family came to possess the estate, the chapel had fallen to ruin and gone to rot. This building that we call the manor house was being used as a hunting lodge. I do not know why the monks decided to leave, when all evidence shows they had put much love and labor into the place. But the fact that they hid these crucifixes hints at dark times. This estate is isolated now, reachable only by that local cow path we refer to as a 'road'. How much more would it not have been so then?"

"Perhaps they feared for their valuables, and built such a place for them."

"It seems so," Henrietta chimed in, "But such a secret place, accessible only if two people know the secret, is in danger of being forgotten – do not you agree? Suppose the friars who knew the secret died in battle or as a result of a plague? They would have taken their secret with them."

"It seems they did so. Yes. It must be something along those lines." Roman called for more ale. "But 'tis good to know it is there."

"When the friars left, they would have taken their library and their records with them. Surely at that great university the records still exist. Perhaps someday I shall go there, or send Ben, and attempt to ferret out the secret."

"Until then, let us put something heavy and immovable by the side of the hearth – I do not want the children playing in such a place until we are certain it holds no more secrets."

"Agreed." Henrietta and Anne spoke at the same moment. Henrietta chose the time to change subjects.

"Speaking of libraries . . ."

"Donaway!" exclaimed Anne. "I wish to hear all about it!"

The late afternoon bled into evening, and as the shadows rose upon the old library walls, Henrietta and Roman finally fell silent. Exhaustion had caught up with them and Henrietta's face, pale even under ordinary circumstances, was almost white with fatigue. Anne rose.

"I have many questions, my niece, but I know the two of you must be more than tired. Rest, and we will resume this discussion anon."

Chapter Nineteen

Ten days later, Anne walked amongst the wild flowers which grew along the road to Coudenoure's gate. After the library, she loved flowers most, and could frequently be found with a small child at her side wandering through the blossoms of spring and summer. The child inevitably carried a knife and a bucket with water in the bottom. As they moved along Anne would point to this flower or that and wait patiently as the child set the bucket on the ground, sliced a long stem for the bloom and placed it in the makeshift vase. The children of the estate jockeyed for this work, for it was well known that Lady Anne carried sweets in her pocket with which she rewarded her helper. As they moved along this day, the child, a wild-eyed girl who whistled as they walked, suddenly stopped and spoke.

"You are very lucky, m'lady." The words were spoken matter-of-factly.

"Oh?"

"You live in a great manor and have beautiful dresses and servants who wait upon you."

"Um, 'tis true. But I am also lame, and in winter, my leg hurts constantly."

"But you have servants to place hot rags upon it to soothe the pain."

"Yes, but it is crooked and unsightly. And the gowns, well, tell me, do you think gowns would make you happy?"

The girl considered the question.

"For a bit." Her reply was brutally honest and Anne smiled.

"Exactly, child. And I have no husband, no children, and when I was very young, the man I loved treated me cruelly."

"So you be no happier than the rest of us." Again, a biting honesty.

Before Anne could reply, a tired old wain appeared on the road just ahead. Behind it were several more, and Anne and her young charge waited in silent curiosity as they approached.

"Now who do you suppose is coming to see us?" Anne asked. "And what do you think is in all those wagons?"

The little girl used the opportunity to remind Anne of payment.

"Perhaps they are full of sweetmeats and sugared figs!" She looked at Anne so matter-of-factly that she could not help but laugh and offer her the contents of her pocket.

"Run along back and tell them we have company. And mind that knife! Put it in the bucket with the flowers before you run!"

The knife plunked in the water and the girl took off, spilling flowers and water every step of the way. Anne returned her attention to the wagons.

"Where are you going?" She asked the closest driver when they neared. The man tipped his cap and turned his head while pointing behind him.

From the back of the train of wagons a rider appeared. He galloped forward, then, with a stiffness which spoke of a long journey, dismounted.

"Madame," he spoke solemnly with a bow, ". . . we seek the estate of Coudenoure."

Anne smiled.

"'Tis quite a brogue you have – I imagine you must Ian Hurlbert, the lawyer for my niece's Scottish estate."

Ian looked upon the woman with interest –
Henrietta viewed the two of them as a perfect
match. She was not at all what he had imagined, for
the picture he had built in his mind (and indeed, the
one he had not changed since Henrietta left
Donoway) was the one sketched and colored for
him by a young and adoring niece. The woman
before him was different in all respects.

While she had lost the flower of youth, a vitality
and wispy beauty remained with her. Henrietta had
spoken of her as kind and sweet, but the pervading
essence which surrounded the woman on the side of
the road was one of intelligence and humor. Her
dark eyes twinkled with a curiosity which marked
her out as intellectual. Her hair, dark and still
luxurious, was bound behind her in what was
surely now considered an old-fashioned caul – small
pearls were sewn into the simple netting, creating a
pleasing contrast with her darker skin tones and
hair. Her figure, too, was pleasing – certainly not
that of a young woman, but pleasing nevertheless.
Henrietta had cast Anne as a gentle soul, one who
was lost and wandered this world in a fog of
womanly and amusing uncertainty. On that
description, Ian had imagined someone else –
perhaps more the artistic type with ringlets and
wide eyes. Maybe a sketch book and pastels. This
was not that woman.

He jerked his mind back to the moment.

"Yes, Madame, I am indeed Ian Hurlbert."

"And I am Anne of Coudenoure. But I am fairly certain you knew that already."

He smiled uncertainly in acknowledgement. She waved her hand and smiled back.

"Do not worry, sir, for Roman has told me all about my niece's scheming. She is a romantic who believes that all souls seek a mate. You are in no danger." She laughed.

Ian had a sudden realization that she had likely been sizing him up as well, and wondered idly how she had found him. He was not one to act on impulse and when an impulsive remark fell out of his mouth, he was appalled.

"And you do not believe all souls seek a mate, Lady Anne?"

"*Isos*", came the reply.

"You speak Greek!"

"Indeed."

They walked along and for the first time he noticed her limp and cane.

"Tell me, what manner of books have you brought for our library?"

Ian was startled.

"Madame, I would imagine any estate to have books, but I did not realize Coudenoure had a library."

"*Malista*," she said with a laugh.

Ian smiled and responded in kind.

"Where did you learn this scholarly language, Madame?"

Anne answered the surprise in his voice.

"I believe there are many things about Coudenoure you will find surprising, sir. And in answer to your question . . . I learned it from my mother, who learned it from hers, who learned it from hers."

A long congenial pause as they turned onto Coudenoure's drive.

"Welcome to Coudenoure."

"Coudenoure," Ian whispered in reply. He did not know if he were surprised, inspired, or simply astounded at what lay before him. In one glance, he took it all in – the ancient monastery turned estate with its gleaming limestone walls and huge windows, the chapel ruins with its stone arches silently beseeching God in his heaven, the great wild flower meadow, and behind it all a rising smoke and distant noise from the tenant and servant quarters behind. Like a well-planned and attractively plated meal, it was glorious in its simplicity and great in its complexity. Ian loved it from the moment he saw it.

As they proceeded down the drive, servants and family ran out to greet them. Again, he was overcome with emotions which left him uncertain – at once, he felt a great sense of warmth, of peace, wash over him. What a strange and wonderful place, he thought, and how lucky I am to have stumbled upon it, if only for a visit.

The interior of Coudenoure was the very opposite of Castle Donoway and again, Ian was taken by surprise at the place and the unexpected feelings it evoked. Light poured in and the great entryway buzzed with activity. Given the size of the structure, he had expected many rooms within, but the old bones of the monastery remained intact, and its rooms were huge and few. Tapestries from long ago hung upon the walls and carpets of saturated hues and deep texture covered the floors. Sound lost its tinny echoes in such a place, and warmed by the textured surfaces and tinted by the glinting light the space became unique. But Ian's biggest surprise was yet to come. Henrietta showed him into the library, the room used by the family for daily living, and he stopped still.

Save for the medieval fireplace and hearth, the entire far wall was covered in books from floor to ceiling. The display was breathtaking and for a bibliophile, more intoxicating than wine.

Anne watched him, amused, realizing that Henrietta had got at least one thing right – the man loved books as much as she did.

Roman came roaring in reeking of freshly mown fields and oats. Even now, Henrietta loved how he looked, how he smelled. He could dance filthy and ragged before the throne and with his roguish grin and sparkling eyes no one would call him out. A small, happy sigh escaped her lips. Anne constantly chided her, for she spoke many languages, and was better at numbers than anyone on the estate. Yet if asked, she would not name those accomplishments as part of her identity. No. For her, as for Roman, identity, self, was to be found in the love and understanding of the other. She cared not a fiddle who knew or what they might think, nor did she particularly care if it was right. It was as it had been intended. Fate? God's will? Kismet, as the Moormen would ask? She cared not. Nor did Roman.

"My good Ian! So you have finally arrived after all!" Roman wiped his hands on the damp towel provided by the kitchen maid and promptly gulped down two quick cups of tea. He had been in the room less than thirty seconds.

"Indeed I did, m'lord . . ."

Ian lifted his hand in a gesture of pleading, interrupting Roman's intended riposte.

"Roman, if you do not mind, for I was not born a gentleman and pray we do not stand on such matters here in your small sanctuary."

Roman nodded for him to continue.

"Well, sir, I am here but 'tis a miracle, for just north of London, there was a great stir and we were forced to shelter beneath our wagons for two nights."

They waited with interest.

"Yes, apparently our good King James was in the area, stopping at some great estate – Theobalds, perhaps? There had been several attempts on his life as he progressed south and his guard were taking no chance of another."

Roman told him of their encounter with James.

"Aha. Yes. There are many who do not wish the kingdoms to be joined."

"Indeed, but the bigger issue is the manner in which our good King James intends to rule," Roman said quietly. "Even here at Coudenoure we hear he has plans for to rule as absolute monarch, ignoring the Parliament we Englishmen hold dear."

"Yes," Ian said, "I am sure you know of his treatise, *Basilikon Doron*, in which he spells out his ideas of just such an absolutist monarchy."

Anne nodded.

"Yes, we have a copy here."

Ian was amazed. Who were these people? What was this place?

After a brief pause, he returned to his theme.

"Tell me, is there such an estate as Theobalds? In the distance I could see spires but nothing else."

Ben had wandered in and listened intently.

"Sir, we have the plans here at Coudenoure. They are in our newly developed architectural section."

Ben was off in a flash to find the volume.

They settled in for small talk and tea.

And thus began Ian and Anne.

Chapter Twenty

Summer 1603

Plague was rampant that summer, and James was loathe to enter London because of it. He lingered at this estate, now that one, putting off his grand entrance into the city. He was king, but not even he could order or discern the means and ways of the apocalyptic disease.

It seemed to feed on the chaos and grime of city life, taking its pleasured toll on nobility and poor alike. From whence did it arise? How did it choose its victims? No one knew, but what was known of the pestilence caused even the greatest in the kingdom to tremble and back away in fear. Physicians agreed that it almost always began with chills, followed by fever, fatigue and the dreaded swelling buboes. Like many, James often thought he would rather have sweating sickness, since it carried you away within a few hours. Not so the plague. As its fingers curled about you and its tongue licked you until you screamed in agony, it declined to finish you off immediately, seeming to enjoy the misery it so induced. And in your time of need you could not depend upon family and loved ones as no one would approach the sick. No one would care for the ill, for the disease leapt from one victim to the next almost as quickly as fire on tinder. Once diagnosed there was no comfort to be had. Death became your only friend and closest ally as you lay, diseased and rotting, begging him to take you with him wherever he might be going.

James arrived at the fabled estate of Theobalds on May 3rd, tired, out of sorts, and concerned about his safety. Two attempts had been made on his life as he had moved south, and while they were generally considered to have been the work of individual malcontents and had not come close to success, still they had colored his mood. Gone was his earlier appreciation of English grandeur and hospitality. What had early in his progress been deemed charming and novel was now found mundane and even boring. Their manor houses were sublime, their treasures fine, but he had come to view the English themselves as oddities – refined heathens, all too ready to wreak harm upon his person. And their manners!

Life at his Scottish court had been informal with an inviting atmosphere. His courtiers knew they were welcome always at his table. He cultivated such ambience. In contrast, he found the English obsession with mannered formality and protocol as stiff and dysfunctional as the starched lace collars they insisted upon wearing far too often. He understood the need for kingly regalia, for pomp and majesty, and greatly enjoyed the robes and clothes he donned for such occasions, but the constant application of such standards to his everyday life had worn him as thin as an old rug.

He had never been out of Scotland, and found himself more and more homesick as he rode ever deeper into England. Oh, the hunting was fine but the weather was becoming too warm for his taste. He longed for the cool, soothing breezes of the highlands, for the wintry blasts from the great North Sea which heralded winter's approach. No, this heat was not for him. For all these reasons, he lingered at Theobalds.

James was no longer awed by the great country estates of the English, and initially, Theobalds was no different. Owned by Robert Cecil and built by his father, the estate had a whimsical quality to it. Great spirals with puffed and swirling caps reached to the sky, while the carefully designed geometric grounds highlighted the skill of their designer.

Gradually, however, as James stayed in residence at the great estate, his longing for home dissipated. He walked in the gardens and hunted in the grand forests of the manor. His body became accustomed to the feel of the mattress upon his bed, the smell and texture of its covers. He looked forward to the contour of the copper and wood bathing tub he used on occasion, the feel of the spoon he always used for supper. The sound of the scullery maids in the early morning hours, quietly moving through the halls and stoking the fires became routine and no longer interrupted his sleep. So too the patterns of the fine carpet which ran the length of the hall outside his bedroom door. It became his home away from Scotland.

The new king was making this journey alone, having left Queen Anne and his children – Henry Frederick, Charles and Elizabeth – safely in Scotland. He wanted to have a feel for England and its people before he subjected his family to such a change. As he had written letters to his new courtiers in the south, so now he sent a steady stream north to his family.

For Henry, his eldest, who had made much of the Stuart ascension to the English throne, he sent a word of warning lest the boy think too highly of his new position and forget who was king:

"Let not this news make you proud or insolent, for a king's son and heir was ye before, and no more are ye yet."

And as Henry always neglected his studies:

"Be diligent and earnest in your studies, that at your meeting with me I may praise you for your progress in learning."

For his beloved Queen Anne, who was prone to womanly angst:

". . . And therefore I say over again, leave these womanly apprehensions, for I thank God I carry that love and respect unto you which, by the law of God and nature, I ought to do to my wife and mother of my children."

Each morning at Theobalds, over a breakfast of ale and meats, Cecil briefed him not just upon the current state of English affairs, but also on the primary matter which informed the ways and machinations of all courts – gossip. Who was the Spanish ambassador's English confidante? With whom did the Polish ambassador sleep? Three generations earlier, this Earl had married that Duke's daughter, but a deep hatred now ran between them. Why? Lady Forthering was a known tart and it was best to avoid even small conversations with her. On the other hand, Davidson's handsome wife was quite stable and could be counted upon to be discreet, unlike her loose-lipped husband.

Cecil briefed him not just on his new noble subjects, but on his administrators as well. It was known, for example, that William Baldridge had difficulties with numbers beyond a certain point, so he should always be relegated to minor accounting necessities. Likewise, Calderon had no eye for detail, but was excellent in strategic thinking. Thomison had no apparent skills but whenever he was absent work tended to drag and not be done by others in a timely fashion.

Tactical and strategic, administrative and clerical, necessary through function or necessary through connections and birth – these were the topics which morning after morning, Cecil drove home to his new king and lord. Over time, James built a mental framework which encompassed the entirety of his new world, the glorious, the vain, the inglorious, all of it.

It was during one of these early morning tutorials that Cecil spoke of the latest plot.

"Another!" James exclaimed. "Pray tell how many heretics and treasonous souls does this kingdom harbor?"

Robert Cecil smiled. Like his father before him, he was touched with the gifts of memory and administration. There had been no difficult transition, for Robert had studied, then practiced, alongside his father for many years. Whereas his father had once held the keys to the kingdom alone, father and son had slowly become the trusted duo to whom Elizabeth turned for information, and when the senior Cecil had died in 1598, Elizabeth had appointed Robert in his place. And now he served James.

He sat patiently this morning as he had every morning since James' arrival at his estate, listening to the king, gaining his trust, telling him what he must know in order to rule England. He neither liked nor disliked his new master – he was neither a

Tudor nor an Englishman, but Robert Cecil placed loyalty to the crown above all else and that meant serving the strange and uncouth Scotsman to his best ability. This unswerving sense of duty was being tested this morning by the new sovereign.

"So, my little man, tell me about this latest treachery."

My little man. Robert Cecil had heard those words his entire life. 'My little pygmy' had been Elizabeth's favorite version, while James alternated between 'my little man' and 'my little beagle'. One would think that as an adult such taunts, thrown out so carelessly and clearly intended to do no harm, would have lost their ability to sting. For Robert, this was not true. He had no physical beauty and in addition to being small had a crooked back which gave him a hunched appearance. His sovereigns' need to draw attention to these attributes was annoying, and in his opinion, petty. And yet they needed him. He took solace in the knowledge that no one, *no one*, could run the kingdom as well as he did. He ignored James' unnecessary remark and continued detailing the conspiracy.

"We believe it to be but a small fraction of a much larger plot."

"A bye plot, then. Well, what is at its heart?"

"I am told that the conspirators intend to kidnap your person and place your niece, Arabella Stuart, upon the throne instead."

"Why?" James chugged ale, burped and stared at Cecil while he waited for an answer.

"They wish for religious tolerance, I believe," Robert continued. "I shall watch it closely before drawing the net. The date I have been told is late June and I wish to identify as many of the traitors as possible before beginning the arrests."

"Well," another burp, "You know best. But these plots are beginning to wear upon my royal nerves."

"Indeed, majesty."

Pause.

"Majesty, we must begin consideration of London, and the festivities to accompany your coronation."

"There is plague about the city, little man! We must be ever vigilant about keeping separate from the masses in order to secure my health."

"Have you determined the date upon which you wish to be crowned?"

"I have left all that with Lord Thomas," James said with evident exasperation. "He is now lord chamberlain and carries full responsibility for the coronation."

He wiped his hands and crossed his legs.

"I have told him that I believe it would be most auspicious to be crowned upon my saint's day, July 25th," he began.

Cecil nodded, but ignored the vexation in the king's voice. Lord Thomas Howard was a friend of his, and a capable man. Both men felt it important to hear the king speak the dates for each stage of the coming events. They were aware of James' suspicious nature, and should anything inauspicious occur during the coronation, they were best served by the king having set the dates himself.

"I agree. And have you a feel for when you would like to enter London? Your subjects are most anxious to see you."

The conversation dissolved into a dithering monologue on the part of James as he gave the advantages first of this date, now of that.

"I believe I shall go when I deem it prudent. Likely soon. Now, I am told they are beating the bushes for me for pheasant. Anon."

He rose and Cecil followed suit, bowing deeply as James left.

"*Anon.*" He spoke the word softly to himself in a plausible and slightly too close imitation of James' Scottish dialect. Cecil was a most serious man, but occasionally, even he had had enough.

"Little beagle indeed." He called for his aides and began his morning's work.

Chapter Twenty-One

In the end, it came to naught. Too many conspirators, too many loose ends, too many dissatisfied with the demands to be made. Surely, Cecil thought wryly, the definition of 'secret' was something told to one person at a time. The average man, including those who would practice treason, has no capacity for discretion, and less for danger, he thought. When consequences began to show themselves, to be felt, there is never a shortage of rats willing to turn traitor against their own. But that was not what disturbed Cecil and kept him up at night.

Like an owl hidden deep within the shadow of a moonless night, he had kept silent watch upon the conspirators. His moles, carefully chosen and well-paid, found their work relatively easy – there was precious little agreement amongst the treacherous group and they turned upon themselves with slight provocation. Two priests led the disparate group, whose aim was fuzzy at best – did they want religious tolerance? Or did they want Arabella Stuart on the throne for other unknown reasons?

Did they want Scotland to remain independent? Were they simply anarchists? From his perch Cecil heard the whispers, read the notes, saw the glances. Regardless of its form and reason, their shrouded purpose had no chance of success. It was never any real threat to James. But Cecil realized early on that the plot itself was not the true peril. The Bye Conspiracy as it was now called, and its larger Main Plot, were transparent, but organized. And therein lay the danger.

As James had progressed south, there had been isolated attempts on his life. These were exposed as amateur and primarily rooted in Scottish clan affairs. But the one before the Bye had also been relatively well-organized and had involved a number of characters. And now the Bye. It had been loose and in the end too large for its primary actors to manage, but the framework showed evidence of forethought and planning.

Cecil was not a suspicious man, nor did he believe that the Fates drove human affairs. In his experience, humans were responsible for most events in their limited world. But he had never seen so much treachery arise so quickly. He would have to be alert, for regardless of their origins, these conspiracies were manifesting ever greater organization and seemed more likely to succeed with each permutation.

He considered telling James of his concerns, but in the end thought better of it. When told that the

Bye Plot was now fully exposed and that prosecution of the traitors would soon follow, the king had seemed concerned, but distracted. In fact, after he was sure of the details he had dismissed everyone from his presence and sat in thoughtful solitude for some time.

Not even Cecil realized that James' thinking was following the very track that his own concerns had covered earlier. So many attempts in such a short time! What was this? Unlike Cecil, however, James' natural and deep suspicion came to the fore and he remembered the first attempt upon his person, just after he had left Scotland.

"And that white witch saved me. Yes."

He rose, stirred the fire, and returned to his musing.

Had she been instrumental in foiling the other plots? Surely she must have played a role, for there had been so many one would surely have succeeded if she had not been active on his behalf! He remembered how she had shown him a poultice, and had stated it was for her leg.

But perhaps that had been a ruse, one perpetrated so that he might not recognize the talisman she had used on his behalf.

Witches. He was annoyed that he might owe his life to one, yet frightened not to acknowledge it. As soon as coronation events were at a close, he would seek the woman out – perhaps she could offer him further protection in the future.

Chapter Twenty-Two

July 25th, the day of coronation, dawned cloudy and cool, with a sky hung low over a diseased-ravaged London. What should have been a bright and glorious triumph would be taking place in the shadows of a gray and somber world. In late May, plague had risen to such a level that the king had been forced to direct his courtiers and the gentlemen of the court to leave the city. Again in June, the Triumph was postponed for the same reason – the plague of death which held London tightly in its claws.

James was already tired of the city and its accompanying problems. The situation forced his mind back to Scotland and cheerier times. He rose early on the morning of his coronation, that great and historical moment when Scotland, England and Ireland would be united under his capable and God-decreed reign, and immediately called for Thomas Howard and Robert Cecil. They arrived at the onset of a deluge which was to continue off and on throughout the entire day.

"Where are your papers? Did I not say to bring them so that we might review today's events?"

Both men bowed and produced papers from the satchels each carried. James nodded for them to sit.

"The coinage? Is it now circulating?"

Cecil affirmed that it was. "Majesty, it is. I must say that the likeness unto you is quite remarkable, and the phrase, 'Great Britain', is well-stamped upon the face."

James rubbed his hands with satisfaction.

"Good. 'Tis important that all my subjects have an image of their new king."

"And the services performed en route? Has the station been prepared?"

Thomas Howard spoke.

"Yes, your Highness, they shall be performed between Westminster Abbey and Westminster Bridge, as you preferred."

A knock on the door interrupted the conversation. A young man appeared with breakfast and left almost as quickly as he had appeared. James preferred ale in the mornings, and Cecil quietly poured himself tea. Howard abstained altogether.

"And the dean of the abbey?"

"Aye, Majesty, Dean Lancelot Andrewes will be
by your side throughout the coronation. Do not fear
or falter, for should Majesty have a moment of
forgetfulness, he shall be there as your prompter."

Cecil seemed to be checking down a list in his
hand.

"The stone?" He asked, referring to the Stone of
Scone.

"'Tis in place," came Howard's quick response.

On and on they went. Cecil began to fidget, for
he knew well that everything was in place. It was
time to dress and be at it. James, however, had one
more question.

"And how many shall attend?"

This was difficult, for most courtiers had
preferred to stay far from London. They would not
be found this rainy morning in the Abbey observing
their new king's coronation. They would be at their
country estates, waiting for the plague to wear itself
out and move on.

Even as Cecil wished to put a pleasing number
before James, he knew better. And much later, after
the ringing of the bells had ceased and James wore
the crown, his worst fears were confirmed: the
Abbey was largely empty.

As the royal heralds, dressed in new, crisp Stuart livery rippled out across the city and the kingdom, they took with them papers proclaiming James' kingship to be hung in town squares and churches across the new United Kingdom. They took gold bezants with an image of James, crowns about his feet as he knelt before God's altar, to give as alms to the poor and as keepsakes for others. And they shouted his title far and wide:

> *"The High and Mighty Prince James, Our sovereign Lord, by the grace of God of England, Scotland, France and Ireland, King, defender of the faith."*

The new era had begun.

Chapter Twenty-Three

Upon the high ridge, they built a fire as of old. Ben carefully made use of each twig of kindling, reserving the main wood until he was certain it would catch. He worked with the skill and knowledge of one whose life had only recently depended on such ability. Across the small circle of flames, Rouster busied himself with his own contribution to the evening's festive reunion. From a large feed bag, easily found hanging on Coudenoure's stable wall, Rouster produced enough food for a small army. First, he pulled two short planks from his sack and placed them carefully before the growing flames. Next, he produced a pair of smaller bundles, made of the clothing he had worn the day he had arrived at Coudenoure. He untied each to reveal bread crusts, cuts of beef and pork long past their prime, and tidbits of sweets he had been carefully and stealthily setting aside since he had learned of Marshall's visit. Cook knew full well what the child was doing, but left him to his own devices – whether the boy would

ever recover from his childhood on the streets of
London was anyone's guess. If he felt the need to
hoard and hide, who was she to tell him differently
when his own experience told him he was right.

For his part, Marshall had feigned illness, stuffed
his covers with hay in the shape of a small boy, and
walked through Greenwich Wood to join his mates.
Roman had seen to procuring him a leave for the
next few days, but Marshall had wanted desperately
to be with Ben and Rouster for an evening on their
own. It represented more than just time with
friends, for the threesome had seen to each other
since their time at St. John's. They were family with
stories to swap and plans to unveil. Children forced
to adulthood in the fevered swamp of hunger and
peril.

As the fire caught and night came on, the glow of
the flames flickered across their faces and danced
eerily in the ebony web of darkness spun by the
moonless night. The ridge rose in the great and
shadowed landscape, a ragged-edged force of
nature. But as quickly as it rose it seemed to decide
against it, and began cascading downward towards
the grounds proper of Coudenoure. From there it
rolled on, flattening itself and smoothing its jagged
contour into a mannered form, one with geometric
lines and calculated gardens. It swept towards the
gravel drive and then, like a wave exhausted and
beaten on some lonely shore, it curled away, leaving
the manicured front of the manor house to its own,
artificial devices. It was there that a second flame

burned and there that others, a couple, sat round about, discussing the day, the future, and themselves – Ian and Anne.

Ian Hurlbert had arrived at Coudenoure in the late spring of that year, faithfully executing the wishes of the previous and current owners of Castle Donaway. He had arrived full of curiosity. What had been, even by his own admission, a stodgy, uneventful life had been transformed into one of adventure. In middle age, he had left Scotland to accompany wagonloads of priceless relics and art to their new home. Contrary to what he had always believed about himself, he found the road refreshing, even invigorating. In the short time it had taken him to reach Coudenoure, he had met more people, absorbed more experiences and learned more than he had in his entire life heretofore. He had slept under a wagon along the way, negotiated tolls with ne'er do wells when forced to take side tracks, eaten questionable vittles and ridden his own horse the entire way. He felt more physically alive than he had in many years. Nothing, he believed, could improve upon the journey. But then he had arrived at Coudenoure.

Was it the jewel-like quality of the place? The library? The family? Or was it the woman, Anne? He had known the answer his entire life, and now he had the questions to match.

What had begun as amused curiosity at Castle Donaway – was this how women approached courtship in England? – had initially given way to further bemusement upon arrival south. Anne was handsome, this was true, and bright – but she was much more than that. The moment she laughed as she confided to him her knowledge of her niece's plan he had found himself at ease, for the situation was more humorous than anything else. But as time went on, he found himself beguiled not by her looks, nor by her intellect, but by the woman herself. She was erudite beyond anything he had ever known. If he had paused previously to consider such a thing (which he had not) he was certain that he would have answered that such profound learning in the female sex would be off-putting and uncomfortable. Now he knew differently. From the moment Ben had raced to find the book containing the architectural plans of Theobalds, he had found it pleasing to talk to a woman at such a level. From that beginning, their conversation had blossomed. He told her of his printing press and how it worked, she told him of the library's history; they discussed possibilities for the two glass houses built by her grandfather, Quinn; the scientific study of botany, of minerals; painting and art and music and sculpture. There was no field too far for them to wander and discuss, turning each topic over and over until every angle had been explored to their mutual satisfaction. He awoke each morning looking forward to the day's perambulations, both mental and physical, with Anne.

Was this love? As a young man he would have scoffed at such a notion. Love was an invented thing, a notion meant to tie two people together economically and physically. If it existed at all (and he had been reasonably sure it did not), then it existed for the sake of society, as the mortar and glue which underpinned civilization. But this was not that. Did that mean, then, that love really did exist, and that he had now serendipitously stumbled across it?

On occasion, as he lay awake at night unable to sleep, he wondered about her feelings towards him. She slept in the bedroom adjacent to his. One evening, as he rolled and tossed beneath the heavy covers he finally snorted, sat up and lit his candle. Without thought, he raised to his knees on the bed, facing the wall between his room and hers. Ever so softly, he placed his hands gently upon its ancient stone and plaster surface. Ever so gently, he leaned in, and pressed his cheek against it and closed his eyes.

After some time, he came to his senses. This would not do. He was Ian Hurlbert, a middle-aged Scotsman with no business behaving like a giddy lad on the verge of, the verge of . . . well, no, this would not do.

*****

On the other side of the thick stone and mortar wall Anne sat up, exasperated. This was not love, she assured herself. The one time she had felt love it had left her hollow and broken, for the man had been a cad. He had loved her not and further, had mocked her feelings and made them known to everyone. It had finished the concept for her and she had made a life for herself amongst other, safer milestones. She had no need now for family beyond what she had – her loving niece and her family, her 'child' Ben . . . no, she was content.

No. She was not. As certain as she was that she had been, she knew that now she was not – it was that simple. And each time she sought to puzzle out this new unrest, this odd need to spend time with Ian Hurlbert, to hear his ideas and gaze into his kind, warm eyes, she felt she was swimming in a pool of, of, something, and only he could swim out and see her safely to shore. What a thing!

Impulsively, and without knowing why, she carefully turned herself to the wall behind her bed which separated her room from his. Carefully she balanced her bad leg against her good, and raised herself up on her knees. She reached out, placing both palms flat against the wall, fingers spread. She closed her eyes and stayed entranced for she knew not how long.

Finally, she turned and lay back down, wondering why she had done such a strange thing.

*****

The days slowly lengthened into the long slow months of summer. At Coudenoure, from sunrise to sunset, time was filled with the high song of a busy season. There were lambs to foal, fields to be ploughed and planted, grounds to be rejuvenated for another season of growth: all of these jobs and more. Bee hives were cleaned and readied; the miller sorted the remaining winter's supply for sale or family; cloth woven in the winter months was put to use now as clothing, bags and other estate essentials.

Roman's parents always visited Coudenoure in the early spring, bringing with them cloth from his father's looms, London and wool trade news, and fleece samples over which Roman and his father would pore endlessly. In the season of '03, however, a new set of eyes began to learn the language of wool – Ian.

Initially, he had made noises and moves to return to his homeland. Roman, in response to Henrietta's not-so-subtle insistence, always found reasons for the Scotsman to tarry a bit longer. Ian had complied with these requests with humor, for it was evident to all what was afoot. But as time passed, Roman found (to Henrietta's great and satisfied delight) that he was less and less in need of excuses. Ian busied himself in the mornings with his work from Scotland, dispatching couriers every few days with documents and directions for their delivery. For her part, Anne spent the mornings with Ben, playing games, tutoring and helping him with his plans for the library. After dinner, inevitably, Ian would find (with no help from Roman) reasons to engage with Anne. Their walks became slower as their conversations intensified. Henrietta had taken Ben as her confederate in the romantic scheme, and was delighted when, one afternoon, he reported breathlessly that Anne and Ian were on their fifth loop around the great meadow walkway. Anne's maid was instructed to put extra healing herbs in her bath each night to soothe the ache in her leg – it seemed she would rather put up with its pain than stop her strolls with Ian.

By supper each evening, they were oblivious to others at the table. They sequestered themselves at one end and their conversation was deep and meaningful. Henrietta, Roman and Ben were left to their own small talk. Occasionally, one of them would venture a question to the two, and it was always answered and followed up upon. Yet inevitably, whether it was Ian or Anne who had responded, the conversation would then lag, develop long lacunas until finally it would cease altogether as the two at the end re-entered their exclusive world. For that was what it had become.

After the third time he found himself on his knees on his bed in the middle of the night, Ian finally understood and could stand it no more. He determined on a course of action. He would bend low in a courtly manner, going down on one knee. He would do this in a quiet moment in the evening after supper, when the candle light lent a dreamy romantic quality to the time. He would quote poetry (he had been hearing good things about that Shakespeare fellow), and then deliver a carefully prepared statement of what he had to offer. After days of preparation, he was satisfied and felt himself ready.

On a sunny afternoon, on their first customary loop round Quinn's meadow, Anne remarked upon the intense color of the lavender that year and how one might best translate it into oil paint for the canvas.

"Will you marry me?" Ian blurted. "I cannot live without you and I do not know how I have done so thus far."

They continued walking at the same pace. Silence. Fear. Consternation.

"I am sorry," Anne said anon, "I do not believe I heard you."

"I want to marry you. You see, I am in love with you."

Walking. Silence. Intense fear. Intense consternation.

"Yes."

More walking. More silence. Intense hope.

"I am sorry," Ian responded, "I do not believe I heard you."

"Yes. You see, I am in love with you as well."

They set a new record for loops that afternoon. From their perch at the library window, Ben and Henrietta correctly and ecstatically deduced the reason and immediately began planning the wedding.

*****

And so on the eve of their nuptials, they sat together on the front drive before a fire. Their chairs were drawn together, and Ian's hand was placed lightly over Anne's. Neither of them had truly believed in personal happiness and joy. Both of them had been proven completely wrong.

Anne looked at the fire upon the ridge.

"What do you suppose those three little imps are discussing up there?"

Ian sighed happily.

"Well, my love, it could be anything from the nature of being to the ingredients in a good shepherd's pie."

Anne laughed.

"You are correct. You know, Ben gobbles up knowledge like no one I have ever known. The child is more erudite than most adults."

"Yes," he mused. "And Rouster, I do not believe that boy will ever be full."

Neither of them laughed, realizing that the child's early life had been desperate beyond anything they had ever known.

"And Marshall?" Ian asked. "What shall become of our Marshall?"

"He will serve royalty all his days I believe, for he has leadership and loyalty. I would trust him with my life, as indeed I once did."

They sat in comfortable silence.

"Dear, we are ready for the morrow, are we not?"

"I hope so, for if ours is not the most beautiful wedding ever seen in Christendom, Henrietta may faint dead away."

As they laughed, Anne looked at him trustingly, watching the flickering shadows on his gentle face as he continued.

"Anne, my one and only love, I believe we have waited for the morrow our entire lives. We shall live as one because we are one."

She pulled her hand out from under his and placed hers on top. There was no need for further words.

*****

Their wedding day dawned bright and beautiful. Henrietta had determined that the ceremony would take place in the ancient chapel ruins adjacent to the manor house. After all, it was here that her ancestors had married one December many years ago. The stone walls with their empty arched windows still spoke a sublime message to those willing to listen. It was carried on the whispered winds which flowed through the spaces carved out from time and place by men now forgotten but whose clarion call sounded yet.

The ceremony would take place at sunset, with candles lighting the aisle and the area round about the ceremony, illuminating bride and groom and the priest. Two fires of yew and pine would burn on either side to ward off any chill which might set in. As always, Anne's leg in winter tended towards throbs and aches. Ben thus determined that she should ride from the manor house front door to the chapel upon a white horse. No other color would do. There was no such horse at Coudenoure, and he spent an entire week combing the neighboring estates and village until he found one. How he had managed to get it to Coudenoure on the day of the wedding was not something he discussed. Many did note, however, that he was most hurried in his efforts to return it afterwards, and that, each time Thomas or Elizabeth brought up the subject with knowing looks, he provided them with sweets and other distractions. For months.

As for Anne, she chose a simple dress, in line with the belief she and Ian shared, namely, that vanity was for those who knew not happiness. A bouquet of sweet pea and lavender, grown in one of the glass houses, adorned her hair. Her only jewelry was a single necklace – the ruby cross. Particularly since Henrietta's travails within the Tower, it had become a talisman of good for all who touched it. Anne wore it because of its familial history, for she knew that with Ian at her side, she had no need of superstitious relics.

Ian awaited her at the altar that day, beaming with a heart full of love and gratitude – one year earlier, as he had sat alone with his books and tea in his small dark dwelling at Donoway Castle, he would have sworn that such a fate was beyond what had been allotted to him.

They were married as the sun embraced the horizon, and that evening, as the musicians played and the children romped and the adults danced, they slipped away from the happy chaos and into their own world. It would be forever thus.

Much later, Roman tugged a laughing, tipsy Henrietta out the front door, leading her lightly towards the now glowing embers of the fires near the old chapel.

"What are you doing?" she demanded. "Do you not want to dance with me?"

Roman's face grew serious and he pulled her close.

"Is this about sheep?" she hiccupped.

"We shall always dance together, Henrietta, you and me."

To the side lay a stack of blankets and woolen shawls, brought for the ceremony to protect against the cold. It was to these that he led her.

"And shall we dance now?" she asked quietly after they kissed.

There was no need for further words.

Chapter Twenty-Four

Sir Robert Cecil was disgusted. Like his father before him, he imbibed little, preferring the sober company of family and books and learned men. And while Elizabeth's court had certainly had its raucous moments, indeed, its raucous years and phases, it had always returned to the solemnity one expected from one's sovereign. Majesty was not called Sloth without reason. Cecil had never seen a royal court such as the one he was being subjected to now. It seemed to have only two fundamental rules upon which it operated: the first was that there was no such thing as too much ale; the second was that there was no shame in observing the first in public.

Time and again over the course of the fall months and into the Yule season, Cecil and the other Englishmen at court were appalled by the drunken stupor constantly exhibited by their now brothers from Scotland. James began his day with ale, supplemented at dinner with more ale, and finished it in the evening by practically bathing in wine for supper. And just when his chief minister thought the debacle could be carried no further, the idea of a masked ball occurred to his royal highness.

It would be performed at Theobalds, Cecil's own estate, which was another growing thorn in Cecil's side. James wanted the manor for his own, and Cecil was loathe to give it. It had led to many an anguished night for him, for at heart he was a homebody and a family man. In the end, knowing he could acquiesce quietly or be set on fire by a confrontation with his new king, he conceded with a forced smile. James would have Theobalds, but in return Cecil would receive Hatfield, an estate he had always loved. The small manor had been Elizabeth's childhood home, and as such it held a special place in his heart.

The masked ball was to take place that autumn, and noblemen from both countries were set to attend. It was determined that part of the evening's entertainment would be an allegorical play, with ladies of the court portraying the seven virtues. From the ancient Greeks would come justice, courage and temperance and prudence. These would be matched with the traditional virtues of St. Paul: hope, charity and faith. Queen Anne, having been in England not even a year, would oversee the event. In the weeks leading up to it, a great stage was built and many rehearsals were called for the fortunate women who had been chosen to play the roles. As the day neared, James' court progressed to Theobalds, and as Marshall later explained to his brothers, Ben and Rouster, there was the greatest excitement leading up to the event.

The three boys had continued their nocturnal meetings as often as their work allowed. When Ben and Rouster found a day when the family might be away at Roman's parents' house in London or busy with end of season accounting or whatnot, Ben would send a note via one of the estate's young children to Marshall at Greenwich Palace where he was permanently stationed. And when the appointed time came, the three would meet upon the ridge, build a fire, and tell their tales. It was at one of these conclaves that the story of the allegory came out.

"But I do not understand," Ben interrupted Marshall. "How came you to be at a great estate other than Greenwich Palace?"

"Because Michael – the son of the Baron of Huntingdon who is apprenticing with the king – was taken ill. I was ordered to accompany the court to Theobalds in his place."

The other two boys considered this while chewing on roast beef wrapped in biscuits, a treat provided for their affair by Rouster. Marshall happily reached for yet another candied fig.

"But you saw the allegory?"

"Yes," Marshall replied, "You see, I taught the cook to read a bit, and in return, she let me slip in through the kitchen and watch."

More thoughtful eating.

"So ladies dress as virtues and each talks about her virtue?" asked Rouster.

Marshall nodded and continued.

"Yes, but you see, they had been at the ale all afternoon . . ."

"*No!*" exclaimed Rouster with a giggle. "I have seen that in the kitchen sometimes. 'Tis quite funny. And afterwards, oooh, it seems to bring on very bad temper."

Marshall was warming to his story.

"Indeed. Well, by the time of the play, I was the only sober person in the room. Faith was sitting in the lap of a gentleman and kissing him . . ."

Ben interrupted.

"Faith? Does she not represent love of our Lord and chastity?"

Marshall giggled and continued.

"But Charity would not have it, for she was in love with Faith's gentleman. Oh, the fight was on and they rolled about the floor screaming and pulling each other's hair."

"What about the others?"

Marshall pulled a piece of beef from the plank before the fire which served as their table. He assumed a matter-of-fact air.

"No one was watching. They were too busy looking at Temperance retching in a corner and Hope sobbing in the middle of the table – no one seemed certain why she was upset."

"But these are the souls who attend our sovereign?" Ben asked in his usual somber style.

"Oh, there are many who stay away now because of the drunkenness. I was glad to get home to Greenwich for the sight was disturbing."

The night ended when the food supply was exhausted, and with a promise to meet again soon, the three boys parted ways.

If Robert Cecil had known that such accurate tales of the debauchery rampant at court had made their way into the common vernacular, his disgust would have been complete.

*****

December 1603

"But we have English translations, Majesty. And as you know, your treasury is in a, um, most delicate state."

James ignored the last sentence.

"We have two translations, my little beagle, King Henry's VII's version, and Tyndale's. But I believe a version more reflective of our Lord's words and intent would be a blessing I can give to my people. We shall call a conference of scholars for this purpose."

Cecil wondered briefly how the king knew the Lord's intent, but decided against bringing the matter to his master's attention. It was a cold day in December, and James had demanded that he ride in Greenwich wood with him. He said he needed to clear his head.

Cecil had always found the wood a gloomy place. Even in the dead of winter, as now, when the trees were as bare as a pauper's cupboard, no light seemed able to reach the forest floor. Only a shadowy dream of it filtered through, seeming to promise illumination but delivering only what the day could wring from the sky. 'Drab' was the word which always came to mind – no subtle hues, no movement, no contrast. Cecil gave an involuntary shudder as his horse plodded along the muddy trail. Only the smell of damp and rotting foliage colored the place. Here and there, mushrooms sprang forth like sole survivors from some great and horrible apocalypse. But they too would wither and die with the evening's frost. He steered his thoughts back to James' rambling monologue.

"And so I direct you to send out a summons to Oxford, to Cambridge, to the great bishops and ministers of our united kingdom . . ."

"Sire, there are many who wish you would not refer to it as a united country, for indeed, many see it as two kingdoms ruled by one sovereign, but not one land."

Again, James ignored him.

"Invite them Hampton Court for a conference, and we shall attend to this most important matter."

"Yes, sire."

"In January."

"Yes, sire."

They rode in silence. Both men wore heavy woolen cloaks over their clothing. James, as was his wont, was dressed as he believed kings and royalty should dress in public – in sumptuous attire. Even his cloak was lined in purple satin and sported fox pelts for its collar and lapels. Cecil's robe was a plain black one inherited from his father. After a moment, he resumed the conversation.

"Majesty, your coffers need replenishing. 'Tis time to consider calling your first parliament."

Silence.

"If we send out the writ, your majesty may summon it shortly."

"I suppose," came the king's laconic response, "But I believe your countrymen have a greatly inflated sense of their responsibilities in the running of this kingdom."

Despite the leather gloves he wore, Cecil's hands were frozen around the reins. In one more moment, he knew he would care about nothing except saving his hands and person from frostbite. Better just to say whatever it took to end this pointless trek across a barren forest. But no sooner had he thought his prayers answered than the great wood ended, and they found themselves in a pleasant and open meadow. The mighty Thames bounded one side while across the way a high ridge isolated the field from whatever lay beyond. James pulled his mount up short.

"'Tis a pleasant place. I had no notion of its existence."

"Indeed." Cecil fought to keep a withering frozen sarcasm out of his voice.

"What do you suppose lies beyond that ridge?"

"I do not know, sire, but as soon as we return to Greenwich, I shall find out for you."

James looked at his minister for the first time since they had begun their ride. His nose and cheeks were bright red, and his breath froze upon the air as he exhaled.

"Why, you are cold!" he exclaimed.

"Yes, Majesty." Lord and God, please do not let him have heard the nuance.

"Let us return to the palace. Yes, I direct you to summon our clerics and the learned of the land to Hampton Court, and also, to summon our parliament." He tittered at his own joke all the way home.

*****

July 22, 1604

"Whereas we have appointed certain learned men, to the number four and fifty, for the translating of the Bible, and that in this number divers of them have either no ecclesiastical preferment at all or else so very small as the same is far unmeet for men of their deserts, we require you that presently you write in our name as well to the Archbishop of York and to the rest of the bishops of the province of Canterbury."

James paused, then continued writing.

"We require you to move all our bishops to inform themselves of all such learned men within their dioceses as, having especial skill in the Hebrew and Greek tongues, have taken pains in their private studies of the Scriptures for the clearing of any obscurities in the Hebrew or the Greek, or touching any difficulties or mistakings in the former English translation which we have now commanded to be thoroughly viewed and amended . . ."

A small knot of courtiers approached him from across the long hall in which he sat at a small desk. Cecil, as always, was at his side. He glanced suspiciously at the approaching men.

"What do you suppose they want, eh?" the king spoke under his breath.

"Majesty, no doubt they wish to discuss parliamentary matters, for there, in their midst, is our courier."

"I do not wish to meet with them. Dismiss them."

"But sire . . ."

James turned with a ferocious hiss to his most capable minister.

"Do you dare cross my words?"

Cecil bowed low and moved to meet the determined looking pack as they neared James. For his part, James ignored them, continuing to write as though they did not exist. Cecil stepped quickly to greet the delegation and with a smooth and practiced flourish shepherded them away from the king.

Many hours later, as they finally cleared Cecil's office, one man remained. In an unlit corner the courier shuffled hesitantly on his feet. He had not even taken off his short cloak or unwound his long knit scarf from about his neck, and Cecil noticed for the first time how young he was – no more than eighteen. What had the lad been thinking when he agreed to that haircut? His dull brown locks had been carefully whittled away near his face while left full and long on his neck. It was hideous, in Cecil's opinion. What was wrong with a nice blunt chop across the front and a matching one in back? Hmm? Alternatively, if one were of a certain age, it might be best just to keep it trimmed and accept one's exposed pate. Clearly courtly fashion trends were on the decline. He glanced at his desk, then back up at the man. Still he stood.

What on earth did he want? Food? His kind knew to go to the kitchens where food would be given. Money? He received a wage and Cecil would not dream of giving additional money regardless of performance.

His back was hurting today, regardless of how many times he shifted his position in his chair, and he was already tired. He glanced outside and saw the shadow of morning receding before the warm embrace of noon. At this rate, he would have no time to ride out and see progress on Hatfield. A day that had begun with promise was now melting away, leaving a small puddle of half-accomplishments behind. He hated this kind of day, days when productivity danced just beyond his grasp regardless of how hard he worked. He looked sharply now at the courier – he was still shuffling and had added a cough to his repertoire of fidgets. Surely the lad did not expect an answer to papers just delivered.

"I have no answer to your documents, lad. Clearly I have had no time to read and consider them."

The young man bowed and began stuttering.

"S,ss, Sir," he finally managed, "I was entrusted with another message for you."

Cecil looked at him patiently – no need to throw the messenger into paroxysms of fear by being angry or hurried. Sure enough, after a moment, he reached inside his cloak and brought forth a thin paper heavily embossed with wax. He passed it silently to Cecil who inspected the seal. Its crest was not one he knew. Carefully he opened it and found within another folded page with only a few lines of text. His face clouded as he read. After some time, he realized the boy was still in the room. From a drawer in his desk, he pulled a small coin and flipped it to him.

"Tell Cook I said to feed you well, and when you are done, you should wait in the small courtyard beyond the stables.

"Thank you, sir! Thank you!"

So much for not rewarding messengers, Cecil thought grimly as he re-read the page. With a heavy heart, he rose and went in search of the king.

Down the long halls of Greenwich Palace he walked, the tap of his cane sounding unevenly on the stone floors. He regretted not bringing his shawl, and noted that even the guards, posted at each doorway, seemed warmer than he. Past the great audience hall, through the library chambers, on through waiting rooms where courtiers and the public, explorers and hopefuls all waited, hoping to catch the king's eye as he went to and fro about the palace. All the great rooms were empty today, however, for James had decreed the day one of hunting – he was not to be indoors and therefore had ordered that none should come looking or waiting for him. Perhaps that explained his moodiness earlier. Cecil did not know and was almost beyond caring.

On the gravel way just beyond the east wing, he located James astride a giant bay, in intense discussion with a groomsman concerning a stag which had recently been spotted on a nearby estate. James was determined that it should be him, not the estate owner, who should bring it down. His displeasure at having to dismount and discuss state business with Cecil was evident.

"Make it quick, man. If this is about that infernal parliament and the nits who people it, you are wasting my time."

Cecil shook his head and drew him farther from the small knot of sycophants which seemed to accompany James everywhere.

"Majesty, there is a plot which perhaps is better organized than most."

James squinted against the sun and beat his crop lightly against his leg.

"What kind of plot?"

"On your life, my Lord."

James again toyed with his crop, this time lightly touching it to his shoulder.

"Are they planning to attack me whilst I hunt today?"

"No, sire, I do not believe they do, but you see . . ."

James walked away, tossing his final comment over his shoulder.

"Then we shall discuss it anon."

The groomsman helped his master into the huge saddle and James, without so much as a glance back at Cecil, galloped away across the newly mown lawn.

Cecil watched him, and keeping his thoughts to himself turned slowly back to the palace.

*****

James was more worried than he cared to admit. He had firmly believed that once England had recognized his authority and his intent to do well by his kingdom it would settle into acceptance of him. At heart, he was utterly mystified by the continuing threats against his person. During the years leading up to Elizabeth's death, and the momentous months which followed it, he had received absolute assurance first from her ministers and then from the hordes of noblemen who rode north to greet him and pledge their fealty. They were with him, they had said; they stood by him, they swore. If that were true, from whence did these whispered conspiracies arise? Each one had been foiled in turn yet more always followed in their place.

As the guards halted traffic on the High Road to London which passed just beyond Greenwich's main gate, the king galloped across quickly, feeling exposed and vulnerable. Who was after him? How could he protect himself? He was accompanied by Thomas Howard on the hunt today and once the wood closed behind them, James pounded along randomly, giving his horse free rein while he allowed his thoughts to wander unfettered through the enigma of the English and their plotting against him. Without warning, he found himself in the meadow at the base of a ridge he recognized.

"I have been here before," he called over his shoulder.

Howard caught up with him, his pale blue velvet cloak flapping in the cool wind. The guards accompanying them remained at a respectful distance.

"I have not," he offered to James, ". . . but I believe that yonder ridge might give a wide view of your kingdom. Shall we?"

"Why not?" James called out, and once again his horse bolted forward. The ridge was steep, and could only be tackled from the side which sloped down to the Thames. They pushed forward and upwards, and James noticed that his animal was picking its way along a well-worn path; the summit was not difficult to attain. He shielded his eyes against the glare of the sun and turned his horse slowly in a full circle.

On one side of the ridge was the meadow and Greenwich Wood. Stretching beyond that he could see the Palace and its grounds, its outbuildings jumbled across the vista like a child's blocks thrown across a floor. The High Road snaked through the landscape and wound its way into the infinite distance before disappearing in a haze of smoke and fog. All these things he saw, and paused to take them in, but it was the far side of the ridge which captured his attention. There, laid out like a bejeweled tapestry, lay an estate of magnificent order and beauty. Its manor house was of aged limestone, and while it was small its symmetry lent it an air of grace. To one side were the ruins of some ancient chapel. Under ordinary circumstances, these would have been torn down long ago, the stone used for other purposes. But the owner of the estate had seen the obvious, stark beauty left behind by time, the faded glory of the place, and had left it intact. From the ridge where James took it all in, the sun gleamed through the abandoned arches and naves of the place, lighting it with piercing glances like God's own sight.

Beyond that lay grounds impeccably groomed, outbuildings ordered and set in thoughtful opposition to one another and the manor itself, and flower meadows skillfully maintained. In the fields which surrounded the place, sheep grazed placidly.

"What is that place?" James asked, nodding.

"Majesty, I believe that is the estate known as Coudenoure."

"Coudenoure . . ." James thought, ". . . where have I heard that name, why . . . yes, of course, Coudenoure. The home of that white witch who saved me on the road south from Scotland. Coudenoure."

"We shall ride in and see this place." Without further words, he wheeled his mount toward the ridge's down-slope. But even as he had turned his horse full around, Howard came astride.

"Majesty, we have hearings this afternoon. If we are gone long, it will be noticed. And already the Parliament is angry. Perhaps we visit Coudenoure at a later date."

James paused, knowing his friend was right. With an angry jerk he directed his horse back toward the meadow and the wood.

"Yes. That is what we shall do."

He made a mental note of Coudenoure, and determined that he would see it soon.

Chapter Twenty-Five

Early Fall 1604

The day was cold and uncertain – it dithered between moments of mist and damp fog, and outright rain. Early on, the sky settled low and at times it was difficult to discern where it drew its boundary. It seemed to roll down to the cobblestone and dirt streets and then, like a cloud on a stormy day, unfold and wrap itself against all it touched.

The man wandered the streets seemingly intent on his own thoughts. To those he passed, he was not noteworthy, just another Londoner about his business on a gray and wintry day. He took care to keep his hat low and his scarf wrapped tight against the lower part of his face. Should his fellow wayfarers be asked at a later time, no one could have identified him. But had they been curious, they would have noted a strange pattern to his ambling walk. Time and again, he walked the quay adjacent to Westminster, where the Parliament met. Each time, his eyes stared intently at the ages old façade. No sooner had he completed that stroll, however, than he would circle round the end of the huge building and eventually, after slight, deliberate detours, would once again walk the quay, staring at Westminster. At times his glance crossed the wide and muddy Thames, seeming to do some mental calculation before being once again trained on the long and imposing structure. This went on for several hours until apparently satisfied, he left the area. This time, however, his ambling had a more decided rhythm in its step, and as the sky let loose yet again, he stooped and stepped inside a deeply recessed door on a street crowded with such doors. Once inside, he removed his scarf and hat, shook out his hair and looked around.

He did not care for the place, this filthy, grubby tavern, but then, it had not been his choice. And as he had been told more than once, no one was likely to recognize him – Robert Catesby – in such a forlorn corner of London. And they were right, for as he moved to the makeshift counter at the far end of the room, no one took notice of him. He had been careful to dress appropriately in dirty worn breeches and vest, but such subterfuge seemed unnecessary now – everyone in the place seemed intent on their own problems and their own drinks. Perhaps they, too, were seeking anonymity for their own dark reasons.

The Duck and Drake was unusually busy today and Catesby pushed his way through the grubby, smelly crowd. After a moment, a short, pudgy man set a cup of ale before him on the makeshift counter – its top fizzed and grew and Catesby quickly drank off the excess foam. The tavern owner did not step away, but waited impatiently for his coin – he knew his clientele well, and to turn one's back was to risk non-payment. Catesby pulled a pence from the pocket on his vest and turned to survey the room. He was a tall man, and he easily took in the others in the crowded space. Only one person glanced his way, a young woman leaning against a doorway beyond the bar. He had only to turn his large, sad, and darkly mysterious eyes upon a woman for her to fall in love with him. He had been known to take advantage of that fact. Today, however, no such thoughts crossed his mind. He sat down on a nearby stool and began nursing his drink. More than an hour later, another man entered, pushed his way through the throng and ordered an ale. He pulled over a nearby stool close and sat down adjacent to Catesby.

The talk at the bar was loud, drunken. After some time, the idea of betting on cards was introduced by someone at the far end. He was immediately taken up on his offer by another and when the man deftly drew a deck of cards he happened to have in his pocket, many at the bar smiled – there was no doubt who would go home the richer man. Catesby seemed in the spirit of the event, and offered to play the man beside him for a bit of coin. After the money was given to the bartender for safekeeping, he in turn passed them a deck of cards. They refilled their mugs and found a quiet table in a back corner. They set up their drinks and whilst one began shuffling, the other spoke. He face was lighthearted as though the ale was speaking through him, and the other laughed. Had anyone been watching, they would have thought a joke had just been told. He leaned in, and while his voice remained gay, his words were otherwise.

"We have quarters across the way, Catesby."

"Excellent!" Catesby began dealing and the two men drew closer yet. "We should not meet here again, for it might be noted."

"We have not been here since May, I would remind you." He was shorter than Catesby, and whether through physical size or sheer magnitude Catesby dominated him. As he took the hand dealt by Catesby he smiled and again spoke in a low, conspiratorial voice.

"Everything is secured and we shall began rowing the gun powder across the Thames this evening."

"Ho ho!" Catesby pretended to laugh and laid down a card. "And the undercroft where it will be stored?"

"Secure."

The second man nodded. He sensed their business was at an end and drained his cup. As he did, Catesby queried him closely.

"And who will keep an eye on our supply? Who is our guard?"

"It will be the man from Flanders – Guy Fawkes."

"And you are sure of him?"

"Oh, aye," came the response. "Indeed I am."

Chapter Twenty-Six

December 24, 1604

To those who knew him, James' had been unusually preoccupied of late. He showed no interest in state affairs other than to rail against Parliament. Time and again he questioned Cecil and others close to him on the possibility of forcing the recalcitrant body to comply with his wishes. But each time he received the same infuriating answer: Parliament might be bound unto him, but they served England. What about monarchs before him, he would query in wrath – Elizabeth and her father – surely they had not found themselves begging before their own subjects. And each time he was reminded that the roles of the monarch and the church had changed. Henry had come to the throne almost one hundred years earlier. Surely, their answers implied, James did not expect the world to have remained static? But he did.

In spite of his fury, however, he could have managed the situation had it not been for a small, nagging fear which daily fed upon his deepest, most morbid thoughts: assassination. Death by a violent turn, unseen until too late, un-sensed until complete. It seemed to loom over him at every turn. Oh, of course there were the usual lunatics, those who ran out from the crowd fueled by alcohol or hunger, plague or madness, intent on doing him harm. No, it was not those who concerned him.

Since the previous summer, Cecil had continued to catch the occasional whispered ghost of an impending plot, one organized and orchestrated by the very people who surrounded him. Like the faint smell of rain borne on a summer afternoon's breeze, it never showed itself – only its shadow. It never came forward but neither did it recede. It was always there, a constant beat upon his subconscious.

Again and again, his mind turned to thoughts of the witch who had saved him before. He knew now where she lived and despite his best efforts, he began to believe that only she could save him as she had before. She was powerful, he was sure, and she was on his side. Despite the cold of the season, he progressed to Greenwich, and on this particular morning, rode out alone. In silence he crossed the High Road and entered the wood. In silence he made the meadow and galloped swiftly across it, skirting the ridge and following an old path of a road until a bramble-covered set of gates appeared. The motto carved in stone spoke volumes to his heart: *To Elizabeth We Pledge All*. Had she, too, been of the coven?

James slowed his mount to a stately walk, taking in the scene before him. The long, straight drive upon which he now trod was banked by a meadow in the deepest repose of winter. The manicured grounds had been cut down, covered in hay against the frost, waiting for spring. The house was unusual in its small size and absolute symmetry. It lay on the landscape like a marble effigy upon a sarcophagus. Smoke curled from a giant chimney, and he knew that it must come from some ancient hearth. No one appeared and a moment of nervousness engulfed him. He was seldom alone. But he had taken pains to dress in royal garb lest they be at all ignorant of the personage who now visited them. The king dismounted. Still no one came forward. He secured his horse to a post, stepped to the door and rang the great bell mounted to the wall . . . and waited. In time, and slowly, one side of the great wych elm doors creaked open.

Before him stood a small girl with flaxen hair and blue eyes. In her hand was a worn manuscript. She wore a simple blue linen frock but over it was a woolen smock, deeply stained and frayed. Standing behind her was another small child, a boy. He held a mortar with both hands.

"Yes? Are you here for Papa?"

James was unaccustomed to being addressed in such a manner but quickly collected himself.

"I am."

"Well, you must see cook for we are busy in Grandpapa's workshop making gold."

James stared at her, thunderstruck. Making gold?

Before he could put a question forward, they ran down the long hallway and through a heavy door, inset at the very end of the way. For the first time, he noticed the exquisite tapestries which graced the walls, the ancient rugs which lay underfoot. A large woman in cap and apron appeared from the depths beyond.

"Aye? Why are you here, sir?"

James was not sure what to say. He had assumed his majesty would render him recognizable regardless of circumstance. In his uncertainty, he stared at the woman silently. She stared back, taking in his splendid riding breeches, his fur-lined cape and be-feathered hat. Before the word 'dandy' escaped her lips, Henrietta entered from the library. A split second later she bowed.

"Majesty." She motioned to cook to bow.

James cocked his head upward slightly with a sniff. He determined to make them wait and only after several uncomfortable moments had passed did he speak.

"I am here to see you," he began.

Henrietta looked askance at the grand figure before her. There was no retinue, no courtiers or guards. What was the king doing here?

"Certainly, Sire," she began, "We are honored that you would visit us at our humble estate."

"Yes, I can see why you would be."

"Majesty, you have ridden a long way to arrive. Would you like tea and a repast?"

"Ale will be fine."

It was hard to know if Cook was more thrilled at being dismissed or more terrified at having met such a personage. Still bowed, and mumbling 'Majesty' over and over, she backed towards the kitchen. As she disappeared through its doorway, shouting could be heard. Henrietta bowed again and she and King James entered the library. Like all first-time visitors to Coudenoure, he stared in awe at the wall of books which defined the room. The medieval mantel, enormous and imposing, seemed small against the backdrop of ancient manuscripts, books, papyri and codices. Henrietta watched his face change from delighted curiosity to deep suspicion. She remarked upon it.

"I see, Majesty, that you wonder about Coudenoure's library."

James took the seat she proffered and nodded at the incunabula which filled one entire shelf. She followed his gaze.

"Yes, we have a significant collection of such works – books printed before 1500. If Majesty would like to review them, I would be happy to read the titles to you or review them with you."

"My understanding was that works of such antiquity were usually in Latin, or possibly Greek – you are familiar with these languages?"

Henrietta smiled a silent laugh.

"Majesty, I read both languages and many others, as does my aunt and my daughter. 'Tis a tradition here at Coudenoure that women be as educated as men."

She did not like the dark look which settled on his face, and quickly added a demurring disclaimer.

"Of course, being the weaker vessel, 'tis not easy and is also quite pointless, but it provides enlightenment for our small minds as we tend to our womanly chores."

James seemed mollified and took a long drink from the cups brought forth by a servant. Henrietta remained quiet, wondering where Roman was and mystified as to why the King of England was sitting in her library. She did not remain in darkness long.

"I believe I met your daughter. And possibly your son – two children answered the door."

"Ah, yes. Elizabeth and Thomas – they are twins!"

"Twins?"

"Born at the same time," Henrietta began to explain.

"Yes, I know what twins are, woman." Henrietta bowed her head and again wished for Roman to appear.

"Tell me, twins are unusual, and surely associated with . . ." James hesitated, not sure how to broach his subject. Should his voice carry condemnation it would surely put the woman off, and he would not be able to get that for which he came.

". . . Twins are usually seen as a sign, are they not?" he finished his statement and looked inquiringly at Henrietta.

"I know nothing of signs," she laughed, ". . . but they are much trouble as you may imagine."

"Hmm. They told me they were making gold in Grandpapa's workshop."

Henrietta laughed.

"They have discovered my grandfather's workshop," she explained. "Do you know of the great philosopher and alchemist John Dee? He and my grandfather spent many hours experimenting on various matters with potions they made and chemicals, too. Elizabeth is quite precocious and when she came across notebooks from Dee and her grandfather, she immediately enlisted Thomas as her aide in re-creating their work."

James listened carefully. This was his moment he was sure.

"Madame, I do not know your name."

"I am Henrietta Collins."

James smiled a thin smile in the hope that it cloaked his disdain for his coming words.

"You remember, of course, that you saved my life on the road south, as I progressed to become your king."

Henrietta bowed her head.

"It was a great honor to do so, Majesty."

"What was that poultice you had at the time? Eh?"

Henrietta thought back, momentarily confused. Then she remembered.

"Oh, that? It was for my leg, and then I used it for my hand – remember, Majesty? I received a cut from the traitor's sword."

"But I do not see signs of that wound now. You seem to bear no scar."

Henrietta looked at her hand. It was true. So completely had the poultice helped heal the wound that no scar was visible.

"No, the poultice was magic," she laughed uneasily, not sure where the man was headed. "When I arrived here at Coudenoure, I made a careful catalog of what I believe was in it, so that we might make use of it here at Coudenoure should the need arise."

"Indeed." He drained his cup and Henrietta rang the bell for more. They sat in silence. Where, oh where, was Roman? The ale arrived and after a long pull, James spoke again.

"Many in my kingdom seem to plot against me."

Henrietta set her cup carefully on the small table next to her chair. She looked down at her simple woolen frock, carefully adjusted the folds of its skirt and folded her hands in her lap. So this was no simple visit. Talk of treason was a dangerous, and talk of treason with the king doubly so, for one never knew how ones' words might be interpreted. He had introduced the topic lightly, but she immediately realized that this was where he had wanted the conversation to arrive all along and the reason for his visit. She remained quiet and a concern arose in her breast.

"Do you have the original poultice yet? Can you make another?"

What did the man want? She was almost shaking. James spoke again.

"Madame, I know of witches, you see, and I know there are good witches – white witches – and evil ones as well. I know you and your poultice saved me once before, and I am here to ask your blessing going forward. I need you to cover me with your magic and give me a poultice that will protect me."

He spoke the words in a low tone, lest they be heard by God in heaven. What he was doing was wrong, invoking some dark art to secure his safety. But the safety of the kingdom depended upon the safety of his person, so how wrong could it be? He leaned back and closed his eyes, letting the ale course through his veins while he waited for the witch to consider his words. But she did not speak. He raised one eyelid and saw that still she sat staring at her folded hands. Why? Why did she not answer? Then it struck him – she must want something in return. So like a witch!

"Madame, in return for your . . . assurances . . . I will grant Coudenoure continued protection from taxes. You see, my man Cecil tells me Coudenoure held special privilege under the Tudor dynasty, and I shall extend that dispensation through my own Stuart line."

Henrietta thought quickly. Clearly, there would be no convincing the king that she was just a simple woman who had benefited from a medicinal pack of herbs given her by another woman. Nor would he accept that her actions on the road from Scotland had been merely serendipitous, not magical. He seemed convinced that having saved him once she could do so again through some dark power she wielded. She began to be glad that Roman had not put in an appearance, for he would have scoffed aloud at what she did next.

"Majesty, come with me. I have some of the original poultice remaining. Let us secure it on a leather necklace that you might wear under your clothing."

She stopped before making any promises about its abilities. The man needed to put his mind at ease and this expedient would surely do that. She led him along the central arched hallway and into Quinn's workshop. There, Elizabeth could be heard and seen happily babbling off some formula to Thomas who dutifully poured various powders, liquids and whatnots into a pot loaned them by Cook. James eyed them curiously.

He was pleased to note that his theory was proven right – where there was one witch there would always be others. They must need one another's strength to survive, and here was a witch clearly passing on her skills in the dark arts to her daughter. The child was beautiful, as was her brother. Twins! Oh yes, he had been right. Having confirmed in his mind that he was in the presence of such creatures, he became suddenly nervous. He had never spoken aloud, knowingly, to one, and he was relieved that Henrietta seemed to take his knowledge of her kind in stride. He had thought to find her secretive, but no, here at this strange estate of Coudenoure, she was in her element. It was he who must be careful, he who for once must show gratitude to her kind, for she clearly had the power to protect him.

Henrietta moved quickly to a back table. From a large drawer she pulled what remained of the poultice given her by the kind old woman at Donoway. She turned and went back to the king.

"Hold this," she demanded, and he dared not do otherwise. She wandered from one area of the room to another, clearly looking for something. The children continued their game, oblivious to his presence.

"Ha, yes!" she ran to a far wall, upon which hung skeins of freshly dyed and twined wool. She selected strands of blue, burgundy and green and quickly twisted them together. James watched, mystified and awed. How many men got to see a witch's workshop, with witches at work concocting their brews and casting their magic on a protective talisman? Perhaps he was the first!

Henrietta returned to him, praying silently that God would forgive her for what she was doing.

"I do it for my family, for the safety of my estate. This man, this *king*, clearly believes me to be a witch. I cannot change that. If I do not help him, he will come against my family, my home. My only choice, dear God in heaven, is to go along with his medieval beliefs and pretend that I can help him. God forgive me for what I do. I do it for my family."

She picked up a nearby awl and drove a hole through the poultice; she threaded the strands of yarns through the hole, mumbling to herself to hurry, lest Roman catch her. He would not go along with her plan, for he would not appreciate the danger.

James heard her mumbling and was satisfied once again.

"Yes," he nodded as he thought, "Now she speaks aloud the dark words of her craft. Now she imbues the talisman with her power."

She placed it around his neck and he carefully tucked it beneath his clothing. It was done.

He glanced once more at the children, noting the intensity with which they worked. A cold shudder ran through him, and he rose and walked quickly and directly to the front door of the manor house. He had what he needed, and he had given the witch what she wanted. The bargain was secured. As he mounted his horse, Henrietta bowed deeply.

"Majesty, you must come again, for we are honored by your presence."

James looked at her and for the first time understood what it meant to be beholden to someone. It was not a comfortable feeling. He turned without response and galloped away down the long drive.

Roman came hurriedly around the side of the estate.

"Cook sent Rouster to find me in the field. Was that the *king*?"

Henrietta nodded, turned, and went slowly indoors. What had she done?

*****

The plague seemed never far away. Having receded during the winter months, it began its monstrous rise once again in the spring of 1605. No one was safe and James left the capital for cleaner, less crowded environs. The government no longer progressed with the king as he moved from palace to palace. But the noblemen and administrators who served as his ministers and parliamentarians feared for their lives as James did for his. They had no intention of risking them by staying in the city when the king himself went abroad for fear of his own. No.

They, too, left London, and the writ went out to counties and cities across the land: Parliament would not meet on October 3rd as originally planned. Plague was too rampant – a frost was needed to slow it down, thus enabling all to return London in relative safety.

Parliament, the writ proclaimed, now had a new meeting day.

*****

November 5, 1605

"And the new casks? Are they in place?" He looked purposefully at those across the tavern table, the strain showing on his face.

Robert Catesby was frazzled and fearful. What had begun as a well-planned conspiracy to put a Catholic on the throne of England, to rid the nation of the hateful, neurotic, Protestant James, had now become an almost theatrical farce. He closed his eyes and for the thousandth time that day, thought back to the beginning.

A year earlier, at home in Chastleton, he had summoned his cousin, Thomas Wintour, and told him of his plans to blow up Parliament, thus ridding the country of the king and his noblemen at one blow. From that night, the plot had grown until now it was all Catesby could do to manage the multiplying mass of men who had come forward to participate. And their sheer numbers scared him, for conspiracies were most often leaked when conspiracies became too large to handle.

And the timing! So many postponements! Why, if Parliament had met on schedule, they would have succeeded already without doubt – James would be no more. But no. It had been delayed, and that delay cost him dearly, for the gunpowder put in place earlier had rotted from the damp and cold of the dank undercroft. Again, then, he had been forced to seek out his Spanish friends, again he had persuaded them to sell him more gunpowder, again he had pledged fealty to some Spanish notion of intrigue once a Catholic was on the throne of England, again he had paid handsomely for the explosives. But that was only the beginning.

Night after night, all was risked as the powder was rowed silently across the Thames from its initial storage place, to the undercroft of Westminster. Night after night, he walked the darkened quay, wondering if this would be the evening when his plans were discovered, when he must ride like thunder and lightning to Woolwich, where a Spanish galleon waited on the tide for such an eventuality.

And Guy Fawkes – even now Catesby shook his head. After the first fiasco of postponement and rotted powder, Fawkes had deemed it a good idea to tunnel deeper under Westminster. What was that, Catesby wondered – a way to pass the time? He had no interest in such a childish approach, and indeed, never asked if Fawkes actually succeeded. Such a scheme lent the whole enterprise a comical air, and Catesby abjured the entire episode. Finally, finally, the eve of Parliament was upon them, and Catesby held a final meeting with his lieutenants. He now repeated his earlier question.

"The new casks of gunpowder are in place?"

"Aye," replied Wintour. He was dressed for a night ride, in dark and woolen cap and cape, as was Catesby. Even as the explosion took place in the south, so the plan went, they would incite rebellion in the northern counties, those areas which seemed always ready to the moment. With no one to rise against them, they would march south and claim the throne in the name of Catholicism and all that they deemed holy. The Pope and Spain were watching, and Catesby well knew that should the enterprise succeed in the initial stages, his success in the long run was assured by their intervention – in a holy war against the Protestants of England if necessary.

All was in place now, and he looked across the tavern table at Guy Fawkes. Here was the man they were leaving behind in London. To him fell the responsibility of keeping the night watch, waiting for the dawn, waiting for the procession into Westminster and finally, for the arrival of King James. He was to light the fuse and escape to the waiting steed tied just beyond the undercroft's small door. For the first time that evening, Fawkes spoke.

"I am ready, and you should leave now. I shall see you anon, when Catholicism is once again in her rightful place upon the throne."

Catesby looked at him. He was a small man, middle-aged, and with a small face. His nose was aquiline and his soft curly hair roiled gently around his face. His hat was fashionable – a stovetop with a narrow brim. In fact, everything about him seemed small, but perhaps that was good. It allowed him to slip in and out of places and situations with notice from no one. Tonight, his small, non-descript presence would not be perceived.

They rose. Each man crossed himself and said a prayer – it mattered not what others in the tavern thought, for it was far too late for anyone to cry havoc. The matter was done – only the results remained to be gathered in. Fawkes tipped his hat, tied his scarf loosely against his vest, nodded, and disappeared into the crowd. One by one, the others slipped away until Catesby was left alone standing by the table. Once again he crossed himself, said another small prayer, and turned to face whatever might unfold.

*****

Of *course* he knew. Robert Cecil was many things – able administrator, loving father and husband, devout Protestant, astute negotiator. Oh, he smiled to himself as he ticked down the list of what he was, I am also . . . intuitive.

When the courier had stayed behind at Greenwich, when the boy had passed over the document with the unknown seal, Cecil had felt the hair on the back of his neck rise. His prescient sense of danger was confirmed by what he read within.

So the Catholics would rise once against. Even as he had watched James ride away that day, he had known what he must do, regardless of the king's approval. The king had the right to turn away from issues with which he did not care to wrestle. Cecil had no such luxury. And so it had begun. He turned now and looked out his window, enjoying the fire in the hearth at Hatfield but still feeling the need for a shawl. He pulled an old one from the back of his chair, wrapped himself in its warmth, closed his eyes and relived the past few months.

There had been no sure way to proceed. Indeed, the note had stated only that a well-planned conspiracy was under way, one which guaranteed the destruction not just of the king, but of England as well. Cecil's problems were confounded by the fact that there was no signature. He was left with what he felt certain was a viable threat, but he had no way to pursue it. Why then, he wondered, had the author bothered to send the note at all? It had to be that some clue was to found within this cryptic, sinister message. For days, Cecil had read and re-read the short epistle, dissecting its every line until finally, a thought occurred to him. He called for the courier.

Two days later, shaking with fright, the boy had appeared.

"I wish to discuss the letter you gave me some time ago."

The lad bowed silently, his eyes the size of saucers.

"Tell me how you came to possess that note."

"I told you, sir, already."

"Tell me again."

The boy struggled not to cry and spoke hesitantly.

"As I was leaving Whitehall, a man appeared from the shadows and told me it was most urgent that you see the note he then gave me."

"What else?"

"He said no one but you should be present when I gave it to you."

Cecil paused and beckoned the boy closer.

"Sit, and have some sweets with me."

This seemed to relax the boy and three sugared chestnuts later, he volunteered additional information.

"You know, sir, I have seen that man since."

"Indeed!" Cecil smiled encouragingly.

"Yes sir. It was when we were leaving for Richmond Palace two days ago. I was behind our good King James, waiting for mail to take to Greenwich, for some other courtiers were going there as well."

Cecil wanted the child to cut to the point, but he dared not interrupt. He only smiled and proffered more food.

"I turned to look behind me, sir, for I thought perhaps Matthew – he is the gentleman who gives me my mail pouch each time I ride forth, sir –well, I thought perhaps he was somewhere in the crowd and I was missing him."

"I see."

"Anyway, sir, when I turned, a giant horse was immediately behind me, and the gentleman was upon it. I was afraid I would be trampled, I was!"

Cecil nodded in sympathy. When oh when would the child make his point.

"Well, sir, as I turned, I overheard him say something to the man beside him."

Cecil leaned forward.

"It was not something I understood – I believe it was the name of some place, but not one which is along any of my routes. You see, sir, each of us couriers has routes for which we are responsible. Mine, for instance . . ."

"Stick to the point, *please*!" Cecil hoped these words spoken as softly and gently as he could manage sounded better than they did when he screamed them in his head.

"What did this man say?"

"Something like 'Castle Town', but there is no such route, sir."

Cecil thought quickly. 'Castle Town, Castle Town'. A thought occurred.

"Boy, did he say Chastleton?"

The child smiled and helped himself to a large slice of ham and half the bread on the tray before them.

"Yes! That was it! 'Tis not a place I know, sir, and I spoke with the other couriers and they do not know of it either."

Cecil let him ramble on – he had his man. Now, it was simply a question of setting the trap.

And so to November 5th, when the idiot Guy Fawkes was found sitting on a pile of gunpowder, holding a watch, a fuse, and matches in the undercroft of Westminster. Indeed.

There was only one loose end, and Cecil sat up in his chair and took off the shawl as he considered it. Shortly after the conspirators were caught, their treachery having come to naught, James had sent for special stationary. Cecil had taken it to him, and had asked if the king would like him to draft a letter, for such heavy paper was used only for the most formal of documents, those normally sent out by Cecil himself and then signed by the king, but not *written* by him.

James had demurred and dismissed his administrator, saying he needed no help with this particular document. After several hours, he had called for his seal, wax, and a courier. Cecil was only too happy to supply him with all three. The letter was already folded and all that remained was the imprint. Cecil took it and handed it to the courier who stood nearby. They left together.

"You understand?" Cecil asked.

The child nodded. He was happy to have made friends with such a powerful man.

"Once it is delivered you are to wait to see if you hear anything, and then you are to report back to me immediately."

He tucked the note safely in his pouch and disappeared down the long hallway. Straightaway, he called for his horse and waited impatiently while it was saddled. Finally, a groomsman appeared and handed him the reins.

"And where are you off to?" the groomsman asked.

"To a place I have never even heard of – but perhaps you have. 'Tis called Coudenoure."

The groomsman looked at him intently.

"Aye, I have heard of this place," he said slowly.

As the courier described the route given him by Cecil, the groomsman laughed and interrupted him.

"Lad, do not bother. Cross the high road into yon wood, Greenwich Wood. Let your horse follow the path and it will lead you to a meadow. From there, skirt the ridge and ride on but a short way. You will be at Coudenoure before you know it."

"Thank you!" said the courier. "You are most kind!"

"If you wanted to tell me what happens there, that would be a fine repayment," replied the groomsman.

The courier was uncertain but only for a moment – it would be good to have a friend in the stables too. He might be able to get the better horses, the faster horses, for his runs from now on. And so he agreed.

"What is your name and I shall ask for you upon my return."

The groomsman smiled.

"Marshall is my name. And I will wait for you so that we may discuss the matter."

The courier turned and galloped from the yard.

"Now who is sending messages to Coudenoure, eh?" Marshall asked himself quietly, then turned back to his business.

"Madame (Lady Henrietta),

I pray all is well with you at Coudenoure. I am sure you have heard by now of the dastardly plot to overthrow the kingdom by blowing up Parliament, and my person as well. It is over, and the traitors have received what they deserved. They are in God's hands now, as is right.

I write to thank you for your, I shall call it assistance, recently. I am sure you know that of which I speak, for had you not intervened, I fear the conspiracy may have had quite a different ending. I owe you much, as does England.

We have our pact, and Coudenoure shall remain as it is today – an isolated jewel of an estate, free of taxes or ordinances or even censures.

Should you ever be in need, Madame, be certain you may call upon me for aid. In that vein, I shall do the same should I need yours.

James Rex

"What on earth transpired that day the king came here? What did you say to him?"

Roman was only half-laughing. Anne, Ian and Ben stood by mystified.

Henrietta giggled.

"Well, 'tis a long story, and I am not sure I believe it myself."

Anne called for tea and they pulled their chairs close in the library.

"We wait, breathless," Roman said drily. A cough from near the door caught his attention.

"Who is that?"

"Sir, I am the courier. Shall I wait?"

"Wait for what? No, lad, be gone."

He had no choice but to leave.

"Now, oh wife of mine, tell the tale."

*****

Late that evening, Ian Hurblert lay next to his wife in bed. The fire across the room burned low in its grate. His nightshirt was one Anne had made especially for him, and he toyed now with the embroidery on the front. His other arm was crooked behind his head. A soft whisper came across the night stillness as Anne curled herself against him.

"What is it?" she asked. "Why cannot you sleep, my love?"

Ian turned to face her.

"King James takes witches seriously, Anne. For him to visit Coudenoure, and then send a letter acknowledging his belief that Henrietta *is* one, well, 'tis very dangerous."

"You worry too much, Ian. You heard Henrietta this evening. The king showed up and she simply gave him peace of mind. That he would write a letter . . ."

"A letter in which he states his belief that she saved him through her witchcraft."

". . . a letter in which he thanks her – it is not a problem."

Anne's eyes closed in a drowsy warm sleep and Ian was left with his thoughts.

"But if it is not a problem now, my dearest, it will be. You may be sure of that, for James is fickle, James is vain, James is suspicious, and he will remember this well. God help us if he ever comes to the belief that her powers have failed him."

Chapter Twenty-Seven

Early Spring 1611

Roman walked alone across the back meadow of
Coudenoure. It was an area somewhat isolated
from the rest of the estate by a large copse of trees
which grew along the banks of a narrow swale.
Before him was a flock of ewes with their lambs. He
had driven them out steadily from the holding pen
which had been their home since lambing. Now, he
moved slowly but deliberately, giving the lambs
time to do that which came naturally – play. In and
out between their mothers' legs they jumped about
and chased one another. One would stop to sniff . . .
what . . . some hint of grass or perhaps an early
crocus? Whenever he paused, those following
behind would barrel into him, then all fell down,
seeming to delight in the chaos of their actions. The
old shepherd dog who accompanied him had no
patience with such folderol and would head-butt
them incessantly until they were once more on the
move with the rest of the flock. They were bound
for a choice location, one where the swale widened

into a small, shallow creek, and the grass grew green and rich. The ewes, hungry after their labors, would enjoy the sweet fodder and the lambs could explore the creek.

Roman had wanted to walk out today. It was the type of day into which his strongest memories were embedded. At such times, he did not remember his childhood, his life, so much as feel it in his bones, in his very limbs as he walked along. He had collected a small branch as he went, stripping it of its sapling leaves and using it to beat a path through the meadow. He brushed it through a patch of lavender, releasing a strong and pure scent – a glorious harbinger of the coming spring. A ewe had begun to wander and Roman almost laughed aloud as the dog bounded forward to get ahead of her. Once in front of her, the dog turned and crouched low, neck stretched out, giving her what shepherds the world over referred to as the evil eye – sheep seemed to recognize the message instinctually and could be counted upon to stop and return to the flock.

How many years had he walked out in this very meadow, enjoying the sunshine, feeling himself fortunate in every way. He began to count: there was the year he arrived, and then of course the birth of the twins. Ian had come into their lives shortly afterwards, and then, when he sheered his first hybrid sheep – a breed of his own making – that had been a time indeed. He laughed aloud as he remembered his father's face, flushed and so full of pride. The old man had personally seen to the fleece being shipped back to London, and in his own workshops on his own looms was produced the first ever Coudenoure woolen cloth. They would conquer the world together, father and son. Dear Papa.

He thought back to the night he had received the news of his parents' deaths and crossed himself as he walked along. His pace slowed, remembering Henrietta's tear-streaked face as she broke the news to him.

"Roman, my love, there has been a fire, a great fire."

She began to sob and he moved to her, wrapping his strong arms around her.

"Shhh, dear, whatever it is we shall see it through together. Do not cry, love." He kissed her eyes.

She sobbed all the more.

"Roman, in the kitchen hearth of your parents' home, a young scullery boy slipped in late at night to fry himself some dinner. He was called away by a friend, and the grease from the meat caught fire."

Roman held her at arm's length – he did not like where he now knew she must be going.

"Henrietta, my parents?"

She placed her hand gently on his cheek.

"They are gone, love, for they were asleep upstairs. The blaze caught the draft of the stairwell and swept onto the second floor – they could not even have had time to awaken."

He stopped walking altogether, remembering the pain. After a moment, he went on – what else could he do.

Where had the years gone? Impossible as it seemed, they were moving even faster now, and as he watched the lambs trip one another up he compared their gamboling frolic to the seasons, bumping into one another, this one pushing that one out of its way, making noise and running amok only to be replaced in turn by yet another.

The ewes slowed, and Roman settled under the canopy of a great oak. He continued to watch the flock, intent on nothing more than enjoying the day. Sometime later, he spied Henrietta tripping along with the children and he sat up, waving gaily. She caught sight of him first and bent, pointing his position out to Thomas and Elizabeth. They left her behind as they ran to him, falling over themselves and giggling along the way. When she finally caught up with them, she threw herself beside Roman, panting with exertion. Roman laughed. From a basket on her arm she gave each child cheese and bread and sent them to the creek to look for whatever hapless critter might cross their inquisitive path. She gave bread and meat to Roman and produced a bottle of ale for the two of them. They sat in silence.

"Have you ever considered . . .," Roman began, ". . . that we might be the most fortunate people in the entire kingdom?"

"I love you, too," she laughed. Roman threw his arm over her shoulders.

"I am serious, Henrietta. We have health, children, Coudenoure . . ."

"Sheep," Henrietta offered.

Roman smiled. The sun was warm and he reached for another bottle of ale while Henrietta continued.

"Elizabeth is very much like her grandfather, have you noticed? She is spending more and more of her days in his workshop."

"And her studies? Is she keeping up there?"

"Yeeeessss," Henrietta spoke slowly as though considering her words carefully, ". . . but she is more interested in what she considers practical issues."

"I do not understand."

"What happens when sheep's wool is died using insects for coloration? What happens when you bake a pie using only sugar as the filling or freeze a flea – these are her primary concerns."

"And Thomas? Our boy? What is his approach to his studies?"

"Scholarly. He and Ben are thick as thieves. This is how it seems to work: Elizabeth declares some grand new experiment to determine God in heaven knows what. The boys immediately run to the library and search every book, every manuscript – every scrap of everything! – until they find something they believe will advance Elizabeth's experiment. Then comes the second phase."

"The second phase?"

"Do you remember last week when a messenger from London arrived?"

"Of course – he had one of those New World creatures with him. The type Anne mentioned had previously lived in one of the glass houses – an iguana."

"Yes, Roman, and why do you suppose he showed up at Coudenoure with such a creature?"

She did not bother to wait for his response.

"It is because Elizabeth had declared that they would hence forth build a catalog of every creature on God's earth, and Thomas discovered Quinn's notebook detailing how to come by an 'iguana'. Sooo, the second phase consisted of pooling their coin, doing chores to supplement the pool, writing a letter to the address in the diary and then, when the creature showed up, paying the messenger. The second phase."

Roman began laughing. "Do I even want to hear about the third one then?"

Henrietta finished her biscuit and meat and took the ale from Roman. The children played in the meadow. A fine day.

*****

While Roman and Henrietta generally went their separate ways during the unfolding of each new day, Anne and Ian did not. They woke together, breakfasted together, and then, rain or cold or heat or sun, they walked Quinn's meadow, observing the minute changes brought by each new day: this flower's petals had been decimated by a finch looking for thistle; that bush was developing a nasty yellow rot on its lower leaves; how long had that rose been in that spot; the great elm on the hill certainly looked fine this autumn day. After exercise, they retired to the library, where they took turns conducting lessons for Thomas, Elizabeth and Ben. All of this was followed by dinner, another round of exercise (usually towards the great chapel ruins and orchard), a short nap, and then letters, study and reflection until supper. To most, such a routine would have seemed stultifying. For Anne and Ian, it was heaven.

They shared each other's enthusiasms, laughed at the same humor, came to the same conclusions. Along with card games and puzzles, they relished opportunities to ply their powers of observation. Ian, why do you suppose Thomas is bending low as he passes by the library window on his way to the children's not-so-secret hideout in the center of the meadow? I smelled bacon and yeast only a moment ago – likely he has purloined the morning's rations from the kitchen for the bandits.

So it was not unusual that the sight on the drive that morning excited speculation. A messenger approached, a large satchel slung over his shoulder. Behind him trailed two horsemen clearly associated with the king. They wore his livery, crisp and clean, and their steeds were groomed and well-fed. The messenger himself was dressed plainly, and yet he had an air which clearly marked him as beyond the common man. Anne and Ian watched from the library window where they sat over tea.

"What is your guess, my dear?" asked Ian.

"Well, I would speculate that the two men in livery are from the court, while the messenger is not."

"Agreed!" he exclaimed. They were close now and Anne rose. "But why send court guards with a common courier? What do you suppose he brings us?"

"Let us go and find out!"

Even as they opened the large front doors, the messenger carefully dismounted and for the first time, Anne and Ian noticed the considerable bulk of his satchel. He treated it with care and came forward.

"I seek the Lady Henrietta." He bowed slightly.

"She is not in the house at present," Ian said, "But is on the estate. We shall answer on her behalf – what have you got, man?"

A look of uncertainty crossed his face. One of the guards coughed and the messenger stepped back to speak to him. Their conversation, sotto voce, was nevertheless overheard.

"What are you doing? Give them the book and let us be gone!"

"But," came the courier's uncertain reply, "They are not 'the Lady Henrietta', and I have instructions . . ."

"Damn your instructions. Give them the book and I will buy you a drink on our way back to London. I am thirsty . . ."

"And I hungry . . ." chimed in the second one.

"Just do it! God's liver you do dither!"

Bolstered by their stern commands, and the promise of an ale, the courier turned once more to Anne and Ian. Handing the satchel to Ian, he unfolded its leather top, and while Ian held it steady pulled from within it a great package bound in linen and tied with purple ribbon. Beneath the ribbon lay a letter sealed with the king's own ring. Ian handed the satchel to Anne and took the package from the courier. From within his vest pocket, he took a coin and smiling at the man, passed it to him. One of the guards pulled sharply on his reins, causing his mount to rear and snort. Without a further word, the messenger turned, re-mounted, and rode silently away. His guards once more trailed behind him, and Anne and Ian watched them go.

The gift was likely from the king himself – otherwise, there would not be a note sealed with the crown's own insignia boldly stamped upon the blood red wax. Such knowledge should have made them giddy with speculation. It did not. Ian had never been able to conquer the anxiety he had felt that day so long ago when the king's letter had arrived for Henrietta. That the monarch chose, for a second time, to communicate directly with her could not be good news.

Over time, Anne had come to realize that he had a legitimate fear of King James – the man commanded a kingdom whose parliament refused to acknowledge his absolutist ideas of monarchy. Angry letters flowed from James to the august body to no avail. This was not the reign of Henry, nor even of Elizabeth. No. A new day had dawned, a new merchant class had arisen, a new sense of power imbued those who sat in deliberation before him. In his mind, they were recalcitrant children and he seethed whenever he could not force them to his will. Whether for that reason or because of natural inclinations, he drank too much, and when he descended into drunkenness, which had now become fairly often, his moods and decisions became unpredictable. Even Cecil, now the Earl of Salisbury, could not convince him to accept the inevitable, namely, that governmental power was now shared . . . absolute monarchy in the kingdom of England would not rise again.

As Anne and Ian carried the newly-delivered bundle indoors to the library, Ben appeared. He did not share their cautious apprehension and immediately pulled one of the ends of the elaborate bow which bound it. It fell open and while they could have stopped him, they did not. As he pulled the linen wrapping back excitedly, a collective gasp arose.

"No!"

"God's knees!"

"Damn!"

"*Ben*! Where did you hear such language?"

Ben smiled proudly.

"Rouster taught it to me – he got it from the stable boy."

Had it not been for the package, a long lecture would have ensued on the importance of words. But Ben was spared.

Before them lay a book seven years in the making, the King James Bible. Encased in the finest calf-skin leather, each corner was braced with a brass guard. A substantial brass hasp and lock decorated the edge, and as Anne and Ian looked on, Ben carefully opened it. Its pages, hand-woven, lay like delicate rose petals waiting to be unfurled. A faint, wispy smell of fresh ink wafted up as Ben carefully leafed through the pages. While the young man stood in place, mesmerized by this new marvel, Ian pulled Anne out of earshot. In his hand he held James' letter to Henrietta.

"Wife, this cannot be good."

"No, I agree – why would he send Henrietta a copy of such a treasure?"

Anne laughed ruefully.

"It is too bad Ben opened the package and not the letter."

"Well, we will have to wait until this evening. She took the children out to have dinner with Roman in the fields."

"Hmm," was Anne's only response.

And so they waited.

*****

"Lady Henrietta,

I pray you are well. Today, I present you with God's holy writ, translated into our English language. I am sure you will agree this solemn undertaking was ordained on high. Hence forward, all in the nation shall read God's word as one body. We shall have one understanding for we shall have one word. I have commanded that this precious work be disseminated across the kingdom, and I send you one as well. Gloria Domino.

Beware, Henrietta, of the danger of inclining toward the darkness. I know personally of your power, as I know personally of your use of it for

England's good. On the day I visited Coudenoure, I saw for myself your daughter's burgeoning abilities, a testament to the power of covens even in this day and age.

Do not forget God's word in your dealings with arts beyond Heaven's boundary. And neither let your daughter forsake the light. For this reason I bless you and your family with this Bible.

Take care, Henrietta, and heed my words."

James Rex

Henrietta looked up. Roman had insisted on having supper before they gathered in the library to hear the king's letter. Slowly and carefully, Henrietta had pried the waxen seal from the parchment and unfolded the page. Moving to the fireplace for light, she had stood and read aloud. Silence filled the room.

"Again, please," asked Anne. Henrietta did as her aunt requested. Again, a stony, cold silence engulfed them.

If any of them had listened carefully, they would have heard a small, grating sound, like stone upon stone, emanating from the hallway side of the room. There, Ben carefully replaced a small chunk of mortar in the stone wall. The niche had provided a listening post since time immemorial – indeed, Ben had stumbled upon it by wondering why the stone floor, in that particular area, had been worn smooth, dipping slightly beneath the plane of the rest of the floor. Having discovered the cause several years earlier, he saw no reason not to follow in the literal footsteps of those who had obviously gone before him. As a result, he knew a number of things which made him the wiser, some frivolous which amused him, and some not. Today's haul of information was of the latter variety.

As Henrietta finished reading her letter the second time, Ben carefully replaced the mortar and along with his two companions crept silently away towards Quinn's workshop. Once inside, Ben set his candle on a nearby table and spoke quietly.

"I believe we should contact Marshall."

"Why?" Thomas newly admitted to the brotherhood, was younger than the others and had no knowledge of life beyond the idyll of Coudenoure. Rouster patted him on the back.

"Thomas, this is not good, and Marshall is stationed at King James' Greenwich Palace. We should find out if he has heard anything about our family. He should hence forward be alert and inform us of any untoward mentions of Coudenoure by the King or his courtiers."

Ben went to a cupboard and produced a small scrap of paper. He scribbled a note. From another table, Rouster produced a block of plain wax and holding the candle near it, dripped it onto the folded letter.

"I will see that this gets to Marshall – when he can get away, we shall meet to discuss it. In the meantime, Thomas, you must not talk of it with anyone, not even Elizabeth."

"Not even *Elizabeth*?" came his plaintive, uncertain question.

"*Especially* not Elizabeth."

They returned to the hall, and went their separate ways.

*****

James was tired. Tired of the struggle. Granted, uniting England and Scotland – a feat no monarch before him had been able to accomplish – was gratifying. It had brought him standing on the Continent, power in both lands, and considerable wealth. But therein lay the problem, for he could sooner pry money from water than from his councilors in Parliament. It was *his* wealth, *his* kingdom and yet time and again they denied him what he wanted, despite his disapproval and what they now knew to be his empty threats; time and again he railed against their obstinacy.

> . . . *"Let not yourselves therefore be transported with the curiosity of a few giddy heads, for it is in you now to make the choice either, by yielding to the providence of God and embracing that which he hath cast in your mouths, to procure the prosperity and increase of greatness to me and mine, you and yours, and by the away-taking of that partition wall which already, by God's providence, in my blood is rent asunder, to establish my throne, and your body politic, in a perpetual and flourishing peace or else, contemning God's benefits freely offered unto us, to spit and blaspheme in his face by preferring war to peace, trouble to quietness, hatred to love, weakness to greatness, and division to union, to sow the seeds of discord to all our posterities, to dishonor your king, to make both me and yourselves a proverb of reproach in the mouths of all strangers, and all enemies of this nation, and enviers of my greatness."*

Even such majestic sentences of such structure as should befuddle their common minds did not sway them – they refused him most of the time, and continued to review his accounts, his spending, his *everything*.

They were insufferable, but he could not ignore them. Year after year, he struggled forward. But this year, 1611, was proving to be a good one. His most favored project, that of translating God's word from Greek and Hebrew into English, was finally done. It had made its way past the hallowed chambers of learning where each word was parsed, discussed and finally settled upon, past the printers and their myriad sub-contracts – necessitated in order to meet his deadlines – and finally, placed into the hands of his subjects. If nothing else were to be known of him in the latter days, let that be proclaimed and shouted from the rooftops.

As a majestic, magnanimous gesture, he had even sent a copy of his new Bible to that witch at Coudenoure. Oooohhh, she had him good. He could not prosecute her for fear of retaliation, but at least he had sent her God's word, and a letter reminding her of his own power, of his own ability to instill fear.

From beside him, a gentle cough reminded him of where he was this bright morning. Cecil stood, regaled as usual in his dark, never-changing, tweedy, medieval gown and sash, his small hat as ever perched upon his brow whilst beside him, young clerks scribbled furiously, taking down each word uttered by the endless stream of petitioners appearing before their king, seeking relief from their conditions.

"What was that?" James asked irritably. "What did you want, old woman?"

Cecil began whispering in his ear, but James had had enough. He waved his hand and rose.

"No more. Get rid of these people. Cecil, manage these petty affairs – 'tis why I put up with you, is it not?"

He strode from the room, all backs bent to his sudden whim.

"I shall ride this afternoon, and I expect ale to be waiting upon my return. See that it is."

Cecil gave a gentle nod and bowed.

"God's knees," he thought to himself, "A king who cannot stop drinking and a Parliament that despises him. How I long for Elizabeth!"

He dismissed all, and returned to his suite with a headache. Where would it all end?

Chapter Twenty-Eight

Summer 1620

Time is linear and forward moving. Troubles, however, are not. Like butterflies on a windy day, they float in and out of view, above and below the straight axis of time. Time is anchored, woven into the fabric of the universe, but troubles float free of that weave. Blown by the fates, chased by the wind, they careen across space and settle in random places, wreak random damage, break random hearts.

*****

Charles was not unlike his father the king in some ways. Since the death of Henry Frederick, his elder brother, had made him England's heir apparent, he had determined that a king's power must and should be absolute, just as his father believed. He had not concerned himself with the matter when it was to be his brother's problem. Now, however, he enjoyed the idea of a world in which his word meant law. He could have what he wanted when he wanted. Ah! What freedom! What power! Of course, there were other less visceral reasons for his late-found belief in autocratic sovereignty. He had watched his father James' struggles with parliament, had been party to his humiliation each time parliament refused their sovereign this whim or that necessity. Was that why his father drank so heavily? Did it account for the cruel streak which seemed evermore apparent in his personality? Charles did not know, but his determination to set things right, unconscious at first, beat a clear and marshal tune in his mind as the day of his own kingship drew ever closer.

He was akin to James physically as well. Like his father, he had inherited deep auburn hair and penetrating, hooded blue eyes. The long leanness of his face mirrored that of his body and it was unlikely someone would not perceive the familial similarities between the two. And, curiously, just as James suffered with a sometimes debilitating weakness in his legs, so too did Charles endure his own Achilles' heel: a stutter which refused to die.

In manner, both were imperious, having come of age in a Scotland that had no tolerance for weak monarchs – if they would rule, then they must needs rule with ruthless strength. But there, it seemed, the likenesses between the two ended.

Charles longed to be a great patron of art. He was not talented himself, but had a keen eye for the work of those who were. He knew his own paintings to be middling despite the praise heaped upon them by his masters and tutors. But his lessons in art did not end with his own efforts. Thomas Murray, his tutor, schooled him well in Greek, in Latin, and in the appreciation of culture generally. Charles was not given to daydreams, but on occasion he gave himself license to plot the timbre of his reign: he would be a king of divine right, obviously, one who ruled firmly but yet was also a gracious patron of the arts. Yes, he would be the intelligent, artistically sensitive king his realm needed. His rule would be grand, he was certain. In history, it would be pointed out as the most enlightened there ever was in the history of England, of Scotland and of Ireland.

Charles differed from his father in other ways as well. In their habits of dress the two men most assuredly did cleave asunder. James preferred loose pantaloons and doublets with a vee-shaped front extending downward. He loved sleeves. The bigger the better in his opinion: billowing, slit, satin, velvet . . . it mattered not as long as they overwhelmed the rest of his dress and were bigger than everyone else's. The same was true of his relationship with collars. He had never moved on from the stiff, starched, oscillating lace ruffles which had defined his youth and had never dressed for state without such a piece. For him, and indeed for his generation, it was the epitome of elegance.

Charles did not share this feeling. His collars, while still made of exquisite lace, lay loosely upon his shoulders. Pantaloons were higher, revealing more leg, while shoulders and sleeves were less flared, more fitted. He wore his hair longer, as dictated by the current style, and his robes and cloaks more fully tailored. He frequently wore a leather girdle about his waist to provide form and shape to his clothing. James accused him of slouching, of forsaking the dress which set him apart from mere mortals. But Charles was accustomed to ignoring his father when he could and *particularly* ignored the old man's fashion advice. Yes, he ignored him, except when it could not be avoided. Today happened to be such a day.

He strode through the halls of Greenwich Palace, oblivious to the courtiers and servants who bowed and scraped as he passed. He was dressed in a fine, pale blue velvet vest and pantaloons cut and pleated with a creamy silk. The lace of his collar lay flat and emphasized the golden chains of necklaces he wore. His outer cloak was grand, a royal blue velvet trimmed in blazing gold. It fluttered out behind him this morning as he hurried on his way to the Stateroom in which King James heard petitions from his citizenry. The summons from his father had been curt, which irritated him, as did having to leave the presence of Alexandra.

Alexandra! Where to begin! Daughter of the newly arrived ambassador from Malta, Alexandra exuded mystery. In a court where pale skin, fair hair and a tiny waist were deemed the hallmarks of feminine beauty, Alexandra's dark, full eyes, olive complexion, ruby red lips and voluptuous body shouted rather than whispered that a new standard had now been set. Men flocked to her warmth and charm, her open sexuality, like children to honey. And indeed, her beauty could be likened to liquid amber, a honeyed gold that poured forth in almost divine brilliance. Despite the innocence of her wide-eyed look, however, she seemed to possess exotic knowledge. Why this was so no one could have said, but it was as certain as a sunrise. As for Alexandra herself, she was rare, and she knew it. She was confident when other women were shy, forward when they blushed, astute beyond her years.

Day to day life at court demanded a suitable, and sizeable, wardrobe, but most women who lived their lives in and out of the royal presence wore their older, perhaps slightly faded gowns and dresses each day. Occasionally, if one looked closely, one could see a slight mend to a worn cuff here, or a stitch to a lace bonnet there. A stain might be cleverly hidden by a patch of identical cloth. One might live at court and travel with the king, but there was still need for economy in gowns and their accompanying sleeves, vests, hats, cloaks under chemises and shoes – these were all expensive and the newer and grander ones not to be worn lightly

when the occasion did not demand. But Alexandra
set this custom, too, directly on its head. Each day,
she emerged from her suite in clothing more suited
for a queen than a mere ambassador's daughter.
Shimmering rose red velvets, deep gold
embroidered vests cut with silver applique, sleeves
slashed with impossibly intricate lace and pearl
insets, skirts so full that other ladies of the court had
to move to allow her passage.

All of these lent her a regal and mysterious
presence which men found intoxicating. The
women of the court . . . less so.

Charles had fallen victim to her overt charms the
very first time he had laid eyes on her. He had been
in attendance upon his father when *her* father, John
Parisot, a descendent of the founder of Valletta and
a member of the ancient order of the Knights
Hospitaller of Malta, was presented at court. Parisot
had brought Alexandra with him and contrary to
the fashion of the day, presented her to the king
even as he presented his own credentials as
ambassador to James' court. Even James, bleary-
eyed with ale and impatient with the length of the
morning's proceedings, had nevertheless been
aware of the woman's outlandish appeal to
members of the opposite sex.

On that particular morning, Charles had not
taken his eyes off Alexandra since she entered the
room. He was smitten and blushed as she bowed
low to the king, revealing an indecent amount of

décolletage, particularly for such a young innocent. His eyes boggled and despite his best efforts he stared – an impertinent, bordering on rude, stare. Unfortunately, his father saw it and worse, understood it.

"Charles!"

Charles was unprepared for speech that morning, especially in front of such an enchanting, otherworldly creature. His stutter rose to the fore.

"Ye . . . ye . . . yes, fffather," he stammered. A deep, crimson blush lit his cheeks. The woman, this delicious Alexandra, had heard him at his worst, had seen him at his least manly as he crouched before his father and tripped upon his own tongue.

James sipped his ale and smiled, pleased with himself. More so than usual, he seemed small and wizened against the throne upon which he sat. Charles felt helpless and enraged. James would never know that the obedient smile his son gave him was actually in response to the image conjured by Charles of his father sliding off the throne and onto the floor like mercury from a phial.

"Stand up straight!" James continued to treat his heir like a trained dog.

Charles shuffled and pretended to suck in his stomach.

"And did you bow? Eh? You are not king yet! Bow!"

Charles bowed.

"Why are you here before me?" James continued on his rant, but that day, something miraculous happened for Charles.

Alexandra had not seemed to notice the raw, humiliating treatment meted out to him by his father. She had ignored it and simply smiled shyly at him. In that instant, boyish, embarrassed infatuation became raw, incandescent passion. His father's control was broken.

Charles' happiness as the weeks sped by was almost unbearable. Initially, he had been amazed at how often their paths seemed to cross. She would encounter him in the hall, be seated behind him at a musical, be found just across from him on the dance floor. On a walk in the garden at Hampton Court, he would find her strolling by herself. As his carriage arrived at Greenwich she might happen to be walking along the drive. He began to take care with his dress and to find reasons for visiting the ladies of the court. And, he decided that there was only one explanation for him and Alexandra being thrown together with such frequency: God intended him to be near her. At that moment, his ensorcellment was complete.

But while James may have lost much of his hold over Charles, he still wore the crown and held the scepter. And seeing his son in such a state, and having given more than a fleeting thought himself to the woman who had put him there, an anger arose in him. He was reminded of his own mortality and resented it mightily.

Today, as Charles entered the hall, angry at having been called away from Alexandra, James demanded to know where he had been.

"Drawing, father, for it is the hour of my lesson." Charles neglected to mention that he was drawing Alexandra as she happily posed for him. James' suspicious mind sensed a deception but could not find a way to root it out. He decided he needed no proof.

"I have work for you, my son."

Charles bowed politely and waited.

"It seems we have many estates, many castles and lands which we seldom visit."

Charles nodded, uncertain of his father's purpose.

"It is true, my king," he stated, "For you manage Great Britain well, and our wealth is great." This was in no way true, of course. The coffers of the kingdom were eternally empty but Charles knew his father would appreciate the flattery.

James sipped his ale.

"I would like you to ride forth and survey them."

"My father, my king, I would be pleased to do so at your bidding. Which ones shall I inspect?"

James giggled.

"All of them."

"Pardon, sire?"

"You heard your king – all of them. I expect you to begin immediately and report back as necessary."

Charles struggled to hide his fury. James knew of his love for Alexandra and this was no doubt a ploy to separate them. A vicious move.

"That is all."

He had no choice but to bow, and accept his father's edict.

*****

"I do not understand," Alexandra had said in her intoxicating, foreign accent. "Why must this be done?"

Charles threw himself into a chair near a window and waved his hand at nothing.

"Because he has so ordered it, my love. It must be done."

It took Alexandra less than a minute to forge a plan. She rose and with girlish impatience ran to his side. Her bending over him was not quite so girlish. Charles smelled her skin, felt her warmth and closed his eyes.

"My Charles, you must of course do as the king demands. But, it is sensible to begin with those closest to us. We are here at Greenwich, so you must begin with your nearby lands and estates. My father wishes me to settle and be tutored – you know I have much trouble reading – and so I will do so here, at Greenwich."

She moved away to the hearth, picked up a bronze poker and stoked the fire before turning back to him with a smile.

"Yes?" she asked, eyes wide.

"Yes," said Charles with a smile. "We shall begin immediately."

Alexandra laughed.

"What is nearby?"

Charles thought for a moment before replying.

"I have heard of a small estate, seldom visited and little known. We shall begin there."

Alexandra clapped her hands.

"I shall ride with you, my lord," she intoned with a sly, provocative bow. "Pray tell, what is the name of the place we are going?"

Charles smiled.

"Coudenoure."

Chapter Twenty-Nine

Henrietta, Anne, and Elizabeth stood in the old chapel ruins. A light snow had fallen the previous evening. As dawn had roused a waking world, a cold snap blew through from the north, bringing with it a heavy morning frost. Between the two, the ancient façade was draped in an elegant cloud of white. The day was cold, but crisp, and the three women stood looking at what used to be the front of the sanctuary.

Despite the differences in age, experiences and clothing, there was no doubt that the same blood ran through all their veins.

Henrietta, as ever, wore a plain, wheat-colored linen dress. Its skirt flared from the deep vee of its waist. A white lace collar hid its simple front. Age had been kind to her, for despite her years her hair was still the color of a ripe peach, blonde mixed with the palest of auburn reds. She wore it bundled in a knitted, blue caul and seldom cut it, for Roman liked it long. She was stouter than before, but then who was not, as Anne was fond of saying.

When Thomas, Elizabeth's twin, had been taken by the plague of 1615, she had thought her heart would break. For weeks there had been no comfort for her. But time had reminded her of what she still had and that there was, if one looked carefully, always happiness to be found. Almost unconsciously she slid her arm around Elizabeth's waist as a silent prayer of Thanksgiving crossed her lips.

In turn, Elizabeth laid her arm gently over her mother's shoulders. She had the slender figure of the women in her line. She was tall, elegant, and accomplished. Despite her best efforts and occasionally those of Henrietta and Anne, however, she seemed always to have a haphazard look about her. Long strands of gently curling blonde hair routinely escaped the confines of her caul and framed her face. She had long since realized that for her work, a simple dress – even as simple as those worn by her mother and her aunt – would not do. She needed long narrow pockets for writing quills and smaller ones for bottles of ink as she worked away in the meadow. A deep wide pocket was necessary for her notebook while the small jars and jugs she usually kept handy needed their own homes as well. She had the milliner for Coudenoure sew her special, smocked aprons which sported pockets almost from top to bottom. These garments were tied in the back, like Rouster's cooking smocks, and provided her with a travelling workroom. For Elizabeth had become what she always had been meant to be: Quinn's successor, a renaissance woman who found adventure in the unknown structure of the flowers of the meadow, who heard the siren's gentle call in the repeating patterns of leaves, of bark, of petals and clouds. She longed for a unifying theory, one which linked everything to some great and boundless tapestry – she knew not if she would find such a universal scheme, but she knew she was made to try. And so she did.

The simplistic drawings of her extreme youth, made with the aid of her childhood companions Ben and Thomas, had become sophisticated mathematical treatises on the world around her. She had been born with a natural ability for drawing, and over time she had honed it for her own purposes. The detail present in her etchings of flowers, in her studies of the feathers of the birds of Coudenoure, were breathtaking in their beauty. She was happiest puttering in the workroom, first Quinn's and now hers, or sitting alone in the meadow, capturing some moment either in formula or in art. She had no need of the world beyond the gates of Coudenoure.

Elizabeth read English, Greek, and Latin. Early on, Ben had come across several manuscripts in the library written in the hand of the Moormen, those mysterious intellectuals from across the Holy Land. Together, they had learned the language and unlocked secrets unknown to the English world.

Together, they had determined to publish works on their findings.

It surprised no one but the two of them when they discovered that childhood pursuits had become adult passions, and that they were part of one another, cleaved to one another, needed one another. Their love was simple and straightforward like the quiet life they built together. Should they be asked about happiness, they would have been puzzled, for they had known nothing else. They were to be married in one week.

Even as she placed her arm over Henrietta's shoulders, she extended her other and wrapped it around Anne's waist.

Anne's road had not been easy – her leg had grown more painful over time. She laughed that it was the bellwether for approaching storms and the onset of winter, for long before the geese flew away to warmer climes, before the trees began their winter slumber, the mended bone would radiate pain. Warm wraps helped, but never cured. But beyond the unhappy years of her youth and the physical pain of her adulthood, she had stumbled across happiness in her dear husband Ian.

Late at night, as they lay together in their room watching the fire die back, they marveled at the circumstances which had brought them together. Such a strange series of events! So much had to happen for them to meet that it could not be mere chance that it had finally occurred. They laughed and fell in love with the notion that their union had actually been decreed at their births, but evil forces had determined against it. And yet, the Fates would not be denied.

Today, as the three women stood in the wintry sun, they studied the chapel thoughtfully.

"Are you positive that people marry in December here?" Elizabeth asked uncertainly. "It seems very odd. Ben is not at all convinced of it."

"Quinn and Bess were artists, Elizabeth, and your gifts come from them and those before them. Do you not want to honor their memory?" A slight chiding was evident in Anne's question.

Elizabeth grinned.

"Guilt, guilt, guilt, Auntie," she laughed. "Ben and I will marry as did Quinn and Bess, right here in the chapel, in the coldest month of the year, December."

Henrietta sighed with happiness.

"The bans have been read – in one week, you will become Elizabeth St. John."

All three smiled.

Across the estate, Roman walked home across the back field and gave a calculating glance at the angle of the sun. With the help of two stable boys, he had driven a portion of the flock out to pasture. Judging by the light, they would only be out a short time, but he had noticed that even on wintry days, should the sheep be given only a bit of exercise, they were physically healthier.

As Henrietta, Elizabeth and Anne all reflected their bloodline, so Roman did his. Occasionally, a sudden turn or a particular laugh, a hand gesture or a glance would cause his wife to catch her breath, for Roman had become so like his father. He had filled out to adulthood, and his hair was streaked with gray. He had become quieter over the years, particularly since the death of Thomas. It had caught him off guard, that, and he seemed never able to understand it. Even now, long after the sadness and the grief, he occasionally found himself thinking of his son.

"Thomas would have found that amusing," he would think, or perhaps, "What is that smell? Raspberry tart? That was my boy's favorite – do you remember when he and Ben stole the whole pie?" Sometimes even now when he rounded a corner, or heard a child laughing he would look up in momentary expectation of Thomas. Thomas. He was always sure to place flowers on his grave in the old cemetery, for he like his sister had always loved them dearly.

In the library, Ben finished a letter to Marshall telling him of his approaching nuptials and asking him to come. He looked out the window, remembering where he had begun his life, grateful for his place now. The three women were returning from the chapel and from the triumphant look on Henrietta and Anne's face he knew he would be marrying in the old chapel. In the cold. In December. He could not even manage a disgruntled sigh, however – he was too content.

The kitchen fires roared as Rouster, now the chef for Coudenoure, railed against his scullery maids and lads. His wife, Marian, rocked their young son nearby and watched the circus in amusement. The backdoor flew open and Ian huffed in pulling it sharply behind him. He made for the hearth and its warmth, slowing only to pick up a hot buttered biscuit from a nearby table.

"Ah! The bookman visits! How does your press advance, eh?" Rouster asked as he whacked a slacker of a potato peeler on his buttocks – that boy was slower than treacle.

"'Tis good," declared Ian. He, too, was now fuller of frame. Tiny spectacles, ground for him according to Elizabeth's specifications in her workshop, perched on the end of his aquiline nose. Rosy cheeks were now ruddy, and only a few strands of white hair clung valiantly round his pate – the rest had long ago given up the fight. But while his physical appearance had changed, he himself had not – he was still jolly, intellectual, and driven to work. In that vein, he had determined Coudenoure should have a printing press.

Once he had made the suggestion, all had seen the wisdom of it. The library, although not known, was one of the largest in the kingdom. It seemed fitting that they might add to their holdings with their own work. Why, Ben was currently working on codifying Elizabeth's writings, Ian was in the middle of a history of the borderlands in which Castle Donoway figured heavily, and Anne was composing a book of sonnets.

The old thatched cottage on the far eastern side of the estate, in the shadow of the Great Ridge, would make an ideal location for the actual press and those employed to run it. There was an excitement about the venture, and as they sat together in the library night after night, the plan began to take shape. Even Roman was pulled from his solitude by the excitement.

"Why not a history of sheep farming in England?"

"Because no one would read it?" Elizabeth hugged him and laughed. "Papa, you are so wonderful and, and, single-minded."

Roman laughed at his daughter's attempts at subtlety and those present were glad to hear it – it was not often that he pulled himself out of the past now.

On this particular morning, as Ian polished off the first biscuit, reached for a second and wandered into the library to greet the women, as Roman came home and as Ben was carefully sealing his letter, a carriage turned through the gates at the far end of the drive. Initially, it went unnoticed but the steady clap, clap, clap of hooves on gravel finally caught everyone's ear.

"A visitor!" exclaimed Ian, "My dear wife, we have not had a guest in some time! Let us play our game!"

Anne moved to the window and studied the carriage as it moved at a stately pace towards the manor house.

"Ah, well, it is royal, but it is not the king's – notice the lack of guards."

"Yes," Ian agreed, "And that suspicious old Scotsman never goes far without a phalanx of them on every side."

Ben looked out the window.

"Well, it may not be the king but it is grand and . . . it is here."

With no further ado, they moved en masse and opened up the mighty wych elm doors of Coudenoure. A freezing wind blew in past them, seeming to reach unto the rafters, and Ian shuddered, whether from the sudden cold or prescience – he was not certain. Roman stepped forward.

A groomsman jumped down from his perch and opened the gilded door. Charles stepped out, blinking in the bright sun.

"I am Charles," he squinted and spoke to no one in particular. Roman stared a second too long.

"*Charles*," the heir to the kingdom repeated. "*CHARLES.*"

Ian was the first to tumble to the identity of their speaker. He rushed forward in a bow.

"Your highness, forgive us, for we have so few visitors and we are enthralled at the richness and splendor of your presence."

"Did he say enthralled or appalled," Elizabeth whispered to Ben, ". . . because I know I have never seen such a peacock in my life . . ."

It was true what they said. Charles and Alexandra had decided to dress in similar colors for the beginning of their grand tour of royal estates. Alexandra had never worn fewer than three colors at once, and this morning, in accordance with their scheme, neither did Charles. His pantaloons and vest were a spring green velvet; his sleeves the blue of cornflowers and his stockings matched. His cape and collar were of a color never seen in nature and a handful of feathers waved gaily from his small cap. In his hand was a gold-tipped walking cane.

Ben stepped on Elizabeth's toe so that she might bite her tongue. Both bowed deep and long, and rose to a strange sight.

Part of a woman's gown – what looked like the side of a very wide skirt – had been wedged and thrust through the golden door of the carriage. As all watched, it continued to emerge from the chrysalis of the carriage in short static bursts. Inch by inch the apparition grew and it became impossible to ignore the determined grunts from within the carriage which accompanied each growth spurt.

Charles, meanwhile, continued facing the doors of Coudenoure, examining his sleeve as though something new and exciting were occurring there. With a final shove, the butterfly freed herself from her golden cocoon.

Alexandra. All watched as she fumed, straightened her multi-colored gown and finally walked to Charles' side. Silence.

"Welcome, Majesty," Roman intoned, "Welcome to Coudenoure."

Silence. Alexandra looked about.

"Well, it is a very nice, but small, estate," Charles ventured. "Tell me – that ridge yonder – what is on the other side?"

"Ah," Roman smiled, "There begins the grounds of Greenwich Palace. I see you took the road to our humble abode, but there is a much quicker, unknown route through the woods. Indeed . . ."

Alexandra looked at him sharply.

"Another route you say?"

"Yes, madam. One has only to cross the Main Road to London, navigate the small wood beyond and one arrives at Coudenoure."

Alexandra seemed to perform some major mental calculation, looking first at the ridge, then at the estate; ridge . . . estate. Charles continued to look about, disinterest evident in every feature upon his face. After a moment, he spoke.

"Well, we have seen Coudenoure, and we bid you good day."

"NO!" exclaimed Alexandra suddenly. "Majesty," she said with a supercilious, sly bow, "We should inspect the interior before we go."

Charles' emotions once again played across his face but if Alexandra wanted to view this backwater tidal pool of algal nothingness, well then. He nodded to Roman and without waiting proceeded indoors with Alexandra on his arm.

He left behind a Gordian knot of perplexity.

"God's liver I do not like this." Ian murmured to Anne.

"Nor I," she responded. "Who is that dreadful woman?"

"The tart? I have no idea."

Henrietta whispered much the same to Ben.

"Yes, it is not good whatever it is. Come, let us see if we can discern their purpose, for surely it is nefarious."

They walked in together.

*****

The contrast could not have been greater, nor stranger. Henrietta, Anne, and Elizabeth were plebeian in their dress and shawls: simple colors, worn fabrics, and utterly lacking in the stays and girdles which defined feminine beauty at court, and for Alexandra. Similarly, one would not have guessed Roman's rank in society, nor Ian's and

Ben's from looking at them in their daily suits –
casual, plain, mended.

There had been no time to ready the formal room
across the great hall from the library – no one had
anticipated visitors of any caliber, much less royalty.
How could they? As a result, the room was closed
and could not be readied on such short notice:
furniture and candelabras were masked within their
linen shrouds; the great hearth was cold and
shuttered against the downdraft from the flue just as
the room itself was shuttered against the cold which
crept in round about its windows.

There was no choice but to entertain Charles and
his guest in the library, the everyday room for the
family. But Charles had entered the manor house
before anyone else, and so even that room could not
be made straight before his entry. Roman's chair,
worn and thrown with blankets, sat near the fire
across from an identical one used always by
Henrietta. Anne normally sat slightly farther away,
her leg propped on an ottoman and wrapped in
warm covers. The table near the window was
always claimed by Ben, Ian and Elizabeth. It was a
happy arrangement, but one which did not lend
itself to company for the simple reason that there
were not enough chairs. Ben quickly drug two from
Elizabeth's workshop and placed them for Charles
and Alexandra near the fire.

Rouster had been alerted and almost immediately trays of cakes, fruit, tea, ale, breads and cheese began to flow forth from the kitchen.

All settled. Charles took a mug of tea but said nothing. His companion did the same. Five long minutes passed in this manner. Finally he spoke.

"'Tis a lovely small estate you have." He spoke to no one in particular.

Roman smiled and nodded but before he could speak Alexandra rose and warmed herself by the fire.

"Tell me," she began, ". . . what are all these books for? I have never liked them."

The hair rose on the back of Anne's neck and before she could answer Ben gave an indignant reply.

"They are for reading, Madam, for those who are *able*."

Alexandra could have ignored the intended slight but did not. She moved close to Ben as she spoke.

"If this were my manor, I should burn them in that antiquated fireplace there. Why, it is too large and medieval for my tastes but before I tore it down I should rid the kingdom of . . ." here she waved her hand at the magnificent shelves which lined the far wall, ". . . of this nonsense." She smiled sweetly at Ben.

But the conversation was not going as she had planned. Normally, men melted in her presence and if she chose to say silly things they only seemed to appreciate her more. But not Ben. He looked at her with thinly veiled disgust, rose, and walked across the room to the books. Roman looked at her in horror while Ian did the same. Only Anne seemed willing to try and salvage the situation. She gave an artificial giggle.

"Oh, Madame, how we enjoy good humor such as you offer! We are indeed honored by your visit, but I must confess, puzzled as well. Why has Coudenoure been singled out?"

Alexandra ignored her, as she was prone to do with other women. Charles finished his tea and responded.

"My father wishes to take stock of all of our royal estates. I have decided to participate, along with Alexandra –"

"So it has a name," whispered Elizabeth to Ian.

". . . and Coudenoure is our first visit."

"But Sire, Coudenoure is not a royal estate," Roman smiled as he spoke, but those who knew him sensed an alertness lurking behind his steely blue eyes. "Indeed, you have caught us so unawares that it would be easy to mistake our place in society."

Roman rose, smiled again and leaned casually against a nearby table. He was dressed in his field clothes as he referred to them – torn and mended stockings, and pants like those worn by laborers on the estate. He had shed his cloak and his shirt, missing several buttons, clearly showed the graying hair of his chest. Indeed, it would be easy to mistake him for a common worker.

"You see, Sire, I am Baron de Grey. These are my family. We are most pleased that you have graced us with your presence, but Coudenoure is an estate which has always been in the de Grey line."

Charles looked at him quizzically.

"Why are none of you at court?"

Roman continued with his fixed smile.

"Sire, we are a simple noble family. We believe we serve best by supporting our good King James through hard work and loyalty."

"In fact," Henrietta interjected, "The King was kind enough to stop here some years ago."

"Why?" Alexander asked. "If it is not a royal estate, why would the king bother with such a, a . . . place."

She was moving about the room now, touching this object, examining that candelabra.

"Why?" she repeated gaily. "Perhaps it was because of your belongings? You seem to have many lovely things. Why, I myself have never seen such a magnificent tapestry as the one yonder." She pointed towards the back wall. "'Tis Flemish?"

No reply was forthcoming.

"Well," Charles finally said, "I do not understand why Coudenoure would be listed as a royal estate if it is not. We must correct this – I will see to it myself."

Alexandra spoke one last time.

"But should it be that the roll is correct, and Coudenoure is of the crown's belongings, I believe I could not be happier with any other home."

They left as they came, and as the carriage moved away, it left nothing but worried anxiety in its wake. Before the others moved or spoke, Ben excused himself and went quickly into the kitchen.

"Oye," said Rouster, "The king's own son! We are rising in the world, my brother!"

Ben shook his head and tugged Rouster aside.

"We are in trouble, I believe."

Rouster looked at him with concern – it had been many years since Ben had spoken with such urgency and he was transported back to the dark days of his childhood on the streets of London.

"What do you mean, Ben? Speak."

"I will, but Rouster, we must get word to Marshall to come quickly, for there is a storm approaching. 'Tis coming on fast. Be quick, and get him here."

Rouster needed no further direction. Within the hour, the word had gone out to Marshall.

*****

"Charles," she said slowly, leaning towards him with an engaging smile. The carriage rocked and jolted along the rutted road. She could have kept the smile for another day, for it was not that which riveted his attention.

"My Charles, did you not sense the warmth of the place, this Coudenoure? I found it to be enchanting."

"Indeed!" came his reply as he looked lovingly at her.

Alexandra let a moment skip by.

"And the proximity to Greenwich – 'tis amazing, is it not?"

"I suppose so," Charles agreed, not having given it any thought.

Another moment.

"And a back way of which no one knows! How positively fascinating!"

"Is it?"

Alexandra's smiled tightened slightly but she maintained it and doggedly continued.

"Ah!" Now a sadness filled her lyrical voice.

Silence. She cut her eyes to Charles. His focus was where it had been the entire ride, indeed their entire relationship.

"Think, my Charles, of how many happy times we could have together if it were not for your father!"

Charles leaned back and looked out the carriage window at the passing fields. They had just turned onto the London road and would be back at Greenwich soon.

"He is king, my love – I do his bidding."

"Of course, but if you were not always in his presence . . ."

"I am where he wishes me to be. It is his ordained right to direct me as it will be mine one day to direct others."

She finally gave up and took a direct approach.

"But Charles, if I were safely at Coudenoure, think of the things we could do! Why, you could slip away from court – go hunting perhaps in the very woods you would cross to reach me."

For the first time, Charles saw her purpose.

"If *you* were at Coudenoure, not me . . ."

"Yes, my Sire?" she breathed almost in his ear.

"I could visit you there as often as I pleased. It is a little known estate – he would never know that I was not simply hunting or riding or even in London!"

"You could teach me art, reading, all of the skills I lack, but so desire in order to please you . . ."

He stared at her bright, full lips as she cast her eyes down.

"And Charles, the things we might learn together . . . you and I, uninterrupted, alone . . ."

Finally, he saw the whole picture she had been trying so desperately to paint.

"And your father the ambassador would approve! Why, I have heard him say many times that a young girl such as yourself needs a stable home in order to learn and grow! And Coudenoure could be such a place! Such a convenient, nearby place!"

He stared out the window, excitement evident on his face.

"But Coudenoure is not mine to command – you heard that yokel – he is actually a baron and the estate is his. That it is on our roll of royal property is a mistake."

She placed her hand on his as they turned onto Greenwich Palace drive.

"I am certain you will find a way."

As they exited the carriage – Charles, Alexandra, her skirt – he gallantly kissed her hand.

"If you want Coudenoure, you shall have it!" He exclaimed, invigorated by the promise in her dark, mysterious eyes.

They did not notice the startled look on the groomsman's face. He took the harness of the lead horse and moved slowly away towards the stables, considering what he had just heard, rolling it over in his mind. As he passed near an outlying hedge, a young girl appeared.

"Master Marshall!"

"Eleanor? What are you doing so far from Coudenoure?" Marshall chided the wide-eyed child. "Does your mother know where you are?"

"She said I am to give you this, and be quick about it. One of the stable boys is waiting yonder with the horse."

She stood still, staring at him.

"I am to wait for a reply," she explained solemnly.

Marshall opened the letter she gave him. So quickly had it been dispatched that it was not even sealed, but only roughly folded. He read the contents with growing consternation. Finally, he folded it and tucked it securely within his livery.

"Go home," he commanded Eleanor. "And tell Ben and Rouster I shall be there this evening."

He continued on his way as the girl disappeared from whence she came. A sudden sound of hooves on gravel told Marshall that she was on her way back to Coudenoure.

Chapter Thirty

George Villiers, Duke of Buckingham, was James'
current favorite. With his boyishly handsome face,
long legs and commanding voice, he had risen
rapidly in both rank and resentment at the Stuart
Court. While those who disliked him, and there
were many, whispered that his relationship with the
king was the reason for his meteoric ascent, others
grudgingly admitted that beyond all of the
innuendo he was an able administrator. The death
of Robert Cecil years earlier had left James bereft of
level-headed governors, men who could and did
keep Parliament in its place. And as the years of
James reign in England had unfurled, the task of
navigating the royal ship of state between king and
Parliament had moved from difficult to well-nigh
impossible. Buckingham was one of the few who
could still command, direct, wheedle and persuade
both sides.

Even in moments of solitude and self-reflection,
James never considered his own role in the
stalemate which was becoming English national

governance. Indeed, whenever the notion of compromise on his part was hinted at in veiled and nuanced language, he lashed out at its purveyor. He was king, and kingship was absolute.

But while he never looked askance at his own attitudes, moments of solitude almost always ended with thoughts of the grand kings who had come before him. Neither Henry nor his father would have dreamed of allowing such power to be wielded by anyone other than themselves. How had such come to pass, then, during his own reign? The lynchpin, he decided, was Elizabeth. She had been a strong sovereign, but she was a woman, like his own mother who had attempted to rule Scotland with such disastrous results for herself and her kingdom. Women were weak vessels, and it must surely have been during her time that Parliament had become the Medusa it now was – threatening him at every turn. His thoughts turned more and more to his early years in his home country. There, he had ruled absolutely. There, he had exercised his intellectual prowess and produced scholarly works of great importance. Why, he had even written the defining tome concerning witches.

Everything seemed always to come back to women and their preternatural powers in this world. He thought of the witch who had saved him from Guy Fawkes – what had become of her and her daughter? He tried but could not remember the name of her estate.

All of that seemed old and gone now. His favorite ally in the fight against the unjustness of his current situation and memories of past accomplishments that were beyond his reach was ale. At first, his consumption had not amounted to much. But as time passed, and frustrations mounted, he found himself frequently alone with a flask and a cup.

This late afternoon was one such instance. He had learned from Buckingham that Parliament was once again refusing to provide him with what he considered adequate funding. How did they expect him to maintain a royal 'presence' without the requisite clothing, staff, food, estates? They seemed not to care about the very matters which he believed to be at the core of his authority. He was glad when the knock on his chamber door revealed Charles. His son bowed and advanced – what was the man wearing, James wondered – peacocks everywhere were surely put to shame. He motioned to Charles to join him near the window which overlooked the great lawn of Greenwich.

"Father, I began my survey of your estates today." Charles proffered. He took the cup offered by his father and sat across from him at the small table. James filled his own cup and then his son's.

"Where are your servants? Your courtiers?" Charles was puzzled at the solitude in which he found his father, not understanding that it was more and more a norm for the old man.

"I sent them away." A long pull on his cup. "So tell me, what estate did you visit today?"

"That is why I am here."

James looked idly out the window.

"Indeed," came his laconic reply.

"Yes, it was a strange place. One whose name I have never heard."

"Get to the point, boy. Where did you go today?" James refilled his own glass, ignoring the empty one beside Charles. Charles sighed and spoke.

"A place called Coudenoure."

A small laugh escaped James as he spoke softly to himself, "Coudenoure. But of course – she sends me the name lest I forget her."

*****

"Alexandra! You are back! How was the ride out with Charles? Eh? Anything to report?"

John Parisot was pacing anxiously in their suite at Greenwich. He had travelled from London in order to obtain a private audience with the king. Here, away from the usual ministers, beggars, courtiers and lackeys, those who seemed to follow the monarch everywhere once he emerged from his rooms, he had a much better chance of making contact.

Malta was small, even inconsequential in the greater scheme of Continental power plays. When the matter of the ambassadorship had been suggested to him, he had initially scoffed – a useless appointment to a cold and northern land. Who would want such a thing? But Alexandra had immediately seen the advantages.

England was suffering an economic downturn. She had no markets for her wares and precious little trade with the outside world. If Parisot could somehow finagle a trade deal with the King – a licensure perhaps, or a writ of passage for quicker sailing – it *might* benefit Malta, but it would *definitely* benefit Parisot: his fortunes had been sagging of late in the small island kingdom, as had hers. The ambassadorship was thus cast in a different hue, and in due time Alexandra and he had arrived in England.

He continued pacing now as Alexandra warmed herself by the fire and sent for ale, bread and fruit.

"I ask again, Alexandra – how was your ride with Charles?"

She only looked at him and smiled. Some minutes later, the servant quietly deposited a tray on the table by the hearth and left. Only then did Alexandra turn to John.

"Well, Papa, do I not deserve a kiss?" she asked seductively. "Of course, that is not the only price I will extract for the information I bring."

"And if someone saw us?" he inquired sarcastically, raising a single brow in askance.

Alexandra laughed and turned her back to him.

"I must get out of this gown." she exclaimed, "It binds too tightly. Help me, *Papa*."

Despite the risk, or perhaps because of it, he moved to her and slid his arms around her waist, kissing her neck, her shoulders.

"What news have you, *daughter*?" he laughed and murmured in her ear.

"I believe I have found the perfect hideaway for us, my sweet."

He began unbuttoning the back of her gown as she continued.

"'Tis an estate no time from here or from London. It sits on the River Thames, and can be reached several different ways. It is small, but well-appointed. And it belongs to the crown, possibly."

"And how will you secure it? And what of Charles?"

"Charles is clay in my hands, darling, and I have already promised him much in return for giving the place to me."

"You wicked girl!" He spun her around to face him.

"No more of this *Papa* and *daughter* deception," she whispered as she stroked his cheek, "I will have the house in my name – a woman of property – and when you visit, no one will know."

She kissed him lightly and backed away towards the bed, grinning as she did so.

"Although . . . you will have to share me on occasion with Charles."

He seemed not to mind.

*****

The fire burned brightly that night on the ridge. As a reminder of how far they had come, Ben, Rouster and Marshall decided to go there once again; once again, Ben kindled the fire; once again Rouster unpacked victuals from his kitchen; once again Marshall waited and kept lookout. When all were settled, Marshall began.

"I bring news."

"No, no, no," exclaimed Rouster, "I do not like thinking on an empty stomach. We eat first – see, I have brought a fine piece of lamb for our dining delight this evening. And the bread is fresh. First, we eat."

He would brook no resistance and they ate in silence, taking each other's measure. There was Ben, a man now bookish, erudite and sure of himself. Rouster, rotund and happy, had developed skills beyond those of most estate chefs, for he never forgot his beginnings, and always, regardless of his good fortunes, planned against catastrophe. And there was Marshall.

Marshall was brilliant, and practical. Well over six feet, his features were those of a nobleman – perhaps his father, or his mother, had been of royal blood. His face, though sunburned and weathered from his work in the stables and training yards of the king, was also sensitive and kind. His eyes were deep and soulful, of the purest emerald green. Time and again in his work, his leadership had been noted, and he had advanced accordingly. But while his life was secure and seemingly on track to greatness within the king's service, something was missing.

Marshall was not unhappy, but neither was he happy. He looked at his friends and knew, as they did, that the two of them had found their niche. He wondered if they realized he had not. He loved them as brothers, and was glad of them and for them.

As they finished the feast, Ben spoke first, telling Rouster and Marshall of the strange visit by the king's son and the woman called Alexandra. In turn, Marshall filled them in on the conversation he had overheard at Greenwich by the same two. They sat in studied silence.

"Well, there is no doubt what it means," Rouster said slowly. "Catastrophe is upon us." His hands were shaking. Marshall pretended not to notice and patted him on the back.

"No, no, Rouster," he laughed heartily, "There will be no catastrophe that puts us back to where we began. But," here he hesitated, "There are coming events, apparently, for which we must prepare."

Rouster smiled at him, trusting him as always.

"Of course! We can prepare!" he found solace, as always, in Marshall's confidence and practical plans.

"Ben?" Marshall asked. "What say ye?"

Ben poked the fire with a stick before speaking.

"I am in agreement. We have not heard the last of this affair and we must prepare. I believe we must tell our family of our discovery."

Rouster was rising from the ground but Marshall pulled him back.

"We will tell them now, but I tell *you* this, my brothers: we will defend these people – they are our tribe, and as I recall, none of them are well-versed in tactics, strategy, or fighting. As before, so now – they have need of us."

Solemnly, they placed their hands one upon the other, swearing an oath together; together, they put out the fire, pulled their cloaks and hats about themselves, and started back down the ridge toward the manor house below.

The bolt had already been slid across the doors of Coudenoure, forcing Ben to clang the ancient bell. Beyond, he heard Roman shouting. As the door opened he saw Ben, Rouster and Marshall. He said nothing. His eyes, however, showed an understanding of the situation, and as he pulled the door behind them, they retired as one body to the library. Anne, Henrietta and Ian and Elizabeth were there, playing cards and laughing by the window. They looked up at the solemn faces, put their cards down quietly, and gathered near the fire. Marshall told his tale, and a great silence enveloped the room. Elizabeth finally spoke.

"They cannot take another man's estate!" she exclaimed. "So why are we worried?" Her brow furrowed as she looked about at her elders.

"'Tis our estate," Henrietta explained, ". . . but since the time of our great King Henry, Coudenoure has not only paid no taxes, but also receives an annual supplement from the crown."

Elizabeth was bright – there was some underlying message, a cipher within her mother's words – that she was not understanding.

"What does that mean?" she asked slowly. "And why would King Henry require no taxes from us on our lands and revenues?"

She caught the look which passed between Anne and Henrietta. Again, silence.

"Why would King Henry require no taxes from us?" she repeated her question more for herself than for the others. The silence grew heavier.

Henrietta changed the subject abruptly.

"It seems Coudenoure shall be very busy in the coming days. The wedding, *that woman* –"

Elizabeth looked at her mother.

"My wedding is in two days, Mamma," she reminded her. "Ben, should we postpone? We know not what is coming."

Ben shook his head as did Roman.

"No, no, my daughter and my future son shall be married as planned." He stood. "Whatever schemes are being put forward at Greenwich and in London, I have faith in good King James. He will not take the property of a nobleman who has done him no wrong, one who indeed saved his life not so long ago."

"But Papa . . ." began Elizabeth.

"No."

She knew her father's tone well.

"Everyone to bed. Tomorrow we shall think more clearly."

*****

Henrietta waited for him beneath the covers of their bed. When he finished pacing, he slipped in beside her and warmed himself against her. They hugged tightly before laying on their backs, their usual attitudes for a chat before sleeping.

"Roman, none of this news bodes well for Coudenoure."

"I agree, my love. In fact, I believe it to be quite dangerous."

"What shall we do?"

He heard the fear in her voice and turned to her.

"Did we, or did we not, Henrietta, survive the Tower? Eh?"

She gave him a faint smile and he continued.

"And did we, or did we not, survive an assassination attempt against King James on our way from Castle Donoway."

She sat up and patted his chest.

"Roman, you are right – together you and I are a mighty force. We will see to our daughter's happiness and we shall protect her heritage."

Now it was his turn to sit up – Henrietta noticed a light in his eyes.

At once, they settled back under the covers and began planning for the next two days.

*****

In the bed chamber across the hall, Ian and Anne lay in the night, whispering together.

"There is a darkness coming, Anne, and I fear it."

She wrapped herself around him.

"Do not, my love, for I am with you."

He closed his eyes, wishing not to remember what he knew of King James and his obsession with witches. Scotland was a long time ago – perhaps the man had left it all behind.

He fell into a restless sleep.

Chapter Thirty-One

The next morning, Charles had demanded much of the King's favorite minister. It had begun with a simple command.

"Buckingham, walk with me."

George Villiers had never known Charles to give orders, making his command highly unusual. What could he possibly want? He dressed quickly in plain garb, threw a cloak over his shoulders, silently cursed the man for interrupting his breakfast and followed him out beyond the Palace proper. There, Charles chose a sheltered, formal garden, one seldom used by courtiers or royals, and only after one entire walk round its outer perimeter did the prince finally speak.

"I wish you to tell me about the estate known as Coudenoure."

"Ah," thought Buckingham, ". . . now I see."

From a window, he had watched Charles' return from Coudenoure the previous day. He had seen Alexandra, the daughter of the Maltese ambassador, exit the carriage with him. Curious, he had followed up and learned of their visit to the nearby estate. He had not seen the angle then, could not figure the dividend which would accrue to her by accompanying the prince on such an out of the way trip. What did the woman hope to gain, for if the rumors were true, she did not waste her time – there must be a prize at the end of the day for her to participate in anything. And so, what was it this time? He had sighed – there were many, many rumors surrounding that woman and he was privy to most of them.

She seemed a bit too old, they said, too old, that is, to be the daughter of the ambassador. He could be no more than forty and while she was certainly young, she did not have the innocent bloom of a young maid. It was tittered about that the only bloom she had, in fact, came from a jar she kept locked in her dressing table. Buckingham had only smiled upon hearing the sly talk, for he, too, had noted the touch of rouge upon her cheeks, the charcoal outlines around her deep eyes. But he nevertheless thought it possible that she was as young as she claimed – it was her attitudes, her mysterious well of knowledge about men and their likes and dislikes which made her seem older. So he had thought.

But then the rumors had changed. Like shadows overtaking the day, they began to come forward from here, from there, creating a form far from the picture provided by the ambassador and his daughter themselves. They had begun in Woolwich, when a package – a large one – had been offloaded from a Spanish barque. It was marked for Alexandra Parisot, daughter of the Maltese ambassador. When the king's men arrived with horses and wagon to transport it to London (at the command of Charles), the Captain had laughed uproariously at the situation: a package for the ambassador's *daughter*, he had exclaimed, laughing. The ambassador *had* no daughter. When told he was mistaken and that the daughter's name was Alexandra, he had laughed even harder, but retreated to his ship when questioned; he sailed shortly afterwards.

Thus began the rumors. They might have died out but for the smallest incidents which seemed to keep occurring. John Parisot, it seems, found danger to be an aphrodisiac. Some said they had seen them in the dark corners of this palace or that; some vowed that after the long walks they took together – far outside any palace grounds – grass stains and straw could be found upon her gowns and his pantaloons. Their defenders said that they were from the hot lands, where the culture was different – perhaps fathers and daughters there always strolled hand in hand, always chased one another through the hedges, always smiled so knowingly at one another. Perhaps.

This morning, Buckingham felt he had the final pieces of the puzzle. So the woman wanted an estate – that was what this was about. If she had a place removed from the court and its incessant gossip, she and her *Papa* would have no problems with rumors. They would be one step removed from it all. Additionally, Buckingham had begun to sense an urgency in the financial schemes put forward by the ambassador. Out of that lust and need was born the idea of Coudenoure – it could only be. Well, perhaps not Coudenoure, he reasoned. Any estate would do, but Coudenoure, with its low profile and proximity to London, to Greenwich, to Hampton Court – Alexandra must have felt she had found the perfect place for her liaisons. And if she could convince the prince to give it to her outright, how much the better for her.

He did not know much about the estate, truth be told, and even less about its reclusive owners. Even as he gave Charles the briefest of histories concerning it, he continued turning over in his mind the advantages and disadvantages of Alexandra being moved to the place. For him, it was not that the woman would suddenly find herself propertied and titled. No. It was that he, Buckingham, would find her gone from court. And if she were not present, Charles could not continue his hopelessly unfortunate wooing of her.

"No one seems to know why Coudenoure was exempt from taxes, and, if the tales are right, receives a royal annuity for its upkeep."

Charles walked in silence, head down, digesting Buckingham's words.

"It seems to stem from the original owner's – Thomas de Grey's – relationship with our good King Henry VII. Without his valor at Bosworth Field, the Tudor line would never have existed. He saved his life, you see."

"Hmm. And the scions of his line chose to honor the Tudor commitment."

"Likely, sire." Buckingham decided not to muddy the water with the legends of great King Henry VIII's mistress, the love of his life, having lived and loved him at Coudenoure. No, it was not necessary. Charles continued speaking.

"I believe I understand. Even though it is the family seat of the de Grey clan, and belongs to them, it has been exempt all these years."

Buckingham wanted to scream that yes, that was what he had just said, but he held his tongue, allowing Charles to ponder further.

"And so there is no way we can force the current baron from his land. Do you agree?"

How much to share with the young prince? His companion remained silent, contemplating the pros and cons of full disclosure. He decided against it.

"Sire, I believe you seek a way to wrest Coudenoure from its current owner, is that correct?"

Charles stopped mid-stride and stared at him.

"You, sir, are a magician! How you fathomed the secret desire of my heart is quite beyond me!"

Buckingham smiled and walked on. Charles hurried to catch up.

"I believe, further, that you may have an interest in gifting it to a certain young woman."

Again, Charles stopped. He let out a long whistle and lowered his voice.

"Do not toy with me, friend, for this is exactly what I want, what I am desperate to have. I need this to happen."

Buckingham smiled at him.

"And the man who should give you such a prize? Eh? What would be his reward, sire?"

Ah, familiar territory at last, thought Charles. They all want something. All of them.

"Sir, should you make this happen, and quickly, you shall rise within my father's kingdom through your merit, but you shall rise through mine because of this."

Buckingham smiled, bowed, and walked away. If not for fear of being seen from the windows of the palace, Charles would have danced a jig there and then.

Chapter Thirty-Two

For the first time in her life, Elizabeth was giddy. She had been unable to sleep, dreaming of the morrow, the day she and Ben would finally be married. She grinned in the dark and almost laughed aloud.

She had never considered how long she had loved him, or when she realized the depths of her feelings for him, or the moment she recognized him as her partner for life. The reason for such absence of introspection was not a lack of interest, but the knowledge that she had always loved him and always would. They were bound by history, by interests, by passion and most importantly by love. It had always been there, always playing itself out even as children. They looked after one another.

When Thomas had left them, she had been unable to cope, nor had Ben. Months passed before they could even speak of their loss, months more before they could acknowledge that their sadness would never pass. Time dulled its edge, but the scars remained. In difficult times, Elizabeth could be found in the old family cemetery seated next to her brother's grave. She realized now that the sun was coming up, and on impulse rose quickly and slipped down the main staircase and out the front door. She ran lightly past the orchard, farther on from the chapel ruins until finally she reached the low stone wall and gate which marked hallowed ground, both for her family and for the monks who had come before them. As she had left the manor house, she had plucked a single red rose from a large arrangement in the library – she grew them in one of the glass houses in honor of Thomas and they would represent his presence at her wedding.

Reaching the small marker beneath which he lay, she knelt and carefully placed the rose on the frozen ground above him.

"My brother, I am to be marri . . ." she choked, and fell silent for a long moment, thinking of the carefree child he had been, and of their times together.

"Oh Thomas, how I miss you! I hope you are happy, somewhere my brother!"

She kissed the ground before her.

"I shall marry Ben today. I have come for your blessing."

Only the stillness of the morning answered her. She knew there would be no omen, no sign that he heard her: no bird flew overhead, the wind did not whistle suddenly, nor did the sun appear from behind a cloud. How she longed for just one sign – anything! – one that would tell her he had heard her. That somewhere he existed yet.

The morning was upon them, and she rose, smiling down.

"I shall fill you in on everything, Thomas. You will always be part of everything I do, everything Ben and I might accomplish together."

She walked away.

Passing the old chapel, she saw and heard the activities of the servants and craftsmen of Coudenoure as they decorated the empty arches of the chapel with the season's greenery, flowers from the glass houses, and candles. Henrietta had been right to order them, for a winter gloom cloaked the land. A great bonfire was being readied behind the altar, providing warmth for all who attended. It would not be long now before she took her vows.

In the distance, she saw Henrietta hurrying towards her.

"Child, what is wrong with you! 'Tis your wedding day and you are wandering about in the cold! God's knees, wrap this blanket round your shoulders and come back in."

"I had to see Thomas, Mamma. I needed his blessing."

"I know, Elizabeth. I know."

*****

The wedding was a great holiday for the entire estate. Ben and Elizabeth were favorites, known for their bookish charm, irrepressible curiosity and kindness. If they could not be found roaming the estate, looking for this insect or that plant, and if they were not in the library pouring over some musty scientific or philosophical treatise, then they were most surely in Quinn's workroom, putting their knowledge to some practical test or application. They were never apart, and those who saw them could only envy such a pure and innocent devotion.

Rouster had awakened his staff early. It mattered not to him that they had been baking, roasting, kneading, pickling and sugaring for the past two weeks in preparation for the day. This was Ben's wedding and all that pertained to it – coming from *his* kitchen – would be perfect.

Even as Henrietta and Elizabeth blew in from the cold, Roman threw open the library door and bowed grandly to allow them to pass. Anne, Ian and Ben awaited them. Across the hall, the great room, so seldom used, had been aired out, its hearth and flue cleaned, its brass candelabras polished and fitted with the finest candles England had to offer. The enormous table in the middle of the room groaned with every imaginable food and drink. For Rouster, food equaled happiness. It meant well-being, success, and security. Today, Coudenoure would not be as it usually was, shy in its good fortune. Today, it would display its love: love of family, love of community, love of place.

Marshall could not escape his duties of the day but would arrive for the feast that evening.

Musicians arrived in a rackety wagon, playing their lutes, beating their drums, whistling their flutes down the long drive. They were led into the kitchen, for who could play on an empty and cold stomach? The day stretched on, with countless preparations for the late afternoon nuptials. It was a grand day, one to be cherished and remembered.

*****

The sun's rays slanted upon the horizon, signaling that the hour set for Ben and Elizabeth to be joined was upon them. Elizabeth twirled in her room before Anne, feeling the soft, luxurious fabric of the new chemise she wore beneath her gown. Weeks earlier Anne had appeared from the attic with a mysterious item wrapped securely in soft wool. Inside Elizabeth found the gown she now wore – a simple yet elegant wrap of cream velvet overcut with rose satin. It was beautiful, and her blue eyes glowed as she prepared for her nuptials. She looked around for her mother.

"Where is Mamma?" she asked Anne. "I want to hug her before we leave for the chapel."

As if on cue, Henrietta appeared at the door, a small packet of linen in her hand.

"This is for you, my darling daughter. 'Tis the talisman for all good things in our family."

Elizabeth carefully unfolded the package. Inside lay the gold and ruby cross of the de Greys.

"Oh, Mamma, it is so lovely. Here – place it round my neck."

Henrietta did so, and kissed Elizabeth before holding her at arm's length.

"Now I know that you and Ben shall be safe all your life long," she smiled, satisfied.

411

"Where did this come from?" Elizabeth asked.

It was Anne's turn.

"Child," she began leading Elizabeth from the room, "There are many stories which you have never been told – about the de Greys, about Coudenoure, about the history of your own line. Tonight, we shall tell you your heritage."

A small moment passed.

"Including the story of that cross – it comes from Henry VIII's grandmother! He stole it for the first Elizabeth, but enough till anon!"

*****

As the bonfire blazed and the candles flickered in the twilight, Elizabeth walked the ancient aisle of Coudenoure's ruined chapel. The light illuminated her face like that of an angel before the divine. A stout baritone voice intoned a passage of holy gospel from the King James Bible. Flowers were strewn in her path, and each citizen of the estate stood in awed silence as she passed.

"Now abide faith, hope and love, but the greatest of these is love."

With simple vows and profound love, before their community and their God, Ben St. John and Elizabeth Collins became one.

But even as the priest finished their first holy communion and bade them rise as husband and wife, a great clatter arose. As it did, so too a cloud covered the remains of the twilight, bathing the scene in the eerie half-glow of the bonfire's flames. A wind arose from nowhere, whipping the flames ever higher, hurling them against God and heaven, perhaps in defiant abnegation of the coming darkness; perhaps in confirmation of its destructive power. A few determined rays of warmth and light hung on the horizon only to slip away as all turned towards the thunder emanating from behind.

Dark and determined, lit only by burning torches, there rode a band of men. On they came, past the great wych elm doors, past the orchard. On mighty destriers they rode, mindful of nothing save their own mission. On and on until finally, those within the chapel ruins were forced back by their fearsome presence.

Roman, Ian and Ben stepped forward.

"Who are you?" Roman shouted above the wind and the snorting, stomping horses. "Why have you come to Coudenoure?"

It was clear that they had come with purpose. Each man carried a heavy lance and, at his waist, a short sword tucked into his belt. No livery belied their origins, only darkness cloaked their forms.

"Again I say – who are you?"

Henrietta and Anne moved silently nearer Elizabeth, taking in the scene unfolding before them.

"Take her into the house," Henrietta hissed to Anne, ". . . for this will not end well."

But Elizabeth shook off Anne's insistent grip.

"No, I am a woman now. I stand with my kind."

From deep within the band stepped the largest horse of all. The man who rode upon it clearly led the group.

"My, my. What have we here?"

Only the horses pawing on the great flagstones of the chapel met his words.

"Oh, I see. We do not want to say what we are about – is that it?"

"Sir, a wedding is taking place here, and we would see you gone so that we many continue our festivities."

A laugh arose among the intruders. From within his vest, their leader produced a sealed writ. He spoke.

"I am George Villiers, Duke of Buckingham, and I am here this evening for the following reasons."

He looked down and began to read:

"I, James Rex, King of all Ireland, Scotland and England, are privy to there being a coven of witches who exercise their powers at the estate known as Coudenoure."

A great gasp arose. Pleased with the response, Villiers glanced up.

"I shall paraphrase the rest. Henrietta Collins! You are hereby arrested on charges of witchcraft and treason against almighty God! Elizabeth Collins! Her daughter! The king saw you learning your mother's spells as a young witch! You, too, are remanded to the Tower!"

A dark fury filled Roman.

"Get off my estate you bastard! Be grateful that I do not pull you from that beast and kill you now."

Villiers looked down at him and smiled.

"Sir. I am here to take the Ladies Henrietta and Elizabeth. I shall do so. They will go to the Tower. And this . . . estate, this land where witches have practiced their occult skills, it is hereby taken from you. As of now, it reverts to the crown, which, kind sir . . ." here he gave a mock bow from his saddle, ". . . shall do with it as it pleases, perhaps passing it to another, more deserving, *baron.*"

Henrietta looked at Anne, and meaning passed between them. Anne leaned into Elizabeth, but before she could speak a mighty change came upon the scene. Within seconds, men were down from their horses, shoving their way towards Elizabeth and Henrietta. A melee of stampeding, frightened, angry, determined, horrified people erupted. Chaos descended.

"RUN! Henrietta, take her and *run!*"

But it was not to be. As Henrietta pushed through the fleeing crowd of servants and craftsmen, Elizabeth's hand slipped from her grasp. She turned, frantically, but already great throngs of wrestling arms separated them.

"I have her – go! *GO!*" It was Anne. She stood between Elizabeth and the approaching men. From nowhere, a hand grabbed Henrietta's and forced her through the crowd. On and on they ran leaving the light behind, entering the shadows of the night. Suddenly, ahead, a door opened and they slipped quickly through it. Rouster pulled it behind them. Only then did her comrade release her hand and turn.

"Marshall!" She gasped. "They are after Elizabeth! We must save her!"

"We shall, Henrietta, but we shall save you as well."

They were on the move now, through the back of manor house, down a passageway seldom used. On and on they fled until they reached the main hallway and entered the library.

"Quickly, for they will be upon us soon."

The two men ran to the great hearth. While Rouster pushed the mantel from below, Marshall felt for the familiar stone on the side. It opened with a scrape and Marshall turned again, frantic now in his pace.

"Get in and do not move or make a sound. Do not come out regardless until we release you – do you understand?"

Numb with fear, Henrietta did as she was told, and the slab closed behind her, leaving her alone in the dark. She sat on the cold stone stair, trembling violently.

Marshall and Rouster ran from the room and threw open the front doors, racing for the chapel. Behind them was darkness; before them was evil. But too late did they arrive, for through the orchard thundered the hooves of twenty horses, pounding hell and Hades towards the gate of Coudenoure. And on the saddle of Villiers, held securely before him, was Elizabeth, wild-eyed with fear, clinging to her assailant for dear life.

They ran on, meeting no one. The fury of the horses disappeared away into the night, and an ominous silence fell upon the place. They ran on towards the bonfire, stopping only when they reached the tiny knot of two who stood deathly still at the altar. All others had fled, only they remained. A strange noise reached their ears: a choking, sobbing sound.

"Roman! Ben! Where is Ian? We must ride for Elizabeth and quickly!"

Roman turned a bloodied face to Marshall and Rouster. Ben turned the same, tears streaming down his face. The choking, sobbing sound continued, but from where? Only then did they see; only then did they understand.

On the cold pavement of the ancient chapel lay Anne, her bruised and bloodied body in Ian's lap. His tears fell on her lifeless form like rain on a winter's field – they could not rouse the life beneath, for it was gone. His sobs rose unchecked, horrible and pathetic to hear.

It was Marshall who broke the spell. He knelt beside Ian.

"My friend, she died saving Elizabeth. We must honor that."

A choking silence was his only answer.

"Ian, hear me, man. We must ride, or they will kill Elizabeth, and Anne's death will have been in vain."

A sudden roar came forth from the grieving man.

"NOOOOOO!!!!!"

A stillness as quiet as a baby's breath filled the chapel. Ian rose, took off his cloak and placed it beneath Anne's head. Roman placed his over her body. The four turned back towards the manor house of Coudenoure. Roman's face was that of a madman.

"Where did you hide my wife? Where is Henrietta?"

Marshall steadied him with a hand on his shoulder.

"Behind the fireplace. Rouster has hidden horses and weapons near the gate. We must get her and go."

Roman slowed.

"I do not understand – how did you know?"

"Roman," Marshall was almost exasperated, "I heard a rumor at the Palace, and when they came for the war horses I knew it must be true. I rode the backway and beat them here. Rouster did the rest."

They reached the manor. Rouster and Marshall released Henrietta from her cell. In one swoop, Roman picked her up, hugged her to him and began sobbing. She pushed him back and stared at him, too frightened to speak.

Marshall spoke gently.

"Henrietta, Anne is dead, saving Elizabeth."

Henrietta turned slowly, deliberately towards him. For a full minute, she said nothing.

"And Elizabeth?"

Roman embraced her again, holding her tightly.

"Henrietta, they have taken her to the Tower."

Like lightening, she raced across the room. She was on the drive before they caught her. Roman spun her around.

"Henrietta! Henrietta!"

Roman had stopped crying now.

"Put this cloak on – it will do no good if we freeze to death before we are successful!"

Henrietta was incoherent.

"Roman!" she screamed. "We must save her! She is all we have now! We must . . . we must . . ."

He held her face in his hands.

"No, my love, she is not all we have."

He kissed her.

"We have each other."

A strangled, frantic laugh escaped his lips.

"Tell me, my darling wife, do we not have one final adventure within us? Shall we ride out once more?"

These were the words she needed.

"Yes, my Roman," she smiled weakly, "I believe we do. Let us go, for we have much to accomplish this night."

She turned.

"And we have our family to help us." She looked round at Ian, at Rouster, at Marshall. A grave determination was written on their faces.

But fate was not with them, that evening, for as they reached the end of the drive, a golden carriage, gaily lit with great torches of light, turned onto the drive. Two horsemen, liveried in the king's colors, rode before it. Stunned and confused, they stood in the middle of the drive, inadvertently blocking its passage.

"Move aside!" a horseman shouted. "Make way!"

"Make way for what?" Ian growled. "For whom?"

"Why the owner of this place. Prince Charles has seen fit to gift it to the Lady Alexandra. Now, step aside!"

They moved en masse to the side, too horrified to respond. As the carriage passed, Alexandra nodded to them, a sly smile upon her lips.

At the end of the drive, two more horsemen waited for them. They passed through in silence and turned, only to see the two men pulling the mighty gates closed against them.

"Move on, you," one laughed, "For Coudenoure is now gone from you. Move on."

They walked on, each wondering what more the coming night would bring.

*****

On and on they rode, Elizabeth barely able to stay in the saddle. Her heartbeat was frantic, but after a long while, she realized that her heart was keeping time with something else. Seeming to set its own course through the dark night which was now lay heavily upon her, as in sympathy with the pounding hooves it beat out its own rhythm against her chest, hung the ruby cross of the de Greys.

*****

[To be continued by Royal Sagas 4: "Kingdom's End"]

44672043R00239

Made in the USA
San Bernardino, CA
21 January 2017